SEVEN RULES
of TIME
TRAVEL

ROY HUFF

To download your FREE copy of *Salvation Ship*, visit Roy Huff at https://royhuff.net/salvationship/.

This book is dedicated to my loving and supportive wife, Rumi.

Don't forget to visit the link below for your FREE copy of *Salvation Ship*.

https://royhuff.net/salvationship/

Seven Rules of Time Travel

"Everything we thought we knew
about time travel is wrong."

– Quinn Black

CHAPTER 1

Saturday morning, August 7th, 2021

Day 1.

7:32 a.m.

THE SOFT PATTER of Quinn Black's alarm clock woke him from the dream.

"Holy crap."

Quinn wished the dream would last forever. He slumped off the mattress and fumbled against the cold metallic bed frame before he found his footing.

Layers of dirty clothes covered the floor in a jungle of disarray, hiding a humble yet otherwise respectable bachelor pad.

That summed up his life: an otherwise respectable bachelor hidden by the clutter of his life.

The next ten minutes blurred together, but Quinn managed to reach his car fully clothed, wrinkled but in one piece. Quinn was able to skate by in an ill-fitting black suit that needed to be dry cleaned because he was a "relatively young" professional. He glanced at the window's reflection and felt as disheveled on the inside as he looked on the outside. His chestnut-brown hair appeared combed, but a few out-of-place strands spoke the truth.

"You gotta be kidding me," Quinn muttered to himself as he stared at his neighbor's expensive new candy-apple colored Beemer. It rested just far enough in front of Quinn's narrow driveway to block a clean exit from his garage.

Quinn stood dazed until the adrenaline racing through his veins forced him to move forward.

"Taxi!" he shouted as a yellow-checkered car approached.

The taxi drove past him. The passenger's rear window silhouette shrunk as the taxi grew more distant. Quinn sighed.

Why did this city have to ban Uber? he thought.

The traffic slowed. Quinn's heart throttled against his rib cage. A bead of sweat trickled from his brow and disappeared into the blades of grass crouching over his feet. Quinn checked the time.

Quinn had left the disorganized jungle of his room for the urban jungle of New York. He was often lonely in the crowds, but the familiarity of the concrete, buildings, and people offered him a kind of safety and security only the city gave him.

Moments later, another taxi approached: an unkempt forty-year-old classic. The driver slammed on the brakes, throwing him forward. It reminded Quinn of one of those vintage crash-test dummy commercials. His heart sank.

Quinn opened the door and pulled out his phone. The screen turned black. He shook his head and took another deep breath. "You don't happen to have a phone I could borrow, do you?"

The short, portly driver nodded.

Quinn dialed a number. "Good morning. Robert's and Son's. How can I help you?"

"Meredith, this is Quinn. May I speak to Logan?"

"One moment, please."

Meredith wasn't Quinn's favorite executive assistant, but he was always polite to her. The glimmer in her eyes and the tilt in her head convinced him she gossiped about him behind his back. She always wore a dark pantsuit and slightly teased her blond hair, which hinted at her Jersey background even though she did her best to suppress it.

All Quinn knew about Meredith was that she had a son who was Quinn's age, midthirties, but Quinn never understood why Logan had hired her. He tried not to think about her. The morning was already bad enough.

"Logan, it's Quinn. I'll be a few minutes late. I've got an issue in my driveway, so I had to catch a taxi. I'll be there in fifteen minutes."

"Fuhgettaboutit," Logan said in his thick, New York accent.

Logan was the kind of boss every employee wanted: kind, understanding, and brilliant with people. He was only a few years older than Quinn but was the most effective networker he had ever seen.

The first time Quinn saw Logan in action, he was inspired. He made the bold move to work free as an intern. Logan said no at first, but Quinn persisted. That impressed him, so he hired Quinn a few weeks later.

At that time in Quinn's life, Logan was everything Quinn wanted to be. Logan had money and style. People fawned over his subtle, half-Japanese, half-Italian features as much as his power. Every suit Quinn bought for work, he modeled after Logan and asked himself if Logan would wear it.

Quinn hung up. The cell phone tumbled from his hand and onto the car floor. He reached for it. Just then, the taxi drove over a monster pothole. The front tire fell into the abyss and lost contact with the pavement. His face grimaced, and his brown hair rocked forward from the impact.

Quinn's stomach sank, just like it had when he used to ride roller coasters as a kid. The front tire hit the bottom of the hole, followed by the rear. The driver's tummy jiggled as they halted to a complete stop. Quinn's head smacked into the seat in front of him. Quinn instinctively grabbed the back of his neck. "Drop me off at the corner," Quinn said.

The driver slammed on his brakes. Quinn grimaced. He felt around his empty pockets. A wave of nausea washed over him. Quinn patted himself down. His wallet was gone. More beads of sweat trickled down Quinn's pale face. The driver stared at Quinn, expressionless. Quinn flinched. The driver shook his head.

"This is going to sound bad."

The driver squinted. Blood pulsated through Quinn's veins.

"No. No," the driver said.

"Wait. I can explain…"

Moments later, the driver signaled to a nearby police officer, wearing the familiar blue NYPD uniform with the badge number 732. Quinn's heart jumped. The officer tapped the window.

"Officer Channing," a faint, fuzzy voice spoke over his walkie.

"Can you step out of the car, sir?" Officer Channing said.

Quinn's stomach turned. His pulse raced, and then he took a deep breath.

"Officer, I can explain. My wallet must've fallen out of my pocket, maybe when I hopped into the taxi. I have cash in my office. If you let me get it, I can pay for the fare. I can call my boss, Logan. He's in that building."

The building stood quiet. A cloud of vapor rose from its stoic foundation and muted the shiny exterior glass.

"He can vouch for me," Quinn said.

Quinn's heart hammered in his chest while Officer Channing ran Quinn's Social Security number through his computer.

"Look. He's right over there," Quinn said as he pointed at Logan who was wearing a stylish pinstriped suit and motioned for Logan to come over once they caught each other's eyes.

After the signal changed, Logan hurried across the street, a tall, lanky figure dressed in black that was hard to miss in the crowd.

Quinn's underwhelming life had preoccupied his thoughts over the past week. Maybe that's why he had dreamed about her. Cameron's perfect lips took shape in his mind.

Back then, Quinn thought he had all the answers, except when it came to people. If someone asked him anything about the card game Magic, it was impossible to shut him up, but put him in front of a girl, and his face heated up like a sauna while his stomach did belly flips.

The first time they met, Cameron smiled at him. They sat on the pier and dangled their feet in the lake. Her white summer dress and the bow she tied around the back of it accentuated her feminine features. Her angelic, auburn hair absorbed the light from the water. Quinn felt awkward by comparison in a plain T-shirt and khaki shorts.

Cameron spoke first. Butterflies swarmed around Quinn's insides. All he could do was stare.

"How long have you lived here?" Cameron asked.

"A while. My dad moved us here when I was five, so like nine or ten years ago, I think," Quinn replied.

"You like it here?"

Her perfect eyes resembled those of a comic book character. Quinn didn't think those kinds of eyes existed, but there they were, beckoning him to say something pithy. Quinn's green oval eyes widened, and his shaggy, brown hair blew in the wind for a beat too long.

"I guess so."

He sensed she liked him, but all he could muster was an "I guess so." He had his chance, and he blew it.

Quinn felt like he always blew it. But in *that* dream, the only one he'd remembered in a long time, things were different. He didn't let the moment hang in the air. He didn't end the conversation with an "I guess so."

Quinn snapped back to the present and forced a smile as Logan stepped onto the crosswalk. Logan walked faster, but it was a wide street and dozens of people surrounded him.

Logan navigated through the sea of arms and legs. Every so often, he caught a glimpse of the officer, whose expression must have told Logan that he better hurry.

The crowd blocked Logan's view. A low-pitched echo reverberated through the air. Vibrations rattled through Logan's bones. And then there was the chatter, which quickly turned into shouts and screams.

Logan froze in place. At first, there was nothing but a hint of smoke and something gray and black just beneath what would have been his line of sight, below the heads of the people walking next to him. A sliver of it would emerge now and again, but not enough to reveal what was causing the commotion.

Rubber and metal squeaked like nails on a chalkboard. By the time Logan noticed the truck, followed by a trailer, it was too late.

People scattered near the intersection. The truck slowed, but not fast enough. It hit the curb. Inertia carried the trailer forward. Logan ran faster, but the truck rolled, flipped, and took turns smashing everything on the sidewalk before it finally launched into the air.

The massive steel rectangle raced toward Logan. Time slowed. Logan couldn't move, and then…it was over.

The trailer touched down in front of them, rolling a few times before it came to a halt, half a block away from their location.

Officer Channing ran toward the scene. Quinn followed the large uniformed, hulking, blue streak as Officer Channing made his way to the scene of the disturbance.

"Logan!" Quinn shouted as he stepped forward.

"Wait, where are you going?" the portly driver asked.

"Logan!"

Quinn walked a few feet more. His heart pounded like it was going to burst through his chest.

A few stragglers ran across the crosswalk unscathed, amid the newly formed sculpture of contorted, lifeless bodies that stretched dozens of yards in a sick display of live art. Smoke billowed from several broken pipes, and water spewed into the air from a main break near the intersection. The faint scent of motor oil and sewage wafted toward Quinn.

"You wait right here," Officer Channing said. "I'll be right back. Don't go anywhere."

The officer's fingers tapped his Taser, and Quinn could

tell this was the kind of cop that loved to use it. Quinn stood, immobile. Blood raged in his inner ear and pushed against his eardrum. Officer Channing surveyed the area. He approached a lifeless body, knelt down, and put his finger on the victim's neck.

Sirens blared. A large fire truck sped toward the area. A half dozen police cars followed. Moments later, a dozen cops rushed over to help Officer Channing.

Quinn failed to spot Logan among the bodies. He stood motionless. A cloud of mist engulfed him. Quinn rubbed his face. His eyes watered. His heart pounded. Sweat poured down the sides of his face and drenched his shirt.

"I'm sorry, Mr. Black, but you're going to have to come with me to the station," Officer Channing said.

CHAPTER 2

"WHAT ABOUT LOGAN? I can't see Logan. Can I at least walk over there and see if he's okay?"

"The police and rescue personnel will handle it from here."

Just then, Officer Channing triggered something in his memory, but Quinn couldn't place it.

"Please. He's my friend."

"Listen, Mr. Black. Just be glad you're not one of those people lying on the ground. I'll take you to the station, and then we'll sort things out. But I'm not going to let you get in the way and slow us down."

Officer Channing opened the squad car's back door and directed Quinn to take a seat. Quinn ducked into the back and fastened his seat belt.

The crowd grew larger, gawking at the paramedics who were assisting the victims. Quinn scanned the pavement, hoping to make out Logan's pinstriped suit and tall figure, but to no avail.

Officer Channing put the keys in the ignition. His imposing biceps popped as he drove in the opposite direction.

Quinn gazed through the back window until the intersection disappeared below the horizon.

Once they arrived at the station, Officer Channing directed Quinn to a cubicle near the back of the room.

Quinn sat down. It was the first time he had ever been in a police station. It fit his perception right down to the jelly-doughnut aroma and burnt coffee stench. He never had a reason to go before. He'd never been arrested and wasn't sure if he was now. He hadn't been cuffed or Mirandized. At least there was that.

"Wait right here while I go talk to my supervisor," Officer Channing said.

If it were any other day, Quinn would've had a heart attack from being taken in, but all he could think about was Logan.

The police station was filled with frantic people asking about loved ones. Quinn stared at the large wall clock and counted the seconds. He needed to call the office, but his phone was dead. He sat next to the booking officer for half an hour until the man finally hung up the phone.

"Is this really necessary? It's all just a misunderstanding. I had the money in my office. I just couldn't get there because of the accident. And I need to know if my boss is okay. He was one of the people who walked out in the street when the truck crashed. I think he's hurt. Can I call the office?" Quinn asked.

"I'm sorry to hear about your boss, and I hope he's all right. Now, about this theft of service—" the booking officer said before Quinn cut him off.

"Theft of service? My wallet fell out of my pocket. Like I told the taxi and the officer who dropped me off, I have the money. I wasn't trying to rip anyone off."

"I see now why Officer Channing brought you in."

"Why's that?" Quinn asked.

"You're a bit lippy."

"I'm sorry. I'm not trying to be rude. It's just been a crazy morning. Would you be willing to let me call my office to see if Logan's okay and if they can bring over some cash to pay the taxi fare?"

The officer nodded, directing him to a nearby phone.

"Meredith, this is Quinn. I'm freaking out now. Did you see what happened to Logan? He was coming out of the office at the same time as the crash. I think he's hurt, maybe worse," Quinn said.

"I'm not sure about Logan. He was in the office earlier, but then he left. Is there anything else I can help you with?" Meredith asked.

"You must know something. The office is right there. It's been a while now, and you must've heard something."

"You'll just have to wait like the rest of us." Quinn heard a click.

"What?" Quinn said before he hung up the phone.

The officer furrowed his brow and eyed Quinn. "You had your call. Now follow me to the back."

"Wait. Please. Just let me make one more call. They can clear everything up for me. I promise." Quinn's heart jumped.

"Yeah, that's what you said last time. You see all these other people here? You got your call. Now let's go," he said, nudging Quinn's arm.

Quinn took a deep breath. Crazy thoughts raced through his mind as he lost track of time. Several hours later, the cops processed him and gave him another chance to make a call.

"Valentino, it's Quinn. You're not gonna believe what just happened," Quinn said as he briefed him on the situation.

Valentino was a born salesman and had worked at Logan's company long before Quinn. Taller and with chiseled features, he was a few years older than Quinn. "That *is* crazy. I'll be right over," he said.

"And Valentino?" Quinn asked, fishing for a favor.

"Yeah?"

"Find out about Logan."

Seventy-three minutes later, Valentino arrived at the detention center. Traffic was a mess. Parking was worse. Valentino looked at his watch: 3:42 p.m. He went through the security check-in, then trotted through the corridors.

Valentino had copper-toned skin that women swooned over. His dark, slicked-back hair was almost cartoonish in style, but he pulled it off.

"Where do I post bail for someone?" Valentino asked one of the officers. His usual suave voice wobbled.

"Around the corner, but you're going to have to wait 'til Monday. It's three forty-eight. They closed a few minutes ago."

"So, there's nothing I can do until Monday?"

"You can make a call and let 'em know," the disinterested, desk-officer replied.

Valentino made the call.

"Quinn. I'm really sorry, but it's just after three forty-five. The cashier's closed, and so they're saying you're going to have to wait 'til Monday."

Quinn's stomach rolled.

"I've got more bad news."

Valentino didn't have to finish. Quinn knew what he was going to say. There was no way Logan could've survived. Valentino broke the news to him.

"Logan's gone. Paramedics pronounced him dead at the scene."

"I can't frikkin' believe it. I just can't. Why did this have to happen to Logan?"

"I'm sorry you have to sit in jail over the weekend for something so stupid, especially now."

Quinn sighed.

"Just hang in there. I'll be here first thing Monday morning. You'll be out before you know it."

Quinn's attention moved to his grumbling stomach. He stared at the feces-stained public commode.

"Sounds like you need to use it," one of the inmates said. This man didn't look quite as menacing as the others—his neck tattoos were notably absent. Still, he wasn't the type of person Quinn wanted to meet on the outside.

"I'll wait."

"Suit yourself, but the weekend's a long time. Better take care of that now instead of holding it in. Guards don't like it when they have to clean up people, and you'll like it even less."

Quinn cringed. Over the next several hours, Quinn took turns counting the seconds and staring at the toilet. He tried to wait it out, but his stomach had other plans.

Quinn made it just in time, and then he relieved himself. He sat there in all his glory and reflected on the day.

He finished up and used the last bit of toilet paper. The hand soap was empty. Quinn shook his head and returned to his seat.

If only Quinn could turn back the clock, relive the day, and do things over again. If only he'd checked his pockets before he hopped into the taxi, he wouldn't have needed to wave Logan down from across the street. Logan would still be alive, and Quinn wouldn't have to relieve himself in front of a group of men with neck tattoos.

Quinn thought about it, focused hard, and imagined it.

His eyelids grew heavy. They weighed down on him like

a truckload of cement blocks. He fought, not sure what to expect from his fellow inmates if he fell asleep.

He lost.

Saturday morning, August 7th, 2021
Day 2.

7:32 a.m.

The soft patter of Quinn's alarm clock jarred him from his dream and forced him to look at the numbers on the screen:

"What the…"

Quinn stumbled off the mattress and grunted as his ankles collided with the bed frame.

He scanned his room. It was the same as yesterday or this morning—Quinn wasn't sure which. He opened the bedroom curtain. His neighbor's candy-apple colored Beemer was in the same position.

Quinn sat on the bed and reflected on what had happened last night. He connected his phone to the charger, then called the office.

"Meredith, this is an emergency. I need to speak to Logan immediately."

"Logan's in a meeting."

"It's an emergency. I need to speak to him now. I don't have time to explain why. Please, just put me through."

"You know Logan doesn't like to be disturbed when he's in a meeting."

Quinn fiddled with his hairline. He wasn't sure if last night had been a dream, a premonition, or what. All he knew was that he wasn't going to take any chances. He remembered hearing once that the best way to survive in an airplane crash is to familiarize yourself with the exits and safety features *before* the accident. And whatever this was, it sure felt like it was going to crash hard.

"Please, Meredith, I'm not playing around. It's a matter of life and death. Please just put me through."

"I'll make sure Logan gets the message." The phone clicked.

Quinn threw on his clothes and made it outside just in time to miss the relic of a taxi that had picked him up the first time. He checked his pockets. His wallet was still there.

Quinn waited for the next taxi to arrive. He thought back on what had happened earlier. Maybe this was just his mind playing tricks on him. But how? A dream? Then he thought back to his actual dream, the one about Cameron. It was sharper than ever.

Cameron smiled. They sat on the pier and dangled their feet in the lake. Off in the distance, the trees gently bowed to the light breeze. It amazed Quinn how different the place felt with Cameron compared to when he was there with his father fishing.

The water's glassy surface mirrored the sky like a flawless reflection punctuated by a few ripples set off by dragonfly feet.

Nature's chorus echoed across the lake. The greenwood surrounding it shut out the rest of suburbia.

"How long have you lived here?" Cameron asked.

"A while. My dad moved us here when I was five, so like nine or ten years ago, I think."

"You like it here?"

Quinn bobbed his head. He kept up with the conversation. He listened and gave meaningful responses. He didn't choke up. And this time, he didn't just say, "I guess so."

A new-model, yellow-checkered car stopped by the curb where Quinn stood. A good start, Quinn thought.

Quinn checked for his wallet when he opened the door, and then reached for his phone in the other pocket. It wasn't there. It was still charging inside. He thought about retrieving it, but there was no time.

"You don't happen to have a phone I could borrow, do you?"

The lanky driver handed him a phone without saying anything.

"Good morning. Robert's and Son's. How can I help you?"

"Meredith, this is Quinn. I need to speak to Logan."

"Mr. Black, I gave Logan your message, but he stepped out of the office. I'm not sure when he'll be back, but I can leave another message if you'd like."

Quinn hung up and called Logan directly. It went straight to voice mail.

The taxi stopped. Quinn looked out the window. Traffic was at a standstill. Sirens blared from around the corner. Quinn judged the distance from his office building, paid the driver, and gave him back his phone.

Quinn flung open the cab door, ran to the sidewalk, and then headed toward the direction of his office building until he arrived at the intersection of the accident.

Bodies lay strewn across the ground. A few stragglers stumbled away, but most lay motionless on the asphalt.

Smoke billowed from broken pipes. Water spewed into the air from the main break.

Quinn pushed his sweaty hair off his forehead. His mouth opened as he gawked at the scene.

"You need to wait right here," Officer Channing said, looking at Quinn.

Moments later, a dozen cops assisted Officer Channing. Quinn failed to find Logan among the bodies. Quinn rubbed his face. His eyes watered. His heart pounded. Sweat poured down the sides of his face and drenched his shirt.

"Screw this," Quinn said.

He pushed his way through the newly erected barricades and scoured the pavement for Logan.

Officer Channing glared at Quinn, then strode toward him. Quinn slipped away.

"Stop right there!"

Quinn ignored him. Officer Channing reached for his Taser. The pins from the Taser struck Quinn on his back-left shoulder. Quinn convulsed and fell to his knees in agony before he collapsed onto the street.

When Quinn came to, he was in the familiar cell, sprawled out on the bench. Quinn's insides grumbled. He stared at the feces-stained public commode.

"Sounds like you could use it," the inmate said.

Quinn didn't wait this time. He relieved himself, and then he sat back down.

Quinn thought about what had happened, the call to Meredith, the cell phone charger, and the taxi. He focused hard on it, imagined it. Quinn's eyelids grew heavy. This time, he didn't fight.

SATURDAY MORNING, AUGUST 7TH, 2021
DAY 3.
7:32 A.M.

The soft patter of Quinn's alarm jarred him from his dream.

Quinn slid off his mattress and scanned the room. It

looked the same. He opened the curtain and stared at his neighbor's expensive new import with the candy-apple finish.

Quinn threw on his clothes, grabbed his wallet, and walked outside.

He flagged down the first taxi that stopped. He gave the driver directions to his office.

"You have a phone I can borrow?" Quinn asked. The driver nodded, then handed it over.

Quinn called Logan directly. It went straight to voice mail.

"You mind speeding it up a little?" Quinn asked.

"You got it, boss." He stepped on the gas.

"Thanks. You won't believe the morning I'm having," Quinn said.

A black-and-white Ford Interceptor turned the corner. Police sirens blared.

"You gotta be kiddin' me," Quinn said.

Quinn took a deep breath. The driver looked in the rear-view mirror and then pulled over to the side as the cop directed him to stop.

The driver rolled down the window.

"You know how fast you were going?" Officer Channing asked the driver.

Officer Channing took his time turning the carbon from his ticket book, and from their pointless banter, it was clear they knew each other.

Quinn folded his arms, cracked his neck, and read the time on the car clock. He took a deep breath, and then pulled out his wallet.

"This should cover it," Quinn said as he flung the cash onto the front seat.

Quinn pushed open the door and bolted.

"Slow down. You might hurt somebody," Officer Channing yelled as Quinn sped off toward the intersection.

Quinn ran faster and ignored traffic signals. He scampered across a side street and dodged the cars that were moving along on the road. Several cars honked, but he made it to the other side, only to have a sidewalk groove trip him up seconds later.

Quinn's face struck the ground. A couple of his front teeth tore through his lips. A sharp pain shot up from his jaw to his skull. Blood pooled out of his mouth. The daylight vanished. The noise stopped. Quinn closed his eyes.

Quinn woke up in a nearby hospital a couple of hours later. An IV dangled from his arm, and wires clamped his jaw shut. Quinn faced an outdated television that was airing reruns of Bob Barker's *The Price is Right*, an episode he had watched as a kid the summer he met Cameron in her white angelic summer dress.

The memory of the dream grew sharper with each trip.

Cameron smiled. They dangled their feet in the serene lake over the pier's wood-stained panels. The day was humid, but the shade took the edge off the sticky air.

Nature's chorus echoed across the lake. The greenwood surrounding the pier's solitary Southern brick structure shut out the rest of suburbia.

The glassy water's surface mirrored the sky like a flawless reflection punctuated by the ripples set off by dragonfly feet.

It was Quinn's favorite spot. He spent much of his youth fishing there with his dad. They rarely caught anything, and when they did, they always threw it back. As Quinn grew up, his father always wore red-flannel, button-up shirts, and jeans when he did work around the house or when he took Quinn fishing. He looked like an older version of Quinn, with beady, hazel-eyes, and well-groomed facial hair speckled with distin-guished, gray-whiskers.

Quinn, however, borrowed his mother's eyes. Sometimes, she would bring out a large blanket during the late morning so they could picnic together for an early lunch. She loved the water, and Quinn was always uncomfortable when she wore her bathing suit to the lake. At that age, Quinn much pre-ferred his mother in her customary mom-jeans and the overt chemistry between his parents nonexistent.

"How long have you lived here?" Cameron asked.

"A while. My dad moved us here when I was five, so like nine or ten years ago, I think," Quinn replied.

"You like it here?"

Her large eyes were perfect, like those of a comic book character. Quinn didn't think those kinds of eyes existed, but there they were, staring straight back at him as if beckoning him to say something pithy. That's what he planned to do.

Quinn smiled back.

The morphine-addled haze blurred Quinn's vision as he writhed in pain in the hospital bed's stiff sheets, unable to squirm out of a wrinkle that rode up his back.

Quinn reflected on the day, the dream, the accident, the hospital room, and everything else from that morning. He focused, imagined it, and then closed his eyes.

CHAPTER 3

THE SOFT PATTER of Quinn's alarm jarred him from his dream and forced him to look at the numbers on the screen.

Quinn jumped to attention, threw on his clothes, and ran out of the house. He wore khaki shorts and sneakers instead of his usual suit and dress shoes.

He tore a piece of paper from his wallet and scribbled a note, "Bike borrowed by Quinn for an emergency. Will return later today."

Quinn lifted the short-wheeled, rusty BMX bicycle that rested in his neighbor's yard. He stepped on the pedals and rode.

The sky was brighter, the scents stronger, his pulse faster.

Curb, drop. Rock, jump. Light, turn. Corner, turn. Hill, brake. Car, turn. Curb, jump.

Quinn pedaled like he had the summer his parents bought him the BMX bike he'd wanted ever since the sixth grade. His parents bought it because of how Quinn had handled things after Quinn's grandparents died.

Light, turn.

Quinn pedaled faster.

Curb, jump.

His office building was visible from a couple of blocks away.

Curb, drop. Kid, brake. Parent on the premises, stop.

"Watch where you're going, freak!" the kid's dad said.

His young son quivered. Quinn's hand trembled. The boy couldn't have been older than four or five.

"Sorry."

Quinn jumped on the pedals.

Cop, stop.

A Ford Interceptor blared its sirens. Officer Channing instructed Quinn to pull over. He opened the door, approached Quinn, then pulled out the ticket pad from his shirt front pocket.

"I'm sorry, Officer. It's an emergency."

Officer Channing's eyes tightened, contorting his face into the resemblance of an overly muscled caveman.

"What kind of an emergency?"

"There's going to be an accident. Someone's about to die."

Quinn realized how that sounded. Quinn's shoulders raised as he sunk down into himself.

"What do you mean exactly? Who's about to die?"

"No, I mean, there's going to be a traffic accident, and a lot of people are going to get hurt."

Officer Channing twisted his lips and squinted his eyes.

"Uh-huh. Let's see, riding without a helmet, riding on the sidewalk, riding on the wrong side of the road, and turning without signaling. I have enough violations to bring you in."

"Please, Officer. It's an emergency."

Quinn's brain finally retrieved the image of Officer Channing, only a much younger version.

"Yeah, I remember you saying that, but that's not helping you any. Better keep your mouth shut and let me take you to the station before you make things worse."

Quinn questioned the point of the rest of the day. It wouldn't help to call anyone. In a few minutes, Logan would leave the office building and get struck and killed. After that, Quinn would end up at the station. He would call Valentino, who would show up past the deadline. Quinn's stomach would grumble, and then he'd wake up again the next day, on the same day.

Quinn took a few slow, deep breaths and reflected on the different scenarios and outcomes. He thought about the situation, how he got there, why the day was repeating, and how he might change it the next day.

Why *was* it repeating? Who could he talk to? If he had been back in high school, that person would have been his best friend, Jeremy, who resembled and reminded Quinn of a younger and smarter version of Valentino.

Back in Quinn's office building, Logan attended a company board meeting. A half dozen men in their late fifties to early seventies wore high-end black or gray suits. They sat at a large oval table adjacent to the penthouse office suite with an immaculate city view.

"I have every confidence in him. Quinn's more than just a friend. He's reliable, hard-working, honest, and brilliant at making a plan," Logan said.

"Then why hasn't he beat sales expectations the last two years? A third of our sales associates have outperformed his numbers. Why should we promote him over any one of them? Most of them are just as qualified and well educated," Robert, his father, noted.

"For the same reason you took a chance on me."

"What did you expect me to do? You're my son. Of course I was going to give you a shot. You just happened to be brilliant at it," Logan's dad replied.

"And Quinn will be brilliant at it, too."

"Then answer the question."

"Quinn clocked in the top three sales five years running, but he took it hard after his friend died. He's just had a couple of unlucky years."

Logan often found himself in similar conversations with his dad, who looked just like him, only a few decades older and more Italian. Robert always made Logan fight for his positions. Most of the time, he was successful. Logan loved his dad but hated looking at the crow's feet around his eyes because it symbolized the long hours at work Robert could've spent with them before his mom died. And after she passed, Robert dove more into his work, becoming distant and cold.

"You know better than that. People make their own luck. Quinn's no different," Robert said.

"Quinn has worked his butt off ever since he was a kid, but he just had one bad break after another. I mean, I could list all the crap he had to go through—from his grandparents' death at the end of eighth grade and Jeremy's, a couple of years back. He's bounced back each time."

"But not high enough. At least not this time. His numbers are flat. Have you forgotten what I've taught you, the most important thing? It's not what happens to you. The only thing that matters is how you respond. Why should we give Quinn the promotion until he shows he deserves it?"

"I know Quinn, and I know what he's capable of. We've put together the perfect team, but it's only perfect if Quinn leads it."

"Logan, you should know better than anybody that the single most accurate predictor of success is a past history of success. We haven't offered him the position yet. It's not too late to offer it to someone else. He's late today, for Pete's sake. What about Valentino? Last year his numbers were through the roof."

"I like Valentino, but if we put him in charge, he'll waste half his time chasing women. Quinn, on the other hand, is a brilliant planner. That's why I hired him, and that's what this project needs. *And* it will give him the motivation he needs to find his footing. I promise you, you won't regret it."

Robert shook his head. "Fine. I'm only going to go along with this 'cause you're usually right on these things, but if Quinn crashes and burns, don't say I didn't warn you."

"He won't. I promise"

Logan hurried out of the office to meet some potential clients. He left the building and navigated through the arms and legs in his way. A low-pitched echo reverberated throughout the area. Vibrations rattled through Logan's bones.

Quinn watched the replay of events, this time from the backseat of Officer Channing's squad car across the street. A massive steel rectangle raced toward Logan. Time slowed. Logan froze, and then it was over.

Quinn gritted his teeth and throttled back. He lifted his legs and maneuvered in the backseat to get his arms in front of him, the best way he could in handcuffs.

An unnerving look overcame Officer Channing's face.

"Officer Channing requesting back up." He turned toward Quinn.

"What did you do, Mr. Black?"

"Nothing. I swear."

"Then how did you know there was going to be an accident that kills a lot of people?"

Quinn paused before he spoke. "I'm not a terrorist. I'm a salesman who's late for work. My boss is right over there, lying in the middle of the street, dead. He's not dead because of me, either. He died because *you* didn't listen."

The words hung in the air. Officer Channing gritted his teeth and balled up his fist.

"You're lucky they banned waterboarding a few years back. I promise you when my team finds out what a scumbag you are, you're going to regret it."

"But you're a cop."

"A New York cop. I've had too many of my family die in 9/11 to let the likes of you get away with another attack. It's not happening on my watch."

"Do whatever you want. It doesn't matter. I'll just come back here tomorrow like I did yesterday and the day before that."

"What are you saying? Are you actually admitting to casing the joint? You have more of these attacks planned? I'm going to give you one more chance to tell me what you did before I put you in a hole you'll never get out of."

In the rearview mirror, Officer Channing watched Quinn lean back and close his eyes. Officer Channing suddenly flung the back door open and placed his hand around Quinn's neck, squeezing.

"You deaf?"

Officer Channing kneed Quinn in the stomach. "What did you do?" he asked Quinn.

It was too much. Quinn was out cold. Officer Channing tried to revive him with a quick succession of slaps, but Quinn lay there, motionless.

"You think I don't know who you are, Quinn? I know exactly who you are," Officer Channing said to the unconscious Quinn.

A few hours later, Quinn awoke disoriented. He forced his eyelids open and lifted his head up from the cold, aluminum desk. Metal chains connected Quinn's cuffed wrists to the interrogation table. A mirror stared back at him. He'd seen enough movies to know they were watching.

Officer Channing walked through the door behind him. The scent of stale coffee and pastries didn't sit well with Quinn's stomach.

"You're up. Good. Now we can start where we left off." Officer Channing tossed a yellow notepad on the desk and sat down across from Quinn. "You said there was going to be an accident and a lot of people were going to die. A few minutes later, a large truck with phony plates just happened to crash into a major intersection and killed dozens of people. How did you know that was going to happen?"

Quinn said nothing.

"You said, and I quote, 'I'll just come back here tomorrow like I did yesterday and the day before that.' That sounds like planning to me, with more attacks to come."

"That's not what I meant."

A younger, moderately attractive female officer opened the door and joined Officer Channing. "What *did* you mean, Mr. Black?" she asked.

"Listen, I know you've got no reason to hold me. I

didn't have anything to do with the accident. I had a feeling is all. Just let me go. I'm tired, and I'm not feeling well," Quinn said.

"Quinn, is it?" the female officer asked. "I'm Kate. You seem like a nice enough guy. You've got no priors. Not even an arrest. If you tell us everything you know, we might just be able to help you. How does that sound?"

Quinn squirmed in his seat.

"You look upset, agitated," she said.

"My friend just died. What do you expect? I'm handcuffed to this table being questioned by a couple of clueless cops. My head's pounding because Officer Scott Channing over there got his rocks off beating the crap out of me in the squad car while my boss was lying dead in the middle of the street. How would *you* be acting?"

Kate glanced at Officer Channing, then caught herself before she looked too long.

"How do you know my name's Scott?" Officer Channing asked.

"Let me go."

"I've got you exceeding three violations, enough to hold you for forty-eight hours. And now I have you on suspicion of terrorism and terroristic threatening. I'm sure we can find a few more charges if we need to," Officer Channing said.

Quinn smirked.

"Well, I hate to disappoint you, but I'm not staying here. Not for long, anyway."

"I don't care what kind of lawyer you have, Mr. Black. We own you for the next two days. That's a long time to find out what we need to know," Officer Channing replied.

Quinn stopped talking. Over the next few hours, several different officers came in and out of the interrogation room.

They used different tactics, attempting to coax Quinn into saying something about the accident.

After a few more hours, Quinn's face turned yellow. "I need to use the restroom. Now," Quinn said.

"You'll get to use the restroom when we finish with you when you've given us what we need," Officer Channing said.

Quinn's stomach grumbled.

For once, Quinn didn't think back on the day. Instead, he thought about the summer before ninth grade and the conversation he would've had with Jeremy if he was there. He thought about what Jeremy would tell him he should do to stop Logan's death without ending up in the hospital or prison. Quinn thought about Bob Barker.

His eyes grew heavy. He didn't fight it.

"Come on down," Bob Barker's voice said through the television, accompanied by the program's magical musical jingle.

"No, not again, not the hospital." Quinn kept his eyes closed. Swallows chirped in the background. A French door opened behind him. A humid gust of wind kissed the back of his neck.

"Hey, can you help your old man with this?" a voice said at the front door.

Quinn opened his eyes. He wasn't on a bed in the hospital. He was on a La-Z-Boy, his dad's favorite, in his childhood home. "Dad?"

CHAPTER 4

Sunday morning, August 15th, 1999
Day 1.

QUINN'S ARMS AND legs were skinnier than they had been in decades. He blinked his eyes a few times just to check to see if he was still dreaming.

"What's going on?" Quinn asked as his voice cracked.

"What's going on about what?" Quinn's dad asked. Frank had thinning hair, a bit of a potbelly, and soft eyes.

"Never mind. I just fell asleep. That's all," Quinn said as he stood up to help his dad bring in the groceries. Childhood memories flooded Quinn's mind. He remembered there was something important about this conversation, but it was a long time ago.

"Quinn, I'm really proud of how you handled things when Mom and Dad died, the way you talked to Amy about the whole thing."

Quinn hadn't seen his sister, Amy, in the last few years, at least not in 2021. She stayed in the upstate area with their parents but then moved to Seattle to go to college after high school. He hadn't seen her since.

"Amy," Quinn said as she struggled to carry a glorious purple-and-black BMX bike over her shoulders. An enormous, shiny, red bow topped it off. Quinn's mind began to clear.

Amy was just as energetic as he remembered, but that was all Quinn's doing, even if he was too humble to admit it. Quinn's parents weren't sure if they could lift Amy's spirits after her grandparents' death, so Quinn took matters into his own hands to cheer her up, spending as much time with her as he could until her mood brightened. The BMX was payback from his parents for helping her through the funk.

Their grandparents' death crushed Quinn, too, more than his family knew. He just hid it better in front of them.

"Just a little something to show my appreciation. I know you've wanted this since sixth grade," Quinn's dad said.

Quinn smiled. "What did Mom say?"

"It was her idea," Kathy said, speaking in third person as she walked in behind Amy.

Quinn hugged her. "Thanks, Mom."

Her face lit up. She looked younger and prettier than Quinn remembered.

"Can I take it for a spin?"

"Why not?" Frank said.

Quinn ripped off the bow, jumped on the pedals, and sped over to Jeremy's. His Chuck Taylor Converse shoes became a blurry mixture of white and blue the faster he pedaled. He forgot all about helping his dad with the groceries, just like he did when he was a real kid.

All Quinn could think about was seeking Jeremy's advice. Even at fourteen, Jeremy would have answers. He was comfortable in his own skin, a typical boy who only bathed if he stunk. He didn't really care what anyone thought about his clothes, but still managed to outshine Quinn's style, even with Jeremy's poverty-stricken sense of fashion. And they complemented each other in more ways than anyone knew.

Quinn neared Jeremy's house. Quinn eyed his front porch, half a block away. Quinn remembered the house after it was painted white with blue trim the following summer. At this point in time, the house had white chipping paint, and the screen door squeaked and slammed loudly when the boys ran in and out of it.

Adrenaline rushed through Quinn's veins.

"Jeremy!" Quinn said.

The screen door slammed behind Jeremy, who hadn't changed much since Quinn had seen him last, just shorter and stubble-free. Jeremy had his summer buzz cut, which made his auburn hair look less red than it really was.

Jeremy smiled. "Sweet bike." Jeremy caressed the frame and glided his fingers across its chassis.

"Screw the bike. Just wait 'til you hear my story. You're gonna wanna sit down for this." Quinn spent the next half hour explaining what had happened from the moment time began repeating until he woke that morning. He didn't have to wait long for Jeremy's reaction.

"You've watched one too many time-travel movies, bro. Which one was it? *Back to the Future*? *Groundhog Day*? You're like Robbie in that eighties Tom Hanks movie, *Mazes and Monsters*, when Robbie couldn't tell the difference between the game and the real world."

"This isn't a joke. I'm serious."

"Did you already fall off the bike and hit your head?"

"Have you ever known me to lie about something big like this for no good reason?" Quinn asked.

Jeremy paused. "What about the time you told me you

went to play for a junior professional soccer league in Russia two summers ago?"

"I forgot about that," Quinn said.

"So, this is two summers ago. What else is new? Now tell me, how'd you convince your parents to buy the BMX?"

"I'm not joking, Jeremy."

"Just let me ride around the block already."

"This is serious. I'm not sure if I'm stuck here, or if I can go back, or what."

"Fine, you want to play this game. Tell me about the future."

Quinn thought about all the time-travel movies and TV shows he had ever watched.

"What if I tell you something and it messes things up in the future?" Quinn asked.

"Well, it's too late for that. You already told me you're from the future, so I guess the damage is done. Now you can tell me the good stuff," Jeremy said.

"No, seriously. What if I say something that causes me to die in the future, and then I don't exist anymore?"

"Are you dumb? Paradoxes are stupid. *You* said that. They can't exist. Otherwise, you wouldn't be here. We have this conversation every time we see a time-travel movie, and you always give the best answer. Remember?"

"Well, that was just an idea I was thinking about when I was a kid."

"When you *were* a kid? Oh, right, you're from the future. Listen, you just told me all this stuff that's going to happen to you in this fake future of yours, so I already know a bunch of things. Plus, you couldn't change anything when you were looping time…if you *were* looping time. What makes you think you can change anything now?"

"Well, that's not exactly true. I could change some stuff, just not what I wanted to change."

Jeremy sighed. "Are we really still having this conversation? Did you start smoking crack over the summer and forget to tell me about it? Should I call your parents? I know your grandparents just died and all. I didn't want to bring that up. You might just be having some kind of brain fart," Jeremy said.

"Just shut up and listen. This isn't a joke. I'm not smoking crack, and I'm not going crazy. This isn't a dream, and I'm really from the future."

"Then prove it."

Quinn rubbed his forehead. "All right. How?"

"Dude, *you're* the one from the future. You think you'd be smart enough to figure it out. Tell me something big, something cool, something I don't know yet that you couldn't possibly know unless you were from the future."

"There's a ton of stuff, but most of that kind of thing won't happen months or years from now, so it's kind of hard. Let me think. What year is it? Nineteen ninety-eight?"

Jeremy rolled his eyes. "Nineteen ninety-nine."

"Okay, there's a few big things that happened, but all those might change if I tell you, and they're still a ways off."

"Fine, what about earthquakes and stuff, or sports?"

"Earthquakes? Yeah. That's a good one. I know there's a huge earthquake that's going to hit in a couple of years near Indonesia and cause a tidal wave that kills hundreds of thousands of people. I can't think of anything closer. There was 9/11, but that's…"

Just then, the reality of what might be happening punched Quinn in the face. He reflected on the iconic words: "With great power comes great responsibility." And yet, like all the superheroes who'd struggled with saving the most lives, Quinn knew he had his limits. Even if time travel had no rules, he couldn't stop everything. He couldn't control human nature, and he couldn't be in two places at once.

"What's nine eleven?"

"I'll tell you that one later, but give me a second. I think I might… What day is it?"

Jeremy shook his head. "August fifteenth."

"There's going to be an earthquake in Turkey in a couple of days, the seventeenth, I think."

"And why do you remember that?"

"Thousands of people died. It was a seven point something. I did a paper about it in ninth grade Physical Science class."

"Fine. Let's say I go along with this story of yours for the next two days—"

Quinn interrupted. "I don't know if I'm going to make it to the seventeenth. Before I came here, I kept looping on the same day. Maybe the same thing will happen here now."

Quinn's face turned ghost white.

"What is it?"

"Today's the fifteenth."

"Yeah, I just said that."

"I can't believe it. I'm so stupid," Quinn said as he jumped on his bike and pedaled off.

"Wait, Quinn! Where are you going?"

Quinn kicked the BMX into high gear, then sped off. The day was hotter and stickier than he remembered. The trickle of sweat on his face morphed into a river.

Quinn pedaled faster, but it was too late. He missed her. Quinn dropped the BMX to his side and ran to the edge of the pier, peeling off his sweaty socks as he plunged his feet into the lake. The water was refreshing but not enough to take the edge off the heat. Quinn sat and took in the scenery.

After he caught his breath, Quinn put on his shoes and pedaled back to Jeremy's.

"Dude, where'd you go? You drop a bomb on me like that and then just dig out."

"I just remembered—I met her today at the lake for the first time. I could've done it all over again, but now I missed my chance 'cause I came here instead."

"Missed what chance?"

"To talk to her. To say something, anything. I had a second chance, but then I blew it…again."

"What girl?"

"Cameron."

"Who's Cameron?"

"You haven't met her yet, but she's in our school this year. She just moved into the neighborhood. The first time I met her today by the pier on the lake."

"You're really serious about this thing, aren't you?"

"That's what I've been trying to tell you. I'm from the future."

"I'm not convinced, but I'll try to play along for the next couple of days anyway, at least until the earthquake in Turkey doesn't pan out."

Quinn smiled.

"Tell me about this girl Cameron."

"She's got the most beautiful lips I've ever seen, and her eyes…her eyes are like—"

"You're gonna make me barf. If what you're saying is true, aren't you like thirty years old or something? What do you want with a ninth grade girl? Shouldn't you be going after someone your own age?"

"That's not the point."

"What *is* the point?"

"She was the only girl I ever really liked. After that, I just kind of gave up."

Jeremy shook his head. "Are you frikkin' serious? That's lame. You're telling me that in all that time you supposedly lived in the future, you never had a girlfriend?"

"Of course I had girlfriends, just none I really liked. No one that I thought I could be with forever. There were a few girls I wanted to ask, but I guess I always chickened out."

"Maybe it's time you changed that. What happened with this girl Cameron?" Jeremy was still convinced it was a joke, but they fooled around like that sometimes.

"It was awkward. She smiled, tried to be nice, but I did what I usually do and psyched myself out. Halfway through the school year, she started hanging out with this douchebag, Scott Channing."

Quinn stopped. "Holy crap. I just realized something."

"What is it?"

"Scott Channing, the cop."

"What cop?"

"The one I told you kept getting in the way of me saving my boss. Maybe there's a connection."

"So, what does your future self know about Scott Channing?"

"Besides the fact that he beefed up a lot, not much. He moved to the city at the end of the ninth grade, but Cameron stayed his girlfriend all through high school. She was never available—always taken by the mysterious Scott Channing. I don't know what happened to her after high school. We weren't even Facebook friends."

"What's a Facebook?"

"Oh wow. It's kind of like a website where all your friends and family hang out. Like a chat room."

"That sounds stupid. Isn't that where all the pervs go? Why wouldn't they just want to hang out for real? I think the future will be way cooler."

"You'd be surprised. In four years, Arnold Schwarzenegger's going to be governor of California."

"Dude, are you really borrowing storylines from *Demolition Man*?"

"Just wait 'til Donald Trump is president."

"Give me a break. If you didn't want me to ride your bike, you shouldn't have come over to rub it in my face. I'm going back inside."

"Wait. I swear. Everything I'm saying is true, and if I'm right, then in a couple of days you'll know I'm telling the truth. If the day starts looping, then I'll learn what's going to happen, and I'll just tell you in the next loop until you believe me."

"Is that a yes?" Jeremy asked.

"Here, take it for a spin," Quinn replied.

Jeremy took the BMX and rode around the corner. He had more fun than Quinn, and smiled the entire time. Twenty minutes later, Jeremy rode up to Quinn and stopped short.

"All right. Let's play this out. I'm really hoping you're telling me the truth because if you are, we're gonna have a lot of fun. I don't believe it for a second, but that never stopped us before, and I've got a long list of things we can do."

"Fair enough. But first I need to know if I'm going to keep looping again. I have an idea. I'll come back and tell you tomorrow if it worked," Quinn said before he hopped on his bike.

Quinn rushed home and spent the rest of the day in his

room, refreshing his memory of ninth grade. He ate dinner with his family for the first time in years. He remembered what a great cook his mother was and the side dishes his father used to make—that only sometime turned out okay. His dad's mashed potatoes weren't half bad. After an exhausting day, he crashed early.

CHAPTER 5

THE SUNLIGHT WOKE Quinn. He inspected the clock, his hands, and the mattress. Quinn threw on his clothes and biked over to Jeremy's house.

"It's tomorrow," Quinn said once he arrived.

"No, it's today," Jeremy replied.

"That's what I meant. It's not yesterday. Yesterday didn't repeat like it did in 2021."

"I didn't think it would," Jeremy said.

"One more day, then. What will you do tomorrow when the earthquake hits and you see I'm telling you the truth?"

"You're still on this thing? I thought you would be done with it by now."

"It's not a thing. I'm serious."

"Fine. *If* it happens, we'll talk about it then. Right now, I still think you're full of it."

"I came here for a reason, and I don't want to waste time. We should get working on a plan together."

"Give me five bucks," Jeremy replied, holding his hand out.

"Why?"

"'Cause if you're lying, I'm keeping the cash."

Quinn reached into his pocket and handed over the money. "So, what should we do, assuming tomorrow comes and I'm right?"

"Write down everything you remember from the future. We'll find out why your day's repeating, how your mind traveled back in time, and why you didn't loop again yesterday."

"I think I figured that last part out."

Jeremy shook his head. "And why's that?"

"Before I time-looped the first time, I was thinking about what happened that day, just because everything went so wrong. I did the same thing before I slept each night. I dreamt the night before about meeting Cameron, so I was already thinking about this point in my life.

"The night before I came here, I thought about why I was stuck in a time loop. Instead of thinking about August seventh, 2021, I thought about yesterday, August fifteenth, 1999, the day my parents bought me the new bike. I think that's why I ended up back here yesterday."

"Why didn't you just ask my future self?"

Quinn changed the subject, hoping Jeremy didn't notice. "I don't think you're hearing me," Quinn replied.

"I heard you. You said you thought about yesterday."

"Exactly. I thought about yesterday. And before I looped in time, I thought about the same day. Don't you get it? All I have to do is think about what day I want to wake up in, and I do."

"That *would* be frikkin' awesome," Jeremy said.

"Let's say I'm right. It still doesn't explain why," Quinn

replied. "I was thinking about that, too. Who knows if or when I can get back or if time will suddenly stop looping. But when I'm ready, I'm hoping I can just think about 2021 right before I fall asleep and wake up there the next day, no problem. And I need to go back soon, just to make sure my last day in 2021 is the same."

"What if you can't?"

"I don't want to think about it. I'm not sure if I would want to relive my whole life again. But *if* I'm stuck here, I'm sure I could use what I know about the future. Maybe make things better the second time around."

"Now we're talking. What kind of things?"

Quinn stroked his chin. With no superpowers, except for time travel, he needed money. It would give him the clout he needed to make changes and convince other people to help him. It was like oxygen, necessary for survival.

Quinn also knew Jeremy's complicated relationship with finance, one forged by Jeremy's poverty-stricken youth, and his later rise above it as a successful entrepreneur. Some people saw Jeremy's persistent money talk as greed or insecurity. Still, Jeremy quashed those notions by building the small business community in his neighborhood as an adult.

Quinn thought the money discussion would draw him in, even if he didn't fully buy the time-travel storyline.

"The stock market drops early next year. The NASDAQ crashes like 80 percent or something. I know Yahoo's stock tanks in the first quarter. If I could buy some out-of-the-money put options, I could make like…a thousand times my money."

"What's an outside-the-money thingamajig?"

"Something people buy when they think a stock is going to go down. If it does, they make money. There's always ways to make money in the market, regardless of whether it's going up or down. You just have to know where to look."

"I hope you're right, but there's a problem. You're fourteen. Don't you have to be like eighteen to open an account?"

"Not if I can get my dad to do it for me. I can give him the allowance money I saved up. If I remember right, I have a few hundred bucks. He'll just think I'm being responsible. He always understood the value of investing and compound interest. He had more of a healthy understanding of personal finance than most people. If I do it right, I can make ten times my money. But I can probably make an investment like that only once or twice because I don't remember that many stock market crashes. I mostly just remember a few long-term trends."

"You kinda sound like you *are* from the future."

"That's what I've been trying to tell you."

"Your idea's good, but we can do better. That's just chump change if what you're saying is true."

"What do you think I should do, then?"

Jeremy smiled. "Finally, you see the value of the Jeremy Meister."

Quinn rolled his eyes. "Don't let it go to your head."

"It's obvious. Isn't it? If you can loop in time, you don't have to remember everything from the future. Just repeat the day over a few times to find the things you can use for cash or influence, like sports matches, stock prices, and other stuff. That's how we can make a killing, get hot girls to love us, and invent cool stuff from the future."

"*If* I can still loop time. I think I should be able to get back to the future, anyway, but what if this was just a one-way trip and I can't?" Quinn asked.

"That's where your future info comes in, the bigger and

more recent stuff the better. Even if we change the timeline, most big things won't change, at least if they're close enough to the present. It won't be as good as time-looping, but it's still huge."

"Things always get screwed up in the movies, though. Time travelers usually find a way to draw too much attention to themselves. They end up getting in trouble with the cops or criminals or something, or they break time, or time finds a way to reverse everything," Quinn said.

August 7th, 2021
Day 1.
7:32 a.m.

Vladimir and two large men lifted the odd-shaped, hefty box. The three of them kept an eye out for onlookers as they carted the heavy container for transport.

Vladimir had olive skin and rough eyes. "This should do it," he said in a thick Russian accent.

He wore an Italian suit that clearly one wouldn't wear to move such an object. The police report would have read: two muscular men in black helped a nicely dressed majordomo move a suspicious object. Still, the Russian knew this before-hand, and he was cocksure enough not to care.

The youngest henchman grinned. "Serves them right," he added in Russian.

"Keep your mouth shut," Vladimir replied.

Inside the box, a chrome sphere with numerous pistons and levers twisted and spun like an old mechanical clock.

"I honestly think the only thing that's going to happen is I'm going to get to keep the five bucks. But if it's true, maybe you were right about what you said the last time we watched *Back to the Future*," Jeremy said.

"You mean about making a new timeline in a brand-new parallel universe, a fork in the multiverse?"

"Exactly. If your multiverse idea is true, then there wouldn't be a paradox because a new timeline would be created, and you would just be surfing the timeline in a brand-spanking-new parallel world. People always talk about not being able to travel back in time and change things because of paradoxes. This takes care of that."

"The 'I killed my grandfather in the past, so how could I be alive to go back and kill my grandfather if I was never born?' problem."

"Exactly. The old timeline would still be there, unchanged. You just took a side street. Problem solved, and you can still change things and benefit from your knowledge of the future," Jeremy said.

"There's still a bunch of problems, though," Quinn said.

"Like what?"

"I still don't know how or why I traveled through time. And what about being able to return back to the same future? If I'm on a different fork in the multiverse, my future will be different in this universe's timeline. I see how I can trace back my steps, but what about switching lanes in the future?"

"What do you mean?"

"If I go back to save Logan, maybe the future will be

different. I might not even work for him anymore. What if I just screwed things up by letting myself move another day forward instead of looping yesterday like I looped August seventh, 2021. Maybe I just switched forks in the multiverse, and I won't get back to my original location."

"*If* you're traveling through time at all. You could just be nuts," Jeremy said.

"I'm not crazy."

"Does a crazy person *know* if they're crazy?"

"That's not the problem, and this isn't a dream."

"How can you be so sure?"

"I know what a dream is like, even a realistic one. You're talking to me right now. You're not dreaming, are you?" Quinn asked.

"No, but…"

"The real issue is *why* I looped and traveled through time in the first place. Will it stop? What if I get stuck and can't go back? What happens if I screw things up, and it just so happens the days don't repeat anymore? I'll be stuck in a messed-up timeline. What if your plans to become rich, famous, and get lots of hot girls puts us in hot water? And what happens if I die?"

"I guess there's only one way to find out. Let's shoot for the moon and see what happens."

"You sure that's smart?"

"Let us assume for a moment," Jeremy said, in his best version of a British accent, "that what you are saying is indeed true."

Quinn shook his head.

"Then the only course of action is to move forward with the best course of action." Jeremy nodded as if to himself, placing the end of his pencil in his mouth as if it were a pipe.

"Which means exactly what?"

"Do I have to spell everything out for you? Make the best choice like each day is your last and you don't get to repeat it. Live it like you would any normal day, but with the knowledge of what you know."

"That's not completely bad advice."

"It's brilliant advice," Jeremy replied.

"What should I do about the future?"

"Here are my seven little rules: one, don't get arrested. Two, don't end up in the hospital. Three, use what you know to benefit you. Four, help other people if you can. Five, don't tell people you can travel through time. Six, have an excuse for every reason you do something. And seven, memorize your excuses before you need them so you don't screw up under pressure."

"What if I still can't save my boss, Logan?"

"You can't save everyone."

Logan wasn't the only person Quinn wanted to save. "Maybe not, but I'm going to find a way to save him."

"You already tried half a dozen times. Maybe saving Logan isn't going to happen. Or maybe the only way you can save him is by living your life in this timeline."

Was that the answer? Was reliving the last twenty-two years the only way to save Logan? Would that be true for each person he wanted to save?

It felt like too much effort. Still, there was something inviting about Quinn's current time and place, not to mention the chance to put things right.

August 7th, 2021
Day 5.
7:32 a.m.

The soft patter woke Quinn from his dream.

CHAPTER 6

QUINN JUMPED TO attention, threw on his clothes, connected his phone to the charger, then hopped onto his laptop to do a quick search of any possible timeline changes. It was time to see if the changes held from the past and if he could finally save Logan.

He lived in the same wrecked apartment with the same computer password. After a few minutes of reading through his emails and web surfing, he saw no recognizable differences in the timeline.

Still, he'd seen too many time-travel shows when characters thought everything remained the same after returning from the past, only to have unknown relatives or newly discovered enemies ambush them a few scenes later.

Quinn dialed the cops while he visited a few historical sites and looked up key events in the last two decades.

"I know this might sound crazy, but I want to report a possible attack. I overheard a couple of suspicious-looking men with foreign accents. I didn't catch everything, but I heard something about crashing a large truck into an intersection."

Quinn waited in silence.

"Go on."

"I heard them say the words 'truck bomb' and the names of a few major streets," Quinn said as he filled them in on the details.

"Anything else?"

"I think you better hurry. I got the sense that whatever they're doing, it's happening now."

"You got all that from a conversation you barely overheard?"

"Yeah. You know, body language and whatnot. Are you going to be able to do something right away?" Quinn asked.

"I'll relay the information to my captain."

"How long will it take?"

"Don't worry. We'll get to the bottom of this, one way or another."

Quinn hung up the phone and made another call.

"Meredith, this is Quinn. I need to speak to Logan. It's about his mother."

"He's in a meeting, but I can take a message."

"Fine, Meredith. Do *you* want to tell him his mother died, or should I?"

The line went silent. Quinn wiped the sweat from his brow. There was some commotion, followed by a series of clanks on the other end.

"This is Logan. What's going on, Quinn?"

"I'm sorry I had to do it this way, Logan, but your life depends on it. No one died—not yet, anyway. Just make sure you don't leave the building for the next half hour," Quinn said.

"You're not making any sense. What are you trying to say exactly?"

"I'm saying that if you walk out of the building, you're going to die. I don't want you to get hurt, I really don't."

"It almost sounds like you're threatening me. Does this have to do with the important meeting I have across the street? Did someone get to you?" Logan asked.

"What meeting across the street? No. Of course not; nothing like that. I can't explain how I know. I just do. You're going to have to trust me. Something's going to happen any second now, and the only way to stay safe is if you don't go outside. Just wait a few more minutes. That's all I'm asking, just a few minutes. Make an excuse or reschedule if you have to. The meeting's not worth your life."

"You're still not making any sense. If this is some kind of joke, it isn't funny. You're not hungover, are you? Valentino didn't finally convince you to go out and get drunk with him last night, did he? If you need to take a personal day, this is a bad time to do it."

"Logan, I'm not hungover. This isn't a joke. I'm dead serious. You're more than just my boss. We've been friends for a long time, and that's why I'm doing this. If I need to cash in some of those chips so that you can give me this one, then I'm cashing in. Please."

"Okay, Quinn. I'll humor you this time. I'll reschedule the meeting and wait this out. But whatever this is, you better have a good reason. I just stuck out my neck for you on this deal. This meeting, and the one across the street's for you, Quinn. You need this as much as I do."

"What deal?"

"I'm putting together a team for a project. I was just in the middle of convincing my dad and the board to let you lead it."

Quinn paused. "I don't know what to say."

"Me neither. I wish I knew what you were going on about right now. I hope you're not in some kind of trouble."

Quinn thought about Jeremy's warning not to tell people he could travel through time. No one would believe him, anyway. Logan would think he was crazy.

"Logan, I overheard something earlier today. I called the police about a possible terrorist attack near the office."

"And you're just telling me this now? If that's true, shouldn't we be getting the heck out of here?"

"No. You need to stay there. It's not that kind of attack."

"It's not what kind of attack? What aren't you telling me?"

"I told you. You're going to have to trust me. I don't have all the details yet. Just stay there. I already talked to the police. Just stay inside the building."

Quinn walked to his window and opened the curtains. He stared at his neighbor's expensive new import with the candy-apple finish. He walked back to his computer and hunted for any information that might be useful if he made it back to the past, things like stock prices and box scores. He still wasn't sure if, or how long, changes to the timeline would stick or if he was surfing different paths in the multi-verse, so he'd take whatever advantage he could grab in the few moments he had.

A few minutes later, police sirens blared.

A couple of intersections uptown from Logan's office, the police erected barricades. Half a dozen police cruisers waited behind the cordoned-off street.

A low-pitched echo reverberated throughout the area. Vibrations rattled through the bones of the immobile officers. At first, all they could see was smoke and something gray and black just beneath their line of sight, and then the top of a large truck revealed itself as it barreled toward them.

"This is it," the police captain said as he drew his gun. The other cops followed suit.

The rubber and metal squeaked, like nails on a chalkboard. The truck slowed, but not fast enough. The wheels hit the curb, and inertia propelled the trailer forward.

"Everyone, get back!" the captain shouted as he motioned his officers to move out of the way. It was too late.

The bodies of blue-uniformed NYPD lay motionless, strewn across the asphalt.

Smoke billowed from broken pipes. Water spewed in the air from a main break.

The shaking rattled Valentino, who leaned against the window one floor below Logan's office and then turned toward the direction of the officers.

On every floor, by every window, from every building in the area, people gawked at the dead officers, who resembled rag dolls tossed aside by a finicky, bored child.

Several police cruisers pulled in front of Quinn's driveway. A shadow appeared from Quinn's neighbor's window between an opening in the curtains.

Officer Channing exited his black-and-white Ford Interceptor. Two officers caught up with him as they approached Quinn's front door.

"Police! Open up. We have a warrant."

The vibration knocked down a picture frame that rested on a nearby table. Quinn's skin turned pale. Officer Channing turned Quinn around, cuffed, and Mirandized him.

"Looks like I already broke one of Jeremy's rules," Quinn said.

"Who's Jeremy?" Officer Channing asked.

Half an hour later, Quinn's head throbbed. He felt like he was on a merry-go-round. Chains tethered Quinn's cuffed wrists to the cold interrogation table. An impersonal mirror stared back at him.

Officer Channing carried in the odor of stale coffee and pastries as he stepped through the door and tossed a yellow notepad on the table. He glared at Quinn, then sat down.

CHAPTER 7

"YOU SAID YOU overheard a couple of suspicious-look-ing men talking about crashing a large truck near your office building."

"That's right. I did what I was supposed to do. I warned you about it, so why are you holding me like I'm some kind of criminal?" Quinn replied.

Officer Channing squinted his eyes and tilted his head.

"You *are* a criminal," he said as he gripped his pen and pressed it against the notepad.

"This is stupid. You know I'm not a criminal. Why are you holding me here?"

"I *don't* know that. But I'll tell you what I *do* know. First, you called to report a truck bomb. Second, the attack took place outside *your* office building. But the third thing is what bothers me the most. How did you know it was going to happen in the first place?"

"I told you. I overheard some guys talking, so I called the cops. It's that simple."

"Don't you think it's a little strange they would be talking about something like that, out in the open, risking anyone hearing their plans? Sounds too ridiculous to believe. And I *don't* believe it. I don't know why you told us. I'm still trying to find out why, but I can assure you I will. So, you better start cooperating."

Quinn thought about the seven rules of time travel that Jeremy had told him the previous day.

"All right. You got me. I'm a time traveler. I've been looping through time trying to save my boss since he died in the attack the first time. I've been trying to save him ever since. That, and not get arrested or sent to the hospital. It's *Groundhog Day*, and I need to fix what happened so I can move forward. At least that's what I think I'm doing."

Officer Channing grimaced.

"You think this is a joke? You think that dozens of my men lying dead on the asphalt is funny? You're one sick guy. You know that? The worst kind of human."

"Then stop questioning me. I told you. I overheard them talking about the attack, and I did my civic duty and called the police. That's it."

"And how did these men look, exactly? Were they Middle Eastern, Asian, Black, Russian?"

Quinn said nothing. The door opened.

"Quinn, is it? You can call me Kate," she said. Her hair was almost exactly the same as the first time they met except that it lacked the curls he'd noticed in their first encounter. He wondered what other changes he'd made in the short time he'd been in the current universe's timeline.

"What he's trying to say is that we have your entire block on camera. Several cameras in the area, including your neighbors and the convenience store across the street, show you in your home the entire morning. How is it that you could hear this conversation without stepping one foot outside?"

Quinn exhaled. "I'm psychic."

Officer Channing shook his head. He reminded Quinn of a gorilla as he dwarfed Officer Kate in size and stature.

Quinn was a slouch by comparison, and he was sure it made Officer Channing want to punch him even more. Quinn straightened up and buttoned his black suit jacket up before he spoke.

"I knew it. You're in on this attack. How many more do you have planned? Who's helping you? The call was just a distraction. Wasn't it? You have something bigger planned, don't you?" Officer Channing asked.

"Listen, you've got nothing to hold me on. I'm tired, and I'm not feeling well," Quinn said.

"You're not going anywhere until we learn what you know and how you know it."

"You can't do that."

"We can hold you for several days if we need to, on suspicion of terrorism."

"Hold on just a second. Is this what I get for trying to save lives, trying to help people? Are you going to sit here and try to destroy me because you're too lazy to go out and find the real criminals behind this?"

"Quinn, that's exactly what we're trying to do. The truck that crashed, it was unregistered with phony plates. We just got word from the sole officer who survived the scene that the truck was empty, that is except for a package that was left inside. Someone used a metal rod to pin down the gas," Kate said.

"What's in the package?" Officer Channing asked. Quinn said nothing.

"The bomb squad has a robot checking it as we speak, but we're still not sure what it is. It doesn't conform to any known design. We can't find a way to open it, and it's covered in an unknown alloy that's blocked our imagers from seeing what's inside," Kate said.

"I honestly have no idea what's in the package. This is the first time I've heard about it. I don't know who's responsible for the truck or the terrorist attack," Quinn said.

"But don't you? Who were the men you were referring to in the phone call? We know you didn't overhear them, but maybe they're part of your crew. If you can give us the names of the people you're working with, maybe, just maybe we can work something out. I'm sure a sensitive man like yourself would feel more comfortable in a nice minimum-security lockup. Copping a plea is the best chance you've got," Officer Channing said.

Quinn had the dumb luck to lie about what he didn't know to elicit a response, only to have his lie match what had actually happened.

"I get a phone call, don't I?"

"You'll get a phone call when we're good and ready."

"You want me to cooperate, don't you? Let me have my phone call now, or I'm going to lawyer up."

Kate gave Officer Channing a look of approval.

"Fine, we'll give you five minutes. After that, you need to start talking."

Kate escorted Quinn to the pay phone down the hall.

"Valentino, is Logan okay?"

"I don't think I'm supposed to be talking to you, but yeah, Logan's fine."

"Thank God. Wait, what? Why aren't you supposed to be talking with me?"

"The office is crawling with cops. They're asking everybody questions about you like you're involved or something.

Logan said you warned him before the truck crash. What's going on?"

"Doesn't matter. Not anymore. At least now I know I can save Logan."

"You can *save Logan*? You're not making any sense."

"I know I sound crazy. The cops don't have a clue what's going on. I don't know everything, either, but you've got to trust me. They're grasping at straws. That's all this is. I just have to learn how to save myself after a few tries."

Officer Channing hung up the phone. The room went black.

Quinn lifted his head from the interrogation table.

The air was suffocating, the light dim, and the wall clock was missing.

Officer Channing gave Quinn a big smile, enjoyed a slow bite of a glazed doughnut, and washed it down with lukewarm coffee.

"Welcome back. You slipped and hit your head. Sorry about that. How ya feeling? Getting thirsty?"

"You want me to talk. Fine, I'll talk. Whatever happened to Cameron?" Quinn asked.

"Cameron?"

Quinn honestly didn't know what had happened with Cameron and Scott Channing after high school. In the short time he scoured the web before he got pinched, he hadn't found out anything about her. It was a long shot, but he hoped he might learn something that might be useful in the past.

Officer Channing stroked his lips and nodded. "So, you finally recognize me. I knew you were a punk in the ninth grade. I just didn't know how much of a punk until you said whatever you said to Cameron that made her want to break up with me."

"I never said anything about you to Cameron. I thought you were a douche, but I never told her that. I wish I had."

"I'm not going to have this conversation with you now. The job you stole from me… Cameron… That's all gone. The only thing that matters is what's in that box, and what's coming next."

"What job? And what do you mean 'stole Cameron'?"

"*Your* job. The same position you have now, that was supposed to be mine."

"Are you serious? It's a decent job and all, but not all that impossible to get. Besides, what do you care? You have a job."

"I guess a punk like you wouldn't understand. My mother arranged an interview with Logan, several years back. But then you went and did some voodoo magic on him, and then he turned me down without even a proper interview. I still can't believe it. She was the best executive assistant he ever had. He should've at least kept the interview out of respect."

"Your mother's *Meredith*?" All of a sudden, the NYPD mug made sense to Quinn even if her Beanie Baby collection didn't.

"Don't play games with me. I know you already knew that. Didn't you? Was this your plan all along? Get in tight with Logan so you can plan your strategy, lay the ground-work with the connections you have in the area?"

"Really? You're the one who sounds crazy now."

"I sound crazy? You're the one calling the police about a terrorist attack by men who you supposedly overheard. *You're* the mental one, and I'm going to nail you to the ground, you janky little punk."

"The only *connections* I have are with a small sales team.

But that doesn't matter. Does it? You're desperate. You going to beat me like you did last time?"

"*Last* time?" Kate asked.

"Ahh, never mind that. Just find out what's in that package, because I have no idea," Quinn replied.

"Then why did you say you would talk to us?" Kate asked.

"I did what I needed to do to get the phone call. You're wasting time with me."

Officer Channing leaned toward Quinn, gritted his teeth, and slammed the coffee cup on the table.

"Tell us what's in the package."

August 7th, 2021
Day 1.
7:33 a.m.

The chrome sphere's levers twisted and spun. It was nearly sixteen years in the making. A secret commission of scientists and leaders who wanted to change the status quo designed it. The device would do it. The only problem was that it didn't work the way they had expected.

It would have, if not for the other thing. That made all the difference.

August 7th, 2021
Day 5.

After dusk.

Quinn thought about Jeremy and the conversation they had the first time on August 16. Quinn had more information this time. Jeremy just might believe him.

CHAPTER 8

QUINN SQUINTED AS the sun's summer rays glared through the sliver in his curtains. He inspected the clock, his hands, and the mattress before he threw on his clothes and biked over to Jeremy's place.

Quinn filled Jeremy in on the details of his trip back to the future and what had happened last time on August 16th. The seventeenth hadn't arrived, so Jeremy didn't get to see the earthquake for proof. He listened to Quinn, and then let loose.

"C'mon. Not good enough. If you really went back to the future, prove it right now."

Quinn thought for a second.

"It's not like there's a list somewhere of what happens every second of every day, so you're just going to have to wait 'til four thirty."

"What happens at four thirty?"

"The stock market's going to close at exactly 11,046.79.

I doubt I did anything big enough in the last few hours to change that, so let's see if I'm right."

"Fine. So, what's the plan now?"

The clasp of the Wall Street gavel on TV alerted them to the market's closing bell. The ticker tape read 11,051.12.

"I knew it. You're wrong. You're so full of it."

"Look again. It takes a minute for the last few transactions to settle and the market numbers to complete."

The closing average read 11,047.11. A few seconds later, 11,046.79.

"Told you. Now, what are the odds that I'd be able to tell you the exact close of the Dow, down to the very penny?"

"It could still be a trick. Just not sure how you did it."

"It's not a trick, but you'll believe me tomorrow when the seven-point-six earthquake hits Turkey and kills tens of thousands of people. It'll cause a seven-foot tsunami that kills another one hundred and fifty-five people."

Jeremy's cheeks flushed, and his eyes widened.

August 17th, 1999
Day 1.

Quinn woke up to a loud commotion in the living room.

Jeremy squeezed his way in after Quinn's mom opened the door. He rushed into Quinn's room and knocked him out of bed.

"Did you see the news this morning? You were right. I can't believe it."

"Come on, man, it's too early for this."

"You know what this means?"

Quinn's mom trotted in behind Jeremy. "What's all this commotion about, boys?"

"Jeremy's just being a goofball."

"Just make sure you're not late for your first day of high school."

"This is going to be awe…some," Jeremy said once she shut the door.

Quinn smiled.

Jeremy's heart pounded. He jumped up and down a couple times before he sat down and caught his breath.

"We still have things to learn. It's not all going to be fun and games."

"I get that, but still… This is unbelievable."

"Just calm down a bit and take your advice from yesterday. We don't want to draw too much attention to ourselves until I discover how to fix things in the future."

"You did that already, didn't you?"

"Almost. In case you forgot, I still got arrested. I need to find a way to save Logan and *not* get arrested, or die, for that matter."

"Can't you just let me revel in the moment for a bit? My best friend is a time traveler. Oh yeah. I can't believe I just said that. And you know about that list you mentioned, the one that tells you what's going to happen every second of every single day?"

"Yeah?"

"You should make one."

For the next hour, Jeremy spouted every time travel fantasy that popped into his head. It annoyed Quinn on the surface, but he wanted to do at least half the things Jeremy mentioned.

After they arrived at school, Quinn looked over his schedule, and they went their separate ways.

Quinn was a convincing ninth grader, given that he had

forgotten most names and the location of his classes, the first one being English.

Quinn always hated how time-travel movies showed people remembering everything from their past. Quinn had trouble remembering things from last week, let alone a couple of decades.

The room was sterile and uninspiring. He sat down in the second-to-last row, right next to her. Quinn fell into his default staring mode and gazed out the window, or at least pretended to.

"Hi. I'm Cameron."

"Quinn," he replied as he held out his hand.

Cameron chuckled, then gave him a firm handshake. She wore her new first-day-of-school clothes. Her auburn hair hung in a ponytail, and even in a pink cardigan and jeans made her appear as angelic as ever. "Nice to meet you, Mr. Quinn."

"He means Doormat," Scott said. "You should probably wash your hands. I saw Doormat digging in his butt after he hopped off his tricycle in the courtyard."

Scott chewed on a toothpick. He looked different, better. He was thinner but looked more like a senior than a freshman.

"Some things never change. Do they, Mr. Channing? What's up with the shades, anyway?"

"Shut your hole, Doormat. And how do you know my last name? Are you some kind of queer perv?"

The one thing Quinn didn't do was waste hours thinking about a witty comeback to Scott's juvenile and cheesy insults, but he almost wished he had, perhaps in the next time loop—if he had the time. "I'm not a perv," was all he could muster.

"So you *admit* you're a queer?"

"Dude, you're a bully, and everything you say is total bunk."

"You're a…"

The teacher walked in and interrupted. Quinn kept his eyes forward, but let his mind wander and play out dozens of scenarios. Quinn thought about how many times he used to think about high school, especially when he was in college. It used to matter, but as he grew older, it mattered less and less.

The trivial events in high school were just that, trivial. But he couldn't help feeling that logic flew out the window when you were stuck in a square cage with a couple dozen infantile knuckleheads and an education system designed to produce drones instead of free thinkers.

Jeremy had grasped that concept long before Quinn, but the reality of human psychology affected Quinn at the moment. You become like the sum of the people you hang around, and at that moment, most of those people were morons.

Before long, it was lunch.

"Oh my god," Quinn said.

"What is it? What's happened?"

"I'd forgotten about these horrid pizza squares. The orange welfare cheese is the worst."

"Did they ever prove the cafeteria was serving horse meat?" Jeremy asked.

"Funny you should ask. It's not horse meat, but it's not a hundred percent beef, either. Parents sued the school district for lying about the menu. Someone discovered it was a meat product."

"Meat product?" Jeremy said before he spat it out.

"You'd be surprised. In the more distant future, people will actually like the stuff."

Jeremy squinted his eyes and changed the subject. "So, did you see her?"

"Cameron? Yeah. I said hello."

"That's it?"

"It was hard to say much else with that douchebag, Scott Channing, in the room."

Quinn eyed Scott, who sat in the adjacent row. He still couldn't get past Scott's shades. Quinn felt they mirrored his attempt to hide his true nature—a dirtbag.

"Who cares about that guy? You can wipe the floor with him with what you know."

"Yeah. I think he deserves it, too, but he's not the worst I've seen, just a bit misguided."

"He sounds like a jerk to me."

"He is a jerk, especially now. But he's lost, like a lot of people. I kinda feel sorry for him, especially after the conversation I had with him in the future. I mean, I'm not sorry Cameron dumped his sorry ass, but he almost seemed like a wounded animal."

"I think you should have some fun with him. Make him fall flat on his face and eat it or something."

"As much fun as that would be, it won't help anything. We've got a job to do, and we can have fun in other ways."

"Suit yourself, but what are you going to do about Cameron? And don't tell me nothin'."

"Not sure yet, but I don't need to do much, just make a few tweaks here and there."

Jeremy thought for a moment.

"Where are you going?" Quinn asked.

Quinn shook his head when he saw it coming. Jeremy

raced over to Scott's table, picked up Scott's food tray, and slammed it in his face. Jeremy ignored the fact that Scott was easily twice his size.

Jeremy smiled. "How do you like them apples?"

Quinn raced over. "Dude, what the heck is wrong with you?"

"It's okay. We get a"—Scott clocked him square in the jaw—"do-over," Jeremy muttered before he was out cold, sprawled out on the floor.

"Want some of this too, Doormat?"

Quinn backed up and rubbed his forehead. Security escorted Jeremy to the health room. Drool spilled down his chin. Once Jeremy was fully conscious, security escorted them both to the principal's office.

"Don't do that. We're not going to get very far with any sort of plan if you keep pulling stunts like this. You're going to get us killed. What happened to all that talk about not doing anything that will get you arrested or put in the hospital?"

"I was talking about you. You've already saved Logan's life, remember? I just wanted to know what it felt like."

"And how did it feel?"

"Besides the pounding headache? Amazing!"

"So, boys," the principal began after she walked into the office. "Starting fights on the first day of school. Off to a great start. I'm sure your parents will be pleased, especially when they find out you're suspended for three days."

"Only three days?" Jeremy asked. "You know, since I have three days off, I was wondering if maybe you and I could go out for dinner. I hear there's this sweet place around the corner."

Quinn sighed.

The principal sneered. "I'm sorry. Did I say three days? I meant five."

Jeremy had the same courage in the future. He just had more of it now when he thought there would be no consequences. Quinn had never understood why Jeremy had dropped out of college and started his solo consulting gig. Quinn wasn't surprised Jeremy had been so successful, just that he had the balls to quit college in the first place.

"And are you sure *you* get a do-over?" Quinn asked, a bit too late.

August 17th, 1999
Day 2.

Quinn woke up to a loud commotion in the living room.

Jeremy squeezed his way in after Kathy opened the door. He rushed into Quinn's room and knocked him out of bed.

"Did you see the news this morning? You were right. I can't believe it."

Quinn was still in his pajamas when he jumped up, shut the door, locked it behind Jeremy, and then pinned him to the wall.

"You better not do what you did last time."

"What do you mean? What did I do? Get off me."

"You slammed the food tray into Scott Channing's face at lunch. You got creamed, and then you hit on the principal. We got a five-day suspension."

"Sweet."

"No, it's not. That's the kind of thing that's going to get us killed. Before you get any more bright ideas like that, make sure you talk to me first."

"Don't be such a buzzkill. How often does someone get

this kind of opportunity? *Never* is the answer. You better believe I'm going to take advantage of it."

Quinn shook his head.

"I might be able to save you in a pinch, but if you bring your crap out on both of us, I don't know what will happen. We need to be smart about this."

"Fine. Whatever. I'll talk to you next time." Jeremy didn't believe what he had just said, at least not completely. "So, what's our next move?"

"Next move with what?" Quinn asked.

"With saving the world and making a gazillion dollars. You went back to the future, right? That's what you said yesterday, or was that the day before yesterday? You looked up stock prices and box scores. Do you remember enough of them to make a killing in the next few weeks?"

"Yeah, and I have an idea."

CHAPTER 9

"SWEET. WHAT IS it?" Jeremy asked.

"I still need to fix things in the future, but while I'm here, we're going to stop 9/11. Not sure if it will stick or if it will be erased, but it would be a crime not to try to save all those people," Quinn replied.

"I remember you saying something about that before. What's 9/11? And why not try to save people from the earthquake? Don't more people die?"

"If I try to save people from natural disasters, they'll think I'm a loon. I won't get very far, and I'll draw way too much attention to myself. One thing at a time," Quinn replied.

"On September eleventh, 2001, terrorists hijacked and crashed planes into the Twin Towers here in New York City. Another plane hit the Pentagon, and a fourth plane that was originally headed for the Capitol building or the White House crashed in Pennsylvania. Thousands of people died, and everything changed forever," Quinn added.

"Wow. That sucks."

"Yeah. It sucks really bad. There was this sick feeling in the pit of my stomach that lasted for months after it happened. A lot of people felt the same way. It was like a cloud just hung over everyone. But that was nothing compared to people who were actually there and lost their lives, or the people who were in the streets under a massive cloud that covered the city after the towers fell. I knew several people who died in those towers. My dad lost a lot. Everyone we knew at school knew someone who had died there."

"This may sound terrible, but I have to ask. Did anything good come out of the whole thing?"

Quinn thought for a moment, then said, "For a second, everyone came together. Politics didn't matter. The country united for the first time in a long time, and then it was gone. Right after the attack, I remember the cost of flag pins shot up on eBay, from pennies to like five bucks. I knew things were back to normal once the price came down."

"How long did that last?" Jeremy asked.

"It wasn't more than a few weeks. Then it was just the malaise."

"Malaise?"

"Just a feeling that everyone was royally screwed and nobody could do anything about it. We came together again when we attacked al-Qaeda in Afghanistan. But then the war spread to Iraq, and soldiers stayed there for years. They called it a quagmire."

"Speak English."

"The year I left, it was the worst it's ever been, maybe since the Civil War. There was the pandemic, and then the riots. The country was so divided. Childhood friends and family disowned each other if they voted for who they thought was the wrong person. It almost felt like living in George Orwell's *1984*. Sad. We have to stop it."

"It should be a piece of cake."

"Don't be so sure. I still haven't fixed the future yet. I don't think it will be as easy as you think. I've been throwing around a few ideas in my head. The safest might be just to send letters to the FBI, the Pentagon, the NSA, along with the airlines of the planes that crashed. We'd have to be careful about what we say and how we send the letters, but it could work."

"What do we have to be careful about?"

"I don't want them getting the idea we're the ones threatening them or blackmailing them somehow. That's happened too many times in the future, and I'm still trying to learn how to get around it. The best way to handle the letters would be to send them anonymously and discreetly, so they can't trace them back to us."

He continued. "And I don't want the terrorists to get tipped off. If they do, they could just change their plans. I also don't want the government thinking that we're the ones responsible for the anthrax letters."

"The anthrax letters?"

"Another attack that happened, right after 9/11. The FBI thinks it was a government expert, some guy named Bruce Edwards Ivins, but there was some uncertainty about the whole thing."

The bell rang. Within seconds of spotting Scott, Jeremy snuck up behind him and clipped both his legs. Scott was lying flat down on his backside.

Jeremy grinned, saying, "This is awesome."

But Quinn sneered, saying, "What the heck, Jeremy?"

Scott jumped up. "Why, you little…"

Jeremy didn't give him the chance. He was already down the hall and had found a custodial room to sneak into. He locked it. Scott caught up fast and pounded on the door. "I'm going to kill you, you little weasel."

From inside the closet, Jeremy grinned. Adrenaline pumped through his veins. His body warmed.

"What are you doing, Scott? Who's in there?" the principal asked, once she saw the commotion.

"This little prick is the one that started it. He's the one you need to do something about."

She knocked on the door. "Whoever's in there, it's time to come out. We're going to take a little trip to the office."

Jeremy unlocked the door, peeked through the crack, then opened it once he saw that the principal had blocked Scott's path to his face.

Quinn, standing by, shook his head. Half an hour later, Jeremy emerged from the office with a smile.

"What the heck, man? Don't you learn?"

"It's okay, Quinn. I got only three days off from school instead of five, and you're in the clear. We can use that time to change things and have some fun."

"You haven't changed much, you know that? And unfortunately, you don't remember the question I asked you last time."

Before Jeremy could process what Quinn said, Scott shoved Jeremy in the stomach, hard.

Jeremy shuffled back. Quinn stared at Scott, who responded with a head fake and a snark.

"You want some of this, too, Doormat?"

Quinn turned to Jeremy. "You all right?" Quinn asked.

Jeremy stood hunched over. "Yeah," he said.

Quinn yanked Jeremy out of earshot of everyone else. "I didn't want to tell you this before because I wasn't sure how it would affect the future, but you need to know. Otherwise,

I think you're going to keep pulling these stunts and ruin everything before we can make any changes."

"What? What is it?"

"The reason I couldn't ask for your help in the future is because you're not in the future."

"What do you mean?"

"You're dead, Jeremy. You were fooling around doing something stupid, and you got yourself killed. Just like you're doing now. You're one of the people I want to save."

"What did I do?"

"Does it matter? You made stupid choices all the time, like the one you just made. You're going to have to stop doing that kind of crap. We've got serious work to do, and if you don't stick to the plan, we're not going to be able to save everyone."

"But you've got endless do-overs."

"What happened to your seven rules of time travel? You know, you have great ideas, but sometimes you're terrible at execution. And we don't know that we have endless do-overs. It could stop anytime. Follow your own advice. And like I said before, we don't know if *you* get the do-overs."

Quinn went on. "We're going to attend all our classes, stay out of trouble, study, and when we get out of school, we're going to save the world. Yeah, we're going to make a little cash on the side, but we're going to keep our heads down."

"What is wrong with you? This is a once-in-a-lifetime opportunity, and *that's* your plan? I get we need to keep our heads down, but I mean, c'mon."

"Do you want to end up miserable and unhappy like Biff or like Marty McFly?"

"Neither. This isn't the movies. We can do whatever we want."

"No. We can't. I'll repeat myself for the last time. I don't know *if* or *when* this time loop is going to stop, so we can't do anything that could keep us from doing what we need to do or get us killed."

"Honestly, Quinn. That could be anything. Did you ever see that episode of *Star Trek TNG* where Q gave Captain Picard his own do-over? Remember what happened? He played it safe, and he ended up a low-ranked nobody instead of the captain. Is that what you want? But that's your life in the future. Isn't it? Did you forget already? No girlfriend, and unhappy with your job?"

"I'm not unhappy. Not exactly, anyway."

"Doesn't sound like you actually believe it."

"Easy for you to say now, but you're the one who's dead in the future."

"You're right. I screwed up. I admit it. I'm sorry, but from what you tell me, Scott deserved it. But fine. I get your point. I won't do something so obvious next time. But let me ask you this. Was I happy before I died? Did I like doing whatever it was that I was doing or was I miserable like you?"

Quinn stood silent. His face told Jeremy all he needed to know.

CHAPTER 10

QUINN ADMIRED CAMERON'S sophisticated updo, her kind eyes, and the way she bit her lips covered in pink lip gloss. Quinn turned to look away when Cameron saw him staring, but she saw him before he could pull it off.

"What happened with your friend back there?"

"Jeremy was just being a goofball. Sorry about that. Hey, I was thinking. What are you doing after school? Maybe you can hang out with us and play cards or something?"

Cards or something? Quinn thought to himself. He was doing it again—the same thing he had always done. But this was different. He wasn't trying to start anything with her. He just wanted to build his courage and become good friends even though he knew he wanted more. He was heartbroken they had lost touch as adults.

"Mmmm…maybe. Not sure what I'm doing yet."

"No problem. Maybe later if you get the chance."

Quinn shrugged it off and biked over to Jeremy's place after school was over. He was careful not to bring up his face-plant moment with Cameron.

"How was the walk of shame?" Quinn asked.

"You mean getting picked up from the principal's office by my parents? Not as bad as I thought it would be. You want to try it again?" Jeremy asked.

"Not a chance. I've got something better planned, anyway. I memorized a few stock prices for the next three months. I'm going to ask Dad to set up the account tomorrow. I'll try to warm him up to the idea later today."

"Think it'll work?"

"I hope so. If not, I could come back and try again, assuming that's possible. If I had a job, it wouldn't be that big of a deal. But we're going to need some serious coin to even get some basic stuff done, like catching a taxi."

Quinn continued talking. "I was thinking about what you said earlier. As much as I tried, I couldn't get it out of my head. I *have* played things too safe. I think I underestimated how much of your luck wasn't actually luck, but balls. I guess I didn't realize it before, but I've resented you for it. I'm sorry."

"I do have big balls," Jeremy replied.

August 7th, 2021
Day 1.
8:10 a.m.

"This better work. If it doesn't, you're both dead."

"You mean we're all dead," one of the henchmen replied in a thick accent.

"Don't worry, boss. It's all here. Everything's been connected and prepared."

"Where's Vladimir?" Smirnikoff asked.

"He said he needed to take care of something and would meet us at the checkpoint, but it doesn't matter. We prepped the truck and placed several backups nearby," the henchman said.

"What about the device?" Smirnikoff asked.

"Take a look for yourself."

It was a bright morning, and only the city's pollution stopped the men from being able to see a few of the morning stars still shining above. They were at the base of a condemned warehouse with a fire escape that gave them easy roof access when needed.

Smirnikoff ran his white-gloved finger across the plain box in a specific pattern. His men in blue coveralls glared as he touched the device.

The cover of the chrome sphere opened and gleamed. An external chronometer ticked in sync with a hollow tube that spanned the diameter of the device, like a handle on the center of a doughnut.

"What's that ticking sound? It shouldn't be ticking," Smirnikoff said.

"I think that's what Vladimir went to check."

The device emitted a blue hue and an electrical current that rotated around the handle. As seconds passed, it pulsed and shuddered, with each vibration increasing in strength.

"Something's wrong. It shouldn't be doing this."

Sweat slid off Smirnikoff's face onto the device. It disappeared as it neared the chrome surface.

"We don't have time to do anything about it. It's already set. That's what the other cluster told us. But everything was in order, boss. They filled the tube. All the exotic matter is there. It's ready to go."

"You're right about one thing. There's nothing we can do about it now," Smirnikoff replied.

He stepped back. The wind picked up as the chopper approached from the southeast.

"I'm sorry, boys, but there's only room for one of us."

One of the henchmen went for his gun, but not fast enough. A bead of sweat dripped from the henchman's brow just as Smirnikoff aimed his semi-automatic at his face, then pulled the trigger. He fell to the floor with a thud. All that was left was a blue jumpsuit, blood, and what used to be the man's face.

"You're safe," he said to the surviving henchman. "I need you to drive the truck. But don't worry. I'll send the chopper for you before it goes off."

The henchman ran down the fire escape as if his life depended on it because it did. Smirnikoff tossed a wad of cash toward him, then climbed into the chopper.

"Where to, boss?" the pilot asked.

"The only place that's safe."

August 17th, 1999
Day 2.
4:30 p.m.

"You've convinced me. I found a place called Ling's in New Haven that lets underage… I should say underage-*looking* boys like myself play for small change. But that's all we'll need. We can win a nickel here and there without drawing too much attention. We'll earn some driving-around money while we wait for Dad to hopefully set up the custodial account, then we can start making some real cash," Quinn said.

"Now you're speaking my language," Jeremy replied.

"The game's Texas Hold'em, no limit. I got good at it in

college, but I didn't have the advantage of looping time. I say we win a couple hundred, then walk away."

"That's it? A couple hundred?"

"Truth is, we may lose a couple hundred the first time. But if we get a do-over, it won't matter."

"Fine. Have it your way."

Quinn and Jeremy caught a whiff of something as they walked through Ling's shop doors. Vintage pinball machines, old arcade games, and dartboards covered the room closest to the entrance.

"What's that smell?" Jeremy asked.

"Not sure, but it was all over Chinatown whenever I grabbed takeout. Some kind of incense, I think," Quinn said as they trotted past a nylon curtain concealing the poker room in the back.

Chinatown was a hundred miles away, but Quinn learned about the other place when Valentino got the idea to drive there one weekend after he had scored a big bonus from Logan. The gambling houses in Manhattan were too scary, and Valentino hated Atlantic City.

Quinn had attempted to fit in when he was with Valentino, who owned every room he walked into. This time, he was with Jeremy, who wore a button-up polo shirt and a bucket hat, as if he were about to attend a boat show in Florida. Quinn felt as out of place as ever.

Jeremy eyed the joint like he was a kid in a candy store. There were games he didn't recognize with cards he couldn't read and round dice covered in Chinese markings.

Quinn trotted over to Ling, who ran the register in a small carved-out section of the dank room. She was in her fifties or sixties and short, but taller than both of them at their current age. She wore her black hair in a bun. Her aged skin still fared like alabaster, and she must have been an unparalleled beauty in her prime. She tilted her head down and waited for them to speak.

Quinn pushed a couple hundred through the small space underneath the bar-covered window that separated them.

"Here you go," she said as she handed them two rolls of chips.

"How are we going to play this?" Jeremy asked.

"I'll give you twenty to get your feet wet, but I'm playing with the rest."

Twenty minutes later, things took an unexpected turn.

Quinn went all-in on a pair of pocket kings, then busted.

"Rack 'em up," the dealer said.

Jeremy had a large stack of chips, and he was taking looks for it. He peeked at his first card—ace of spades. He was the first person to make a bet on the hand and raised. Fellow players sneered at the move.

"I'm getting sick of this," one of the regulars said. He was hefty, midfifties, and carried a distinctive odor that complemented his grumpy mood.

Half the table called Jeremy's raise out of curiosity, while the other half folded.

The dealer flopped over the first three cards. Jeremy won four grand on the hand with four aces. He looked at Quinn.

"We should get going," Quinn said.

"Where you off to so quickly, boys?" Ling asked as she walked by the table.

"It's a school night. We really should be getting home. Our parents will be pissed if we stay out past our curfew," Quinn replied. He didn't know what to do with his hands and was worried Ling picked up on his tell.

"You're big enough to play at the adult table. I'm sure

your parents won't be too upset, especially considering how much coin you're walking away with," she replied.

"That's kinda the point. We wouldn't want to lose it all on the next hand," Quinn said.

One of the players from the table stood up and blocked their path.

"What kind of crap are you boys trying to pull? You got cards up your sleeve or something?"

"No. We wouldn't be that stupid. I swear," Jeremy said.

Jeremy's hands trembled. This wasn't the ninth-grade locker room, and the man in front of him was three times Scott Channing's size.

"I'm not letting you go so easily."

The man reached for his pocket and revealed the silver handle of a semi-automatic pistol.

"Hey. You're not supposed to have those in here. Check them at the door. Remember?"

"Sorry, Ling. You never know what kind of help you're going to need from dirty scrubs like these."

Ling pulled out a vintage Smith and Wesson revolver.

"Hand it over right now, and leave those boys alone."

He stepped back.

"Slowly," she said.

He flipped the position of the gun and gave her the handle, barrel face down.

"The man has a point. Just to put his mind at ease, why don't you take off that jacket and empty your pockets," Ling said.

Quinn and Jeremy complied and dumped their keys and some folded piece of torn notebook paper with scribbled numbers on it.

"What's this?" Ling asked.

"Just guesses on a few games."

Ling squinted.

"Very detailed guesses," she said as the room fell silent.

"I'm going to take these numbers, just in case. But come back anytime. Old Stevey won't bother you again," she added.

Jeremy exhaled and glanced at Quinn. Both stood frozen until Ling prodded the chips from their hands and exchanged it for cash. Quinn sensed Jeremy's relief, but he couldn't help but remember *Back to the Future II*. He knew the rules were different or at least thought they were. But still, the butterflies in his stomach and rising pulse worried him.

Jeremy stole a glance in both directions. Then they slipped out the back exit.

"Holy shit. I can't believe we just did that," Jeremy said. "And we didn't even need to time travel."

Quinn worried that he just might have turned future Jeremy into a serial gambler.

"We might not be so lucky next time."

"But like you said, we don't need luck."

"As long as we don't get killed. It was looking dicey there for a while," Quinn replied.

"What do you think happens if you die?"

"Don't know, and don't want to find out. Not even by accident."

"What are we going to do with all this money?"

"Not sure yet, but I need to put some feelers out, and see if I can stop a few things from happening. 9/11 wasn't the first time terrorists blew things up. There's a ship called the *USS Cole* that was bombed in 2000. If we can stop that from happening, maybe that alone will stop 9/11. If they can catch the guy first, things might take care of themselves."

"How do you plan on doing that?"

"I have an aunt who was in military intelligence, or I should say *is* in military intelligence. She's a civilian contractor and used to be in the Navy. Dad said her commanders always passed her over for promotions, which is why she left. She's the perfect person to help."

"So now you want your dad to open up an account for your investments *and* talk to his sister about military intelligence?"

"I was hoping we could avoid the asking part. I think we should talk to her directly."

August 17th, 1999
Day 3.
4:57 p.m.

Quinn almost let it go after they cashed out the first day of the loop, but he wasn't sure how Ling's discovery of his numbers would impact the future. He couldn't risk her becoming Biff.

Quinn pushed a couple hundred through the small space underneath the bar-covered window that separated them.

"Here you go," Ling said.

Quinn took the chips.

"How are we going to play this?" Jeremy asked.

"I'll give you twenty to get your feet wet, but I'm playing with the rest."

Quinn still used the odds and made the right statistical calls. The men at the table, though, were just better at reading Quinn's face.

Twenty minutes later, Quinn busted, this time with pocket aces instead of pocket kings. It was harder than it looked to cheat at poker as a time traveler.

Every small action—from a squirm in a seat to words that hung half a second longer on players' tongues—changed things. Those differences influenced the movement of the dealer's hands and the precise moment he shuffled the cards, which in turn changed the order of the cards on the flop and in the players' hands.

Jeremy had beginner's luck, again. He raised on the big blind and played for an outside straight, which he didn't even know at the time. It didn't matter.

"All in," Jeremy said after the dealer flipped over the next card.

This time, they walked away with fifteen hundred, enough to annoy the players, but not enough to draw their ire.

"Not bad. Fifteen hundred bucks," Jeremy said.

"I need to talk to my aunt," Quinn replied.

AUGUST 18TH, 1999
DAY 1.
3:30 P.M.

"So, I hear there's this terrorist named Osama bin Laden."

"What do you know about Osama bin Laden?" Aunt Lisa asked.

"Just that he's a really bad guy."

"And how do you know that exactly?"

"I've heard of the ninety-three Trade Center bombing. I have to do a paper on military conflict and the impetus for war."

"Sounds like a pretty heavy topic for ninth grade," Aunt Lisa replied.

After his conversation with Aunt Lisa failed to make enough progress, Quinn returned to the future and looped nearly two dozen times just to find a specialist that could tell him everything about the terrorist communications network surrounding the *USS Cole* attack.

"So, I hear there's this terrorist named Osama bin Laden."

"What do you know about Osama bin Laden?" Aunt Lisa asked.

"I've been doing some research online. The ninety-three Trade Center bombing came up in a class discussion, so I decided to see if I can find anything out about it."

"You probably should be careful when doing that. Online information isn't exactly the most reliable, or safe. You could find yourself in some serious trouble."

"I know. I get that lecture from Dad all the time, but I came across something, some chat rooms on the dark web."

"Wait. What do you know about the dark web?"

"That's what I'm trying to tell you. I came across this bizarre chat group, so I followed a link pathway. I noticed a disturbing subthread written in code. It wasn't hard to crack, and you won't believe what I found."

Aunt Lisa squinted her eyes.

"You just watched *Hackers* again, didn't you?"

"I haven't seen that movie in over twenty years," Quinn replied.

"So, I hear there's this terrorist named Osama bin Laden."

"What do you know about Osama bin Laden?" Aunt Lisa asked.

"I've been doing some research online. The ninety-three Trade Center bombing came up in a class discussion, so I decided to do a character study. Figured I could take care of two class assignments with one.

"Anyway," he continued, "I found this thread after I clicked on a few links and ended up in some underground forum. It looks crazy, but what scared me the most was a few pictures I found. Here. Take a look for yourself."

Aunt Lisa glanced at the screen. She scrolled down one forum, and then another, picture after picture, and rant after rant. It was a hub of terrorist discussions and clusters of cells planted all across the globe.

"This is serious stuff," she said as she scribbled down the URLs of the site and a few subthreads. "I'll look into this, but I don't want you visiting this site again. This is the kind of thing that can get you killed, what your dad warned you about when surfing the web."

"I know, but I was just doing research, and I'm worried something bad is going to happen. I didn't believe it at first. It looked too bizarre to be real, but after a while, I started noticing that whatever they mentioned in this thread started happening in real life. There are things about future events and plans."

Lisa paused a few seconds before replying, "Show me."

Quinn sat down next to her, scrolled, and clicked until he found an implicating thread involving bin Laden that suggested a future attack on a military target in the Middle East.

"I'm going to have to tell your dad about this. I hope he doesn't have a heart attack."

CHAPTER 11

August 7th, 2021
Day 26.
7:32 a.m.

AS SOON AS he awoke, Quinn dialed Logan's number, intent on finding out more about the explosion and saving Logan's life.

"You need to sit down and listen closely to what I have to tell you." Quinn filled him in on the near future. After the last few loops, Quinn grew more convincing.

"Fine. I'll stay in the building, and I'll call the police to tell them what you told me."

Quinn ran two blocks and stole a senile neighbor's unlocked brown Datsun with keys in the ignition. He stepped on the gas and dropped all pretense of safety. He dented mailboxes and scratched cars in his mad dash to find the truck Officer Channing had mentioned during the interrogation.

A truck appeared after the last turn. Quinn felt something was off about the license plate and suspected it was fake. Three burly men locked up the back, and one of them walked toward the driver's side with a piece of plyboard long enough to reach the gas pedal.

Quinn's office building was a straight shot from where the truck rested. He inhaled, his pulse racing. He still wasn't sure what would happen if he got killed, but he couldn't wimp out forever.

Quinn approached the truck. "Hey, what are you guys doing?" Quinn asked.

The man closest to the driver's side aimed his gun at Quinn, then fired.

Quinn fell. He heard the gun again. Quinn laid motionless. The truck picked up speed, and the men ducked out into a side street.

Quinn grunted and pushed his body off the ground. He ripped open his white button-up shirt and removed the bulletproof vest he'd discovered in the prior few time loops. The impact had formed large tender red areas on his chest and torso. He lightly touched his skin, grimacing, happy he wouldn't stay there long enough for them to bruise.

He needed to leave earlier next time.

AUGUST 7TH, 2021
DAY 27.
7:32 A.M.

Quinn dialed Logan's number and explained the situation.

"Fine. It's completely nuts, but I'll take your advice," Logan said.

Quinn arrived at the intersection a minute earlier and hid from view. The extra time revealed that the men spoke Russian and gave Quinn a closer look at the box.

One of the men closed the back of the truck. The other took the plywood to the driver's side.

Quinn needed a gun.

August 7th, 2021
Day 28.
7:32 a.m.

Quinn dialed Logan's number, improving his explanation.

"Fine. It's nuts, but I'll do it," Logan said.

Quinn never thought MacGyver reruns would be useful, but one idea stuck with him. He used the last time loop to double-check his idea's effectiveness.

Quinn patched together a crude device he hoped would clear out the area. It contained smoke canisters with a mixture of chemicals to obscure the street and incapacitate the Russian goons. It also contained a secondary centrifuge activated by a revolver that could launch shrapnel and shoot bullets should he need the extra firepower. He had tested it, but it needed real-world application.

Quinn arrived thirty seconds earlier, put on a gas mask, grabbed one of the makeshift devices, and tossed it toward the rear of the truck.

The men scampered. Quinn unloaded the second device, ran up to the rear, and jumped in the back. He ran his hand across the device's smooth metal alloy.

Vladimir dialed an encrypted cell phone from a hollowed-out bunker near the subway, then spoke in a mixture of Russian and Farsi.

"Hashim, the device is in place. I made the modifications. The explosion is set on a sixteen-hour time delay, eleven thirty Eastern. By then, I'll be in Tehran."

"Excellent, Vladimir. After all this hard work, things are finally in place to level the playing field, and we couldn't have done it without the American donors. I still can't believe you pulled it off. How did you get them to give us the money?"

"Simple. I explained how it was in our mutual interest. They are followers of The Way. We all want the same thing, an end to American colonialism. I just left out the part about the centrifuges and exotic matter," Vladimir said.

"What about Smirnikoff?" Hashim asked.

Mechanical noises and loud bangs filtered into the conversation from the background behind Hashim.

"Another useful idiot. That's why we have the clusters in place, so we can use them and leave them behind. Speaking of clusters, do you have the rest of the team assembled in Tehran?" Vladimir asked.

"They'll all be ready before you arrive."

"You've done a tremendous job, comrade. Putin will be pleased," Vladimir said.

"You know I'm not in this for money. I'll see you in Tehran."

August 7th, 2021
Day 29.
7:32 a.m.

Quinn dialed Logan's number. "Fine. I'll take your advice."

Quinn launched the smoke bombs near the truck and waited for the men to disperse, then inspected the device.

What he needed was a sonic screwdriver, but he wasn't Doctor Who or a Time Lord. He was just Quinn Black.

August 19th, 1999
Day 1.
6:30 p.m.

"I'm stuck. I've tried to learn what's in the device, but it's like something straight out of *Stargate SG-1*. It's like the Asgard made the darn thing," Quinn said.

"I love *Stargate SG-1*," Jeremy responded.

"I have no idea how to open it. I don't speak Russian and don't have the patience to learn. There's got to be a better way."

"What did you do at night? You said you saved Logan. How did you get back here?"

"Just some basic research. I looked up more history on 9/11, stocks, tried to learn some computer code but got distracted with old Jean-Claude Van Damme movies I was watching for inspiration. The last couple of nights, I actually studied Russian. I didn't get very far. These guys aren't asking for simple directions. It's going to take a bit to find out what they're saying."

"What time do you fall asleep?"

"Sometime around eleven thirty. That's when I fell asleep

during the first time loop. There was a clock on the wall, so I remember. I'm afraid of what will happen if I wait much longer, but it's easy to fall asleep by then. Each loop, I'm always exhausted towards the end, and I can tell I'm about to pass out. But I always make sure to think about when I want to wake up."

"Maybe you should see if you can stay up later and make it to the next day."

"I don't want to take that chance until we've fixed everything."

"Didn't you say all you want to do is save Logan without getting arrested or sent to the hospital? It sounds like the last few times you've done that. Why not just stay?" Jeremy asked.

"You're right. I did, but I could at least stop the accident before moving forward, so all those people don't have to die."

"I don't think there's any reason why you wouldn't be able to come back. You've done it each time before, even after switching back and forth between 1999 and 2021. What's one more day?"

"Honestly, I don't have a good feeling about it. I don't know what's in the device, but something is off. What if it's nuclear? I could be toast, along with everyone else."

"Why don't you record their conversation?" Jeremy asked.

"I'd have to find recording equipment. Then I'd need to get the equipment to the truck in enough time to record them. I barely have enough time as it is."

"What do you usually do before then?"

"I throw on some clothes, call Logan, and then I steal a neighbor's car."

"You steal cars now? Looks like I'm having a positive influence on you, after all."

"Borrow, I should say. I brought it back each time."

"Joyriding still counts," Jeremy replied.

"And then I drive over to the truck as quickly as I can, knock over a few mailboxes in the process, and get rid of them with a couple of souped-up smoke bombs. I learned that from MacGyver," Quinn said. "Since I couldn't understand their Russian, I decided to focus on the device, but so far, I've gotten nowhere."

"What time do you find the truck?"

"Last time I got there around eight twelve or so, about forty-five minutes after my alarm wakes me up."

"Here's an idea; don't call Logan."

"I told you. I don't want Logan to die. And besides, it doesn't take that long. I've gotten it down to about a minute."

"That's another minute you can use to learn what you need to, and there's no reason to think you won't be able to save him again since you did it before. Once you get each thing down, it will be easier, but you're getting distracted doing too many things at once. Just drop everything else and focus on one thing. If you don't, you're going to waste each loop," Jeremy said.

Quinn sighed. "You're probably right, but it's a lot harder than it sounds. I'm just so worried if I do that, everything will change, and then things will be screwed."

"Dude. You've got the best opportunity that's humanly possible, maybe even *inhumanly* possible. But you're still managing to waste it. If you really want to change things, get over it, and grow a pair. Focus."

Quinn realized why he thought Jeremy's advice would be useful when he first discovered the time loop. Jeremy was impetuous but possessed a profound insight into things, even at fourteen.

"You're probably right."

"I am right," Jeremy replied.

Quinn threw on a pair of dark khaki shorts, made a quick batch of modified smoke bombs, and headed out for Manhattan.

The truck wasn't there yet. He checked the time until they were to arrive, 8:07 a.m. Quinn used the extra time to plan his strategy when he made extra smoke bombs in the back of the truck. He visualized the device and thought about the possible ways it could open. It could be a pattern of some kind. If it required an external sensor, he'd be out of luck, but hopefully, he didn't need it.

Quinn thought he might be able to stop the accident if he could block the truck. He'd try it in the next loop. He needed this loop for something else.

Quinn took most of the day off since he wanted to see how it turned out in the end. Time travel had its perks, but it put his brain in overdrive. He had to quiet the unnerving thoughts in his head. The first thing he did was put in earphones to block the outside noise, then slept for an hour. When he awoke, he returned to his minuscule desk to continue planning.

Several hours and a couple of Jean-Claude Van Damme movies later, Quinn watched the clock creep toward eleven thirty p.m. His eyelids weighed on his sockets like lead blankets. It took everything he had to keep them open. He stood up, shimmied, then walked in circles while he watched the time.

At 11:33, a loud bang rattled Quinn's ears. He didn't know if it would work, but he plopped down on the couch, closed his eyes, and thought about 1999.

CHAPTER 12

"WE'VE GOT A bigger problem. I almost didn't make it. This is my second loop today. Last time you told me to chance it and see if I could stay up until the end of the day. It didn't work out so well," Quinn explained.

"There was an explosion. It shook everything. It felt like a massive quake. If my eyes weren't already heavy like a rock, I doubt I'd be alive. I don't think I can cut it that close next time. I need to find a way to stop the explosion. It's gotta be related to the device somehow."

"Why don't you go back one day earlier?" Jeremy asked.

"I wish I could if I could remember it, but even if I did, I wouldn't know where to start. I doubt they have posted signs saying, 'Terrorists live here. Come kill us.' The main thing is that I don't remember the day before, so I can't go back if I can't remember. I think that means my time traveling is limited to only days I've lived that I remember."

"That still sounds like a lot."

"A lot less than you think."

"That's a minor problem. You still have endless do-overs, assuming you don't die. And we're still not sure about that one. You already know that certain things won't kill you. You can stay in your apartment in 2021 and learn everything you need to know. You've got the internet and a phone. What else do you need?"

"If I'm going to stop those guys, I'll need more than that. It's not like they just advertise where they're going to be on the internet."

"Didn't you say they use internet chat rooms or something, the… What did you call it… The underweb?" Jeremy asked.

"The dark web, and yes. They still do. I'm not an expert, but they're a lot more careful than they were in 1999. The NSA is watching. We know that, thanks to Edward Snowden."

"Who's Edward Snowden?"

"A former CIA guy who defected to the Russians, or at least moved there, after he blew the whistle on the government spying on American citizens."

"You think he's involved somehow? You said the guys at that truck were speaking Russian."

"I'm not sure if the guy's a hero, a traitor, or both. But at least now they're watching. I have no idea if he's involved. That would be a big coincidence. Still doesn't help with a plan."

Quinn remembered watching a TV episode where a CIA official said he didn't believe in coincidences. It *was* an intriguing idea.

"Since you keep forgetting everything, why don't you start by researching how to remember things? Didn't you tell me about a book that you read to raise your IQ and score high on those tests? I guess it didn't work out so well." Jeremy said.

"It would have *if* I had used it. But you know how most things are. Knowing and doing are two different things."

"First order of business, find out more stock tips and box scores. Second order of business, research some future tech, so we can invent it in the past," Jeremy said.

"I don't think the last one is going to help us out very much."

"Really? Because it sounds like you've got a big problem in the future with a bomb that's going to go off and you don't know how to open it. Maybe inventing stuff early could help."

"How? I can't even pick up the stupid thing—it's so heavy. I'd need help and a lever or something. Otherwise, I'm stuck looking at it and trying to see if I can move my hand in the correct pattern, if that's even what opens it. That could take forever," Quinn replied.

"You've *got* forever, but it's not the box that's got you worried. It's why you're moving through time. Maybe you can make the future happen faster. I know you can't bring anything back with you, but you could memorize stuff, like parts and things. Maybe big ideas would be easier, too. You know, like the cure for cancer and stuff," Jeremy said.

"Now you're the one who isn't focused. Aren't we trying to discover what's in the device? And they still haven't cured cancer, just improved treatment. *Way* too complicated."

"Well, there you go. Why don't you learn as much as you can about simple but big ideas that you can get people to start testing out? Maybe time travel and physics would be a good place to start—and throw in a few phasers for good measure."

"What about the device?"

"What about it? Why not just change the timeline, so it doesn't happen in the first place. Isn't that what we talked about in the beginning?"

Quinn thought for a moment, sighed, and rubbed his chin.

"I'm still not sure I want to relive the last twenty-two years."

"Then what about 9/11? Isn't that the only way you stop it, by reliving the past? Otherwise, things will just reset when you send your mind back to the future."

Quinn sighed again. "Phasers aside, it couldn't hurt. But no one's going to listen to me as a kid. I'd have to do my own research. And I'm still not giving up on the future. At least not just yet."

"If people think you're a genius, they'll listen. If you have millions of dollars, people will listen. I know it wasn't the original plan, but what other choice do you have unless you want to sit around for another ten years until you get old enough to start your own lab?"

After Quinn thought about what Jeremy said, he realized he wasn't thinking big enough. In reality, his only limitations were that he couldn't move past 11:33 p.m. on August 7, 2021, and he needed to stay alive.

Quinn decided to stop wasting time, and for the next hour, he planned out the rest of the day.

Later that evening, Quinn finally decided to ask. "Dad, I've been thinking about an idea for a while. I researched different methods, and I have a few strategies I want to use in the stock market. You can open up a custodial account for me. I'll use my allowance money and make all the stock trades myself. I have a couple hundred saved up. I just need your permission to open the account and to withdraw funds."

Frank inspected his face, squinting his eyes.

"Those are some big words. Glad to know you're learning something at that school of yours. And it's only been a few days. Must have good teachers this year."

Quinn smiled, and so did his dad.

"I don't see why not. I think it's a great idea. As long as you know there's risk involved."

"Everything has risk, Dad, including doing nothing."

His dad smiled. Quinn knew about hidden risk. That's part of what Quinn learned in his sales job. Most people were mainly aware of the dangers associated with action, but inaction was usually much more insidious. People often let inflation decimate their meager savings instead of investing it, or succumbed to the health consequences of a sedentary lifestyle due to the fear of social interaction.

"That's some elevated insight. I'd be interested in knowing exactly where you picked that up." He then cocked an eye and stroked his facial hair.

"I've done a lot of reading lately, *Think and Grow Rich* by Napoleon Hill."

Quinn wasn't sure if his dad had heard the title, but he looked impressed. And then Jeremy's words just struck Quinn. Quinn remembered someone in the future once said that most people weren't living their dreams because they were living their fears.

"Fair enough. I'm not sure if that's really it. I get a sense there's something more going on, especially after the conversation with your Aunt Lisa, but I'll set up the account tomorrow."

"Can we do it now? I've done my research there, too. We

won't be able to fund the account just yet, but we can get the application completed online. There's a couple of brokerage firms that just opened up online portals," Quinn said.

"You're really motivated to do this, aren't you?"

"There's no time like the present. Wait… You talked to Aunt Lisa?"

"Yep."

Over the next half hour, Quinn walked his dad through the online application process. Frank was impressed. Quinn was a different boy than he had been the previous week. He sounded different. He acted different. He *was* different.

August 7th, 2021
Day 31.
7:32 a.m.

"Screw this. What good is Netflix if I can't use it?" He pushed his hair back off his forehead. His flannel robe was open, and his dingy socks needed to be changed.

Quinn remembered reading somewhere in a book about beings who lived billions of years. There were two main personality types—those who learned everything they could and were super productive and those who did absolutely nothing.

Quinn thought about it and decided to work on his nothing skills. He scrolled through his queue for movies and shows that had gathered dust over the past year. It was time to do some housecleaning. Sometimes before one could focus, one had to rest, reflect, and clear out the distractions.

Quinn finished the last A-movie in the queue and searched for something else to watch. A memory flashed in his mind from a daydream in his youth. He used to fantasize about what he would do if he could freeze time.

He would read every library book, watch every movie, walk down every block, rob every bank, and do everything he could possibly think about until he ran out of things to do. He remembered the first time why he thought it would be pointless: he would be *alone*.

It was getting *too* easy to withdraw. Quinn knew if he didn't stop soon, it would become a habit, and the time loop would consume him like a junkie looking for their next fix.

Then he remembered if he stayed in the loop too long, he would start to forget. Memories of his distant past would fade even more. His family and friends would recede into the background until they disappeared altogether. It was the curse of the immortal.

AUGUST 20TH, 1999
DAY 1.
7:00 A.M.

"You're right. I need to stay focused. I took a few days off, and then it dawned on me. I should set up a schedule where I loop the day and learn as much as I can about everything. Or I should concentrate on one thing until I become an expert. But I'll do it every other loop, or two out of three, so I can spend time in this past and move my timeline forward slowly, taking detailed notes in the past and studying them so I don't forget."

"Sounds perfect. You should do it. That's what I've been saying. And the first thing you should do is make a killing in the stock market. Create your millions, then hire some experts to do your research," Jeremy said.

August 7th, 2021
Day 42.
7:32 a.m.

Quinn threw on his clothes, hopped into his neighbor's Datsun, and drove to the intersection. Quinn lay in wait for the men to arrive, half a block away from where the truck would appear.

One of the men walked toward the driver's side with the plywood. Quinn stepped on the gas and drove forward. His heart raced. Quinn stopped in front of the truck, yanked the keys out of the ignition, then ran down the street.

The men barreled after him, but Quinn ducked into the entrance of a neighboring building.

Quinn rode the escalator up the first floor. Then scrambled for the elevator before riding it to one of the top floors of the building.

He watched through the window and after a few minutes, he saw one of the men exit the building, then double back toward the truck.

By the time the men returned, Officer Channing was standing in front of the Datsun, writing a ticket. The men hopped in the truck and threw it into reverse. Quinn waited until they were out of sight, then approached Scott Channing.

"Officer, I was walking by, and I heard those guys in the truck talking about a bomb. I took down their license plate."

Officer Channing took down the information, then called it in. Seconds later, shell casings peppered the ground. Quinn turned. Multiple bullets pierced his chest. The force of the bullets brought Quinn to his knees and then to the ground, landing on his back. His skull hit the ground with a dull thud.

When they finished with Quinn, the men sprayed the rest of the bullets into Officer Channing's chest.

CHAPTER 13

"HOLY CRAP!"

Quinn flew off the bed, double-checked his stomach to see if the holes were still there. He looked outside. His neighbor's car still blocked the driveway. At least now he knew what would happen if he died. He would wake up again on August 7, 2021.

Quinn took the current loop off. He still didn't want to tempt fate and push the clock past 11:33 p.m. There was no guarantee anyone would come back from *that*, but it still eased his fears a little.

Quinn spent the evening reminiscing over old photos and memories of his childhood and the years leading up to the present. He thought about the choices he had made and the different paths he and Jeremy took after college.

Quinn wondered if he could save Logan *and* stop the explosion, or if it was a one or the other proposition.

At eleven, Quinn focused his mind on August 20, 1999. He'd have to open the account all over again.

August 15th, 1999
Day 2.

Quinn's arms and legs were skinnier than they had been in decades. He blinked his eyes a few times just to check if he was still dreaming.

"What the…." Quinn asked as his voice cracked.

"What the what?" Frank asked as he walked through the door.

It took a few minutes for Quinn to process what had just happened.

"What day is it?"

"August fifteenth," Frank replied.

"This can't be happening."

"What can't be happening?"

Quinn shook his head. "I can't believe it's today again. This doesn't make any sense."

"You're not making sense yourself, Quinn. What's going on?"

Quinn stormed out of the house and ran over to Jeremy's.

He'd forgotten how much stamina he had as a kid. In the last time loop, he had used his bike most of the time. But now he ran all the way to Jeremy's house and didn't even break a sweat.

Quinn pounded on the door. "Jeremy, open up. This is serious!"

"I'm coming. I'm coming. What's so important?" Jeremy asked.

Quinn explained what had happened in the last timeline

and how his death had somehow caused him to travel back to August 15 instead of the day he intended.

"I call BS on that. What's your deal today?" Jeremy asked.

"What sucks most about living in a time loop is having to repeat myself every time something goes wrong."

"I'm sure I could learn to live with it," Jeremy replied.

"I'm sure you could. We've had this conversation before."

"I guess I'll have to take your word for it."

"I can't figure out what happened. If I did it wrong, I thought I would reset again in 2021 either on August seventh or August eighth. That part at least happened. But after that, I should have woken up on the day I was thinking about before I went to bed. That's about a week away. I don't get why I came back today."

Jeremy eyed Quinn. The worried look on his face told Quinn he hadn't been convincing enough.

"I get it. I know you don't believe me. Not yet, anyway, but you will. I just need to find out what the heck happened."

Jeremy sighed and twisted his lips.

"Just humor me for a bit, will you?"

"I'm trying."

"Wait. What time is it?" Quinn asked.

Jeremy looked at his watch. When he looked back, Quinn was running in the opposite direction.

"Where are you going?"

Quinn ignored him and kept running. He arrived just in time. Cameron was still there, her shoes off and legs dangling in the lake.

Quinn hurried down beside her, then smiled. She didn't have the expression on her face he'd hoped for.

"Hello. I'm Quinn. Did you just move here?"

Cameron smiled. "Yes. I'm Cameron. Nice to meet you. You live here, too?"

There was a sweetness in her voice without a hint of skepticism.

"Yes, for a while."

The run was good for Quinn since he didn't like to over-think things. The last time he was in that position, he had his bike, which was a topic of conversation that broke the ice. Usually, he would have frozen in place without an icebreaker or at least some common ground.

"Are you looking for someone? You're out of breath."

"I just like to go for a run sometimes. I was talking with my friend Jeremy, then got bored, so I decided to come over here. My dad and I come here a lot. He likes to take me fishing sometimes. What about you?"

"I've never been fishing, but I do like the water. It's my first time here, but I think I'd like to come again."

"Are you going to the high school up the street?" Quinn asked, already knowing the answer.

"Yeah. I'll be starting ninth grade."

"What a coincidence. I'll guess we'll be classmates," Quinn replied.

"Great. At least I'll know somebody. I hate moving to a new school and having to learn who everyone is. Maybe you can help me."

Quinn's face reddened. "I'll be happy to help. I know a lot of people who'll go there, and I can tell you who to avoid." Quinn hesitated a moment before continuing. "I can tell you one right now. His name is Scott Channing."

"Scott Channing?"

"Yeah. He's a troublemaker. Likes to bother people for fun. He's new, but he's already got a reputation. I hear he got into trouble at his last school for beating up some kid with asthma."

The last part was a lie, but in Quinn's mind, Scott might as well have done the deed.

"I'll keep a lookout for him. So, what kinds of things do you like to do for fun besides fishing?"

Quinn thought for a moment. Time travel almost slipped out.

"I like to travel when I can, but we don't do it that often."

It wasn't his first choice, but he went with it. He wasn't going to tell her the truth, which at that time in his life was playing the card game Magic. In the present, he'd upgraded to binge-watching episodes of the *Battlestar Galactica* reboot.

Quinn took a deep breath. "What about you? What do you like?"

"You're going to think I sound like a dork, but I love science. Recently, I've started reading up on black holes and dark energy, and lots of other cool stuff, like time travel."

"Wow. I love that, too."

"Really?"

The first time they met, Quinn's conversation barely lasted more than a couple of sentences. Cameron's stark beauty paralyzed him. Her piercing eyes contrasted with her hair's soft locks that curled past her shoulders. He was upset with himself for never pushing past his initial feelings of inferiority and embarrassment to learn more about her.

"We should hang out sometime. I know there's not an awful lot to do around here, but I could show you the places I know. And I'd love to pick your brain on some of those ideas of yours, especially time travel."

Quinn yammered on, growing lightheaded during the exchange. His recent conversations with Jeremy and the run-in with the Russian thugs made his words flow like a spigot.

"Why don't we start with time travel?" Cameron asked, interrupting him.

"My favorite subject, and I'm glad you asked," Quinn replied.

Cameron went into a long diatribe, which Quinn interrupted every so often just to hold his train of thought. He was interested, but she knew more than anyone her age would know.

"Here's what I understand," she said, after building up to that point with more arcane foundational physics principles. "There are a few cool theories out there. One is about the holographic mind and how your current thoughts in the present influence your opinions and beliefs in the future."

When Quinn heard those words, his first thought was that she sounded like a motivational speaker. What you put into your mind obviously influences your actions and the future, but then he understood—there was something special about the thoughts and words themselves creating a link between the present and the past.

"You think it goes both ways?" Quinn interrupted.

"If you don't think of time as linear, I suppose. The other theory is that our universe is part of a multiverse, and every decision creates a new universe. Not so much that you're creating new stuff and worlds with your actions, but that the infinite number of universes already exist and provide an alternate reality for each choice."

"I don't follow."

"Think of our universe as a maze. You're a rat in the maze. Every time you find a new intersection, you can go back to that same point, but you're free to look at other paths to find the exit. Once discovered, you can always go back because you know where it is."

"Holy crap!"

"What is it?" Cameron asked.

"What happens if you die?"

"That's a good question. I'm not very religious, but if you're talking about space time and the multiverse, think of the maze as three-dimensional. Each time the rat reaches one intersection, a new maze is created in a new dimension stacked above it. Then, the rat is free to travel, not just any other path in the original maze but each new maze as well," Cameron replied. "The rat can always go back to the original maze, assuming he can remember where it was, but the events in one maze are separate from the other. His mind and his actions are the only links between the two."

"Wow. Do you think it's possible someone could discover a way to hop from one maze to the next due to something like say, a nuclear bomb? And if they die, the maze will reset somehow?"

"Honestly, I have no idea, but I don't see why not. I doubt a nuclear bomb would do it—maybe something like dark energy or exotic matter."

"How would that work exactly?" Quinn asked.

"Dark energy makes the universe expand. Exotic matter can form stable wormholes, at least in theory. If someone was able to access both just before the point of death, their holographic mind might be able to traverse the multiverse."

"So, they would never die?"

"Hard to say, but my guess is like the rats in the maze, they could trace back each intersection in each maze up until the point of death. But each time they died, the maze would reset only to what had existed up until that first point when their holographic mind intersected dark energy and exotic matter."

Quinn thought about the last part of what Cameron said. It fit what had just happened, and why he had ended back in the original August 7th and August 15th timelines.

"That's it, then?" Quinn said.

"What is?"

"If someone traveled this three-dimensional maze, every time they die, things would reset to the first time they jumped into the second maze, and they'd be free to do it all over again. They'd just have to relive each timeline."

"Maybe," Cameron replied.

Quinn's head was spinning over the implications. "Screw it. I'm going all kinds of crazy over this stuff. I have to tell you something, but you're not going to believe me."

"What is it?"

"I told my best friend Jeremy this fifteen minutes ago, so if you believe me, at least I'll have two people to talk with about it now."

"All right, I'm really interested now. What is it?"

Quinn hesitated, then spoke. "I'm from the future."

CHAPTER 14

THE LOOK ON her face said it all. During the last few minutes, Quinn thought he had made a connection. Cameron was brilliant. He didn't know how she knew what she knew, or why. He only discovered how brilliant she was just then, but she was more amazing than he realized. But now he worried that she thought he was a raging lunatic.

Cameron took a deep breath. "Let's pretend I believe you. What do you want me to do? What do you expect me to say?"

"I need to come clean about something. I don't want you to find out later and then hate me for it, so I better tell you now."

Cameron averted her eyes and waited for Quinn to finish.

"I wasn't exactly truthful about Scott Channing. He *is* a prick, but he didn't beat up a kid with asthma. The reason I hate him so much is because of what he did to me in the future and what he prevented me from doing in the initial couple dozen time loops on my last day in 2021."

"So, you're from 2021?"

"That's right, and I can prove it. The first time I came back, I had to wait a couple days until an earthquake hit Turkey, but I know some sports stats now. During my time loops, I researched things I thought might be useful if I needed to prove my ability or if I got stuck in the past with no way of returning."

"I'm definitely interested. Let's see where this takes us," Cameron said.

Quinn thought it was more likely she thought he might be a loon, just harmless enough for it not to worry her.

"How did you learn about physics and time travel? Why aren't you going to a special school for geniuses or something?"

"My father's a physicist, or *was* a physicist."

"I never knew that."

"Why would you? I don't tell most people. My dad's the brilliant one, but he has severe autism. It's usually too much work to explain everything. The conversation always moves in that direction when I start talking about him, so I stopped doing it."

"I'm sorry. That must be tough."

"My life is always so different from everyone else's. My mother left a few years ago. She couldn't take it anymore. He would start working in his room, then would never leave for hours, sometimes days," Cameron said. "I heard them arguing right before she left. He was quiet. She did all the talking. Or yelling. I get why she left. I just don't understand why she married Dad in the first place. It's not like he was that much different when he was younger. I think he might have been even worse—more antisocial."

"Is that why you love science so much?" Quinn asked.

"I love my dad even more, but it's not because of him. I just love science. But he helped me understand it."

"Do you believe me?"

Cameron took a deep breath, her eyes darting back and forth. "I have no reason not to. I want to, and I'm sure I'll find out soon enough."

"You think I could talk to your dad?"

"I'm not so sure that's a great idea, but I can ask him later."

"That would mean a lot if I could. I know it's a lot to ask since we just met, at least for you, anyway."

"It's okay, Quinn. I like you."

The statement made him feel like a champion boxer holding up a victory belt. He stared straight at her, soaking in her words before he replied.

"I like you, too," he said, careful not to wait too long. "I wish I could stay longer, but I need to talk to Jeremy. I left him hanging, but we're going to finish this conversation later." Quinn walked a few steps then craned his neck back. "And by the way, the Mariners beat the Red Sox four to three."

Cameron's eyes widened. The game was only a few hours away. She wouldn't have to wait long to see if Quinn was telling the truth.

One thing about the autism spectrum is that once someone on it gets stuck on a topic, they tend to fixate on it. Her dad was like that with baseball. She said he got the bug when he was five, and it stuck with him. He never moved past it. Cameron never met anyone who was fanatical about both baseball *and* physics, except herself.

"Oh, wait," Cameron said, just as Quinn resumed walking. "You said you hated Scott Channing because of what he stopped you from doing in the future. What was it?"

"I worked for a sales company. My boss, Logan, was killed in a truck crash. I completed a few dozen time loops and traced the crash to some Russian guys. They had some kind of bomb in the truck," he explained. "The first few times I tried to save Logan, I kept getting blocked by Scott. He's a cop in the future and an annoying one. I eventually saved Logan, but I haven't been able to stop the truck or the bomb. It's too big, too heavy, and I can't open it. It's connected somehow to another explosion later in the evening. I think that's the one that triggered my first time loop."

Quinn continued talking. "I wasn't able to investigate much further because I died in my last loop. I came back to 1999 and have been back and forth between both timelines, but the timeline reset after I died."

Quinn waited for her reaction. Her eyes told him she just might believe him, and any doubts might be put to rest after the game had ended.

Twenty minutes later, Quinn returned to Jeremy's house.

"Sorry for leaving in a rush. I couldn't screw things up again with Cameron this time around."

"Who's Cameron?" Jeremy wanted to know.

"I'll tell you later. Let's just watch the game now. If I call the winner, you owe me a Diet Coke."

Quinn sat and listened to Jeremy rant about the summer. He missed most of what Jeremy was saying, deep in thought about the conversation with Cameron. The idea of being immortal was too overwhelming to process in one sitting, especially if all his hard gains were lost with every reset.

The umpire called the final strikeout, and the game was over, just as Quinn had predicted.

"How the heck did you do that?" Jeremy asked.

"I told you. I'm from the future. We've been through

this. I thought I had things figured out the last time I was here, but things keep getting more complicated."

"Tell me the short version."

"When I first returned from the future, I needed to save Logan. Now, I need to stop another explosion that's going to kill me and everyone else in New York City. I don't know how bad it is, but I have to stop it," Quinn said. "I think the only way to do it might be to live through this timeline, the slow way. It might be the only way to make the changes stick since each change creates its own universe. Or more accurately, accesses a different one. I just happen to be able to shuttle my mind back and forth between each timeline I have created. At least that's the working theory."

"You're smoking crack, aren't you? I was worried something like this might happen after your grandmother died. You have always been kind of fragile."

"I'm not fragile, and I'm not smoking crack. You saw for yourself I called that game."

"That could've been just a lucky shot. It's baseball, anyway. Basketball would've been more convincing since there're more points."

"Fine, but get ready to be blown away," Quinn said as he took out a list of stats he had written down earlier.

Over the next several hours, Jeremy watched as game after game ended precisely how Quinn had predicted. He had no doubt. Quinn *was* from the future.

August 7th, 2021

Day 44.

7:32 A.M.

Quinn stumbled from his bed and pushed away the clothes piled on the floor. He flipped open his laptop and spent the better part of the morning researching everything he could about Cameron.

She was a ghost on the internet. In the prior dozen loops before he died, he searched one site after another. She had no social media account, no deep-dive search accounts, no arrests, purchases, or anything else viewable through public records.

Scott Channing's words stuck with him. What did he mean by what Quinn had said to her? Why did Scott think Quinn had said anything in the first place other than that they happened to know each other and they both wanted to work there?

It dawned on Quinn that maybe he was searching for the wrong person. He should be searching for Cameron's father. He'd have to ask for his name first.

August 7th, 2021

Day 45.

7:32 A.M.

Quinn stumbled from his bed, pushing the clothes piled on the floor out of his way. He flipped open his laptop and spent the better part of the morning researching everything he could about Cameron's dad, Dr. David Green.

Dr. Green wasn't the mystery she was, but there still

wasn't much of a record. A few searches turned up his prior employer, Lawrence Livermore National Laboratory.

An article mentioned Dr. Green, alongside several other prominent physicists. A peer-reviewed paper linked him to two additional publications on temporal displacement and causality.

Quinn intensified his search. He entered every phrase he found in each article for several hours in different combinations through several search engines. He was about to give up when one article caught his eye. One of the researchers who worked with Dr. Green was injured in the World Trade Center bombing in '93. It couldn't be a coincidence.

The article went on to say that their grant was shut down after an investigation showed there had been some impropriety in how the grant was funded. Initially, there was concern that the grant was connected to the bombing. One of the researchers on the team was a Saudi national.

The investigators found nothing on Dr. Green except for a single innocuous purchase at a baseball game. He used a debit card from the grants account, which he paid back that day.

It was one of those things Dr. Green did. He knew he wasn't supposed to do it, but he figured since he would pay it back, it wouldn't matter. If it hadn't been for the investigation, it would've been no big deal, but the government panel needed a scapegoat. Dr. Green took the heat.

Quinn put the pieces together and assumed that was why Cameron's mother left a couple of years later. After the article, Dr. Green's paper trail vanished. There was, however, a last known address.

CHAPTER 15

August 16th, 1999
Day 3.
7:00 A.M.

JEREMY POUNDED ON Quinn's front door like it was
Noah's Ark. Quinn expected it this time and opened it after a
few seconds. Jeremy's face beamed as he shoved his way into
the entrance.

"What are you boys up to?" Quinn's mom asked.

"Jeremy's just being a doofus."

Jeremy pulled Quinn out of his mom's earshot.

"Jesus. I get you're excited, but calm down."

"No, you don't get exactly how excited I am. You know
what this means?"

"Of course. I've been through this already. It means we
can make a lot of money, get a lot of hot girls, play pranks on
everyone who's ever given us any grief, and invent cool stuff
from the future, that is, with a lot of hard work."

"Exactly," Jeremy replied.

"I have other things to worry about right now."

"What could be more important than getting hot girls?"

"How about saving the world?"

"The world can wait, but I'm only going to be in ninth grade once."

"You sound a lot like my friend Valentino."

"Sounds like we could be good friends."

"Won't happen."

"And why is that?"

Quinn hesitated. He remembered that in this timeline he hadn't told Jeremy about his death in the future, and he wasn't sure if Jeremy was ready to hear the news.

"Let's just say there are things that prevented both of you from ever meeting. And seriously, things aren't as exciting as they sound. If I die, things will just reset, but I'm not sure about everyone else."

Quinn could see the elation bottled up in Jeremy like he was a kid the morning before a trip to a theme park.

"That's amazing. That means you're immortal. You get to do everything over and over again, and try everything in different ways forever."

"If that *is* what happens, at some point I'm going to get sick of it, just like Bill Murray did when he killed himself over and over until he realized it was pointless. Sure, I can do all kinds of cool things, but I get the feeling that life is lonely as a Time Lord."

Jeremy smiled.

"I like the sound of that, *time lord*."

"One thing at a time. Let's find a way to stop the explosion in 2021, or at least what caused the time looping. And while I'm working on that, let's devise a plan to stop 9/11. I need to talk to my aunt, and I need to talk with Dr. Green."

"Who's Dr. Green?"

"Cameron's dad. He's a physicist. He was indirectly

connected to the '93 World Trade Center bombing, and it can't be a coincidence. My guess is that he knows something. Cameron certainly did, at least about time travel."

"Forget about '93. Forget about 2021. You're in 1999, and you can time travel, loop time, and do whatever else you want. What difference does that other stuff make?"

"It makes all the difference. I'm convinced it's the reason why I'm looping. Cameron suggested I could be stuck in a longer loop between 1999 and 2021 if I keep dying, so I need to find a way to stop it."

Jeremy sighed. "Can't we at least have a little fun?"

"Have you ever had something but you couldn't completely enjoy it until you were finished? My brain wants to solve this problem. I want to solve this problem. I'm not saying I won't enjoy myself along the way, but unless I stop the thugs who killed my boss and blew up Manhattan, it's going to make it a heck of a lot harder."

"Fine, have it your way. What's your plan?"

"Funny thing is, I returned to the past for *your* advice. You gave me a few good pointers with your seven little rules for time travel, which we both keep breaking, but I'm still waiting for that big idea."

Quinn watched the initial approval fade into disappointment as Jeremy's face went limp.

"Let's assume for a moment," Jeremy began with his fake British accent, "that the sum of all requirements is less than the least of all requirements."

"What does that even mean?" Quinn asked.

"You asked for a plan, and by golly, I'm going to give you one," Jeremy continued as his fake accent degenerated.

"So, let's hear it."

"I haven't formulated one yet, but I promise if you let me

have a little fun, my head will be in a better place to come up with one."

Maybe it was time for both of them to start living their dreams. Quinn pursed his lips, thought about it for a moment, then sighed.

"Fine."

"Yes!" Jeremy cried in victory.

"I know this place not too far from here. We'll be a little early, but why not? I should warn you—the last time we went there we almost had to dodge bullets."

"Sounds exciting. I would say be careful, but since you're immortal, I don't think it matters anymore."

"It does matter, unless I want to keep rehashing everything each time I get killed. It should matter for you, too, especially if you're stuck in the timeline without me."

"You know, Quinn, most people only get one life. How many have you had already?"

"Fair enough. And since *you* brought it up, I'm taking Cameron."

Jeremy's eyes widened. "She agreed to go with you?"

"Haven't asked her yet, but I don't see why not."

After school, Quinn met with Cameron and Jeremy. Jeremy wore his polo shirt and bucket hat. Thankfully, Cameron was in a more inconspicuous yellow cardigan and modest blue skirt. They took a taxi to Ling's, and each sat at the table with fifty dollars in chips.

Quinn lost everything on his first hand with a pair of tens. Jeremy was low on chips by the end of the first half hour, but Cameron was on a hot streak. She had five hundred in chips with fifteen hundred in the pot. The dealer revealed the ace of clubs. The player to Cameron's right raised, all-in.

"Call," Cameron said.

The player was bluffing. He had a pair of fives and four of the same suit.

"Full house," Cameron said as she lay her hands on the table. The man next to her grumbled.

"I think it's time we cash in," she said.

"Just be glad you're a little girl."

"Why is that?" Cameron asked.

"Because if you weren't, we wouldn't be having this conversation," the player said as he reclined back enough to let her see the gun barrel near his waist.

Jeremy sighed and shook his head.

"Why'd you have to bring her? I'm sure I would have done better if I weren't so distracted," Jeremy said to Quinn.

"Don't be a prick, Jeremy," Quinn replied.

"No, it's okay," Cameron added.

"Sorry. I didn't mean it. I just hate losing. That's all."

Cameron smiled. "Everyone hates losing, but that's what makes it so much fun when you win."

Quinn eyed the door when they left to see if the man would follow them. They walked a few more feet. A noise startled Jeremy and drew Cameron's gaze. Quinn stepped forward.

They walked a few more feet. A chill ran down Quinn's spine. Then the alley fell silent. Aside from a slight ringing in his ears from the echo of the boisterous gambling house, the area was quiet.

Quinn stopped. The silence made him squirm. "Let's get out of here," he said.

They hastened their pace until they reached the corner, in view of streetlights and several passersby. A hand touched Cameron's shoulder. She looked back.

"How'd you get so good?" Quinn asked.

Cameron exhaled.

"Physics and baseball weren't my dad's only hobbies."

Quinn's cheeks lifted. "Mind if we split the haul? I know we didn't talk about it before we came, but I'd hate to reset the day and do it over."

She handed over a grand before he finished his sentence.

"I still can't believe it," she said.

"Me neither," Jeremy replied. "I thought for sure I was going to win."

Quinn chuckled. "I'm sure you'll get your chance. What's important is that we're all together and on the same page. Hopefully I won't have to reset the day anytime soon."

"I think I have a plan. Y'know, the one you had asked for," Jeremy said. "Have you ever read *Ender's Game* by Orson Scott Card?"

"I saw the movie," Quinn replied.

"They made it into a movie?" Cameron asked.

"Yep. Not a very good one, either. I was disappointed," Quinn added.

"Do you remember what the movie was about?"

"This kid and a group of other kids were training to fight an alien race, and the main character ends up killing all of them."

"Yeah, but do you remember the part about where they were in the simulation?"

"Vaguely."

"Well, the point is the kids were told they were in the game the entire time. During the final battle, they were still told it was a simulation."

"Okay, where are you going with this?"

"You could do the same thing in the future to try and discover what's in the box."

Quinn thought for a moment.

"How exactly? It's not like I have months to find a team of gamers. I have less than an hour."

"You have more than an hour. Remember? You said you found the box after you knocked out the men with the device. After that, you had until eleven thirty-three p.m. You just need a location to drive the truck to, then you can find a group of gamers who think your objective is to finish the game."

Quinn thought the idea was farfetched, but the more he thought about it, the more it made sense. There would be enough time to find some people willing to at least try. He could loop forever until he did.

Quinn could experiment with different individuals and groups of people to see if their interaction would create synergy and lead to a solution.

"It's a plan, all right. Not sure if it's a good one, but it's something," Quinn said.

"I think it's brilliant. I'm sure there are tons of places in Manhattan where you can find gamers. All you need is the right bait," Jeremey added.

"What do you suggest?"

"What all gamers love—a chance to get noticed."

"You want me to do what? Tell them they'll be in the new game or something?" Quinn asked.

"Sounds good to me. Give them some money up front. Tell them it's for their time participating in a beta version. The goal is to find a mysterious porcelain orb and then discover what's inside. Whoever wins, they get to be the main character in the game," Jeremy said before pausing to breathe. "You can insert yourself as part of the game lore. Say that the owners of the orb have handlers that need to open it so you can track their progress. If one of them does, you congratulate them and give them some cash."

Quinn nodded. "One of the irritating things about shifting back in time is that if I want to move forward, I always have to repeat at least one day."

"What do you mean?"

"My mind can only think back to the days I remember. I need to have already lived that day if I want to return. If I have a good day and want to move forward in the new timeline, I'll have to think about nothing when I fall asleep, so I can wake up the next day instead of repeating one I've already lived. Then I can think about 2021 tomorrow before I go to sleep, so when it's time for me to return, I don't erase the day."

"Okay, now I'm starting to get it. You only wake up in the morning, not at night. That means when you're in 2021, and you're ready to return to 1999, you can't return to tomorrow from our perspective because it hasn't happened yet. If you don't wake up tomorrow in this timeline, you'll return back to this morning. It will be like the day never happened to us."

"That's it. I guess the day is still there, but I'll never have access to it again unless I live one more day in the future, because in the first timeline, I never lived the next day. I can't think about tomorrow because it hasn't happened yet. I'm not sure what will happen if I try. I suppose I'll just end up repeating the same day in 2021. Then I'll have to relive the day over again."

"So which day will you live now?" Jeremy asked.

"It should be obvious. This was a good day. We made some cash, and I don't feel like rehashing everything again if I loop the day. That's getting irritating, so I'll think about nothing, wake up tomorrow, and probably just spend time researching. Then I'll return to 2021 and do my best to find and convince a bunch of complete strangers to go on a gaming quest to solve the mystery of the porcelain orb."

August 7th, 2021
Day 46.
7:32 a.m.

Quinn, half-naked with no robe or dirty socks on, threw open his laptop and dropped a note on Craigslist, Meetup, and a few more sites. It read: *Gamers wanted to beta: Cash reward. Big money. The game starts now.*

Quinn populated the sites with the details he had planned in the past. He hopped onto several chat rooms and a few other sites—4chan, Reddit, and several underground sites he'd normally have been wary of visiting.

Within a few minutes, several text boxes opened up, and threads started to trickle in. Quinn looked at the clock. He was too slow.

August 7th, 2021
7:32 a.m.
Day 47.

Quinn, half-naked, threw open his laptop and dropped a note on Craigslist, Meetup, and a few more sites. It read: *Gamers wanted to beta: Cash reward. Big money. The game starts now.*

Quinn decided to stick with one site—where he had gotten the most responses in the previous loop. He shaved off a few more minutes and got his first bite.

Quinn gave the details to the gamer, who was close

enough to meet him outside his apartment. Quinn realized his plan was more limited than he thought since the gamers that played would not only have to read and agree to his terms, but they'd have to live close enough and have the time to meet him in the short window available. At the moment, that was a total of one person.

"Hey, Gary, here," the gamer said. Gary had on a tattered, EverQuest T-shirt with torn jeans and Converse shoes. He looked more like a guitar teacher than a gamer, and his form-fitting shirt gave away his unexpectedly ripped body.

Quinn slid an envelope in his hands and handed over two makeshift smoke grenades. Gary peeked in the envelope to confirm the cash was there.

"Good luck on your quest," Quinn told him. "The clock is ticking."

Gary returned to his ancient vehicle, a Buick, then followed the instructions Quinn had left in the envelope with the cash.

Within minutes, Gary found the intersection. He tossed the grenades, waited for the men to disperse, then swooped in to inspect the orb.

Gary had planned out the entire process in his head. He was perfect for the task. He had won three different gaming tournaments in the last two years, and several game-company scouts had approached him to work as a developer. Each time he had turned them down. If he took the job, he feared there'd never be enough time to play the games he wanted. That was his main goal: to play as many games as possible and win. Everything else was just an obstacle in his way.

He didn't fit the gamer stereotype, either. He spent the bulk of his time training physically and mentally for each game. He'd also inherited a lot of money from his grandfather who'd passed away a few years before, but spent it frugally in pursuit of the gamer's dream.

People were usually shocked when they met Gary in person, but he always explained that the ability to focus in a game required energy, and he wouldn't have that if he sat on the couch all day long eating potato chips. He needed to be in top physical shape. He was the ideal candidate for Quinn.

Gary ran his hand alongside the edges of what Quinn called the *Orb of Truth*. Quinn thought the bit of lore he had stolen from elements of fantasy novels and old D&D games would help in the quest.

Gary slowed his breathing and repeated the process. Nothing happened. He took a closer look at the truck and where the device was placed. He told Quinn he thought Quinn's idea of using a lever could work.

A few minutes later, Gary's friends, all team members, arrived with the needed equipment. They pulled up to the back of the truck and positioned their equipment in place. The device was heavy, but they secured the device, then left the truck in less than sixty seconds after they arrived.

Twenty minutes later, Gary and his team took turns attempting to open the device. Its smooth surface challenged them. They used touch technology, magnets, electricity, and a few other techniques to elicit a response. The orb remained quiet.

"I have an idea," Gary said to one of his team members. "Grab me the box."

CHAPTER 16

GARY'S TEAM HAULED over a massive cardboard box brimming with radiation detectors, gas masks, and other carefully curated, scientific supplies. From a distance, the group gave off the vibe of the most epic, live-action, role-playing sessions of all time, which masked their more serious purpose.

"This can't be right," Gary said.

The device gave off no radiation, none. Gary took out another device that measured radio waves.

"What is it?" one of Gary's team members asked.

"The orb isn't giving off any radio waves, either. There should be something. Everything gives off radiation. When did you last check the equipment?" Gary asked.

The other member of his team grabbed the detector and waved it over Gary's face.

"Does that answer your question?" the team member replied.

The detector flashed and beeped in all the right frequencies.

"The only thing that I know in the universe that doesn't give radiation is dark matter. You think the shield may be reversing the readings by emitting waves that cancel out what's inside?" Gary asked.

"About as possible as the orb filled with dark matter," the team member replied.

"This is just a game, but let's think like we're in the game. The developers obviously must have some type of shield that cancels it out, but do they want us to think it's dark matter? What should we do, and how do we open it?" Gary asked.

"I have an idea, but we're going to have to lift it out of the truck," the team member replied.

Gary and his team used a professional hand truck to slide the device into their rusty, oversized Buick. The car had seen better days, but the back seat was the perfect size to hold the device.

An hour later, Gary's team hauled the device into Gary's apartment bathtub and filled it up with water.

"What's the idea?" Gary asked his team member.

"If there's an opening, we'll see some air bubbles."

"You think this thing is going to float?" Gary said.

"Who knows. Maybe it's water powered, or the opening is triggered if it's submerged."

"This isn't going to work," Gary said.

"You have a better idea?" Gary's team member asked.

"How about fire?" Gary asked.

"Just give it a chance. It's not going to—"

Before he could finish, a brilliant light glowed from the center edges around its circumference. The orb opened like a plastic shell. A chrome sphere gleamed a brilliant, shimmering light. The chronometer attached to the outside of the sphere ticked. A hollow tube embedded within the device ticked in unison with a chronometer.

"We did it!" one of the team members said.

"Look at that," Gary said as the water poured into the orb and vanished before it reached the center.

"What do you think it is?" Gary's team member asked.

"I don't think this is a game. It looks like some weird kind of bomb."

Back at the intersection where Gary's team had smoked out the Russians, the Russians regrouped in their nearby warehouse.

"What are we going to do about it, boss? They stole the device," the henchman said on the cell phone.

Smirnikoff laughed. "It doesn't matter. None of it matters. It's programmed to go off at eleven thirty-three p.m."

"What do you mean?" the henchman asked.

"There are two devices: the external bomb, and the real one—the outside device is just a distraction," Smirnikoff replied.

"I don't get it. A distraction for who? For what?"

"You, the police, Vladimir, and everyone else."

"I don't understand."

"Don't you see? I needed an excuse to get your cooperation to import the bomb into New York City. Once the bomb explodes, it will annihilate the entire Eastern Seaboard and everything else within a thousand-mile radius," Smirnikoff replied.

"What? How are we supposed to get out in time?"

It took a few seconds for the henchman to register what Smirnikoff was telling him. When he did, his mouth dropped. His eyes drooped, and he hunched down.

"Don't worry. You'll meet your seventy-two virgins in heaven for carrying out God's will."

"I'm not Muslim."

Smirnikoff laughed.

"Why would you do this to us?"

"Why wouldn't I? The world has gotten so disgusting. We've polluted it with our existence. It's unnatural. We're all unnatural. The only way to stop it is to kill everyone," Smirnikoff said.

"What are you saying? That doesn't make any sense, and it wouldn't kill everyone, anyway. You just said it would wipe out anything within a thousand miles of the Eastern Seaboard. What about everyone else?"

"That's just the initial blast. Then comes the massive worldwide tsunami. But that's nothing compared to what will happen once the dark matter explosion rips a hole into the center of the Earth and causes it to collapse in on itself."

"What! You're a fool. Why would you do that?" the henchman asked.

"I told you. The human race is an unnatural metastasized cancer that can't be excised. The only way to rid the universe of the sickness is to purge it from the system."

August 7th, 2021

Day 47.

9:23 a.m.

A few minutes later, Gary called Quinn.

"We did it. We opened the orb, but something really freaky is going on inside. What did you hire us to do, really?"

"What does it look like on the inside?" Quinn asked.

Gary snapped a photo, then texted it to Quinn.

"What the heck is that? I'll be right over," Quinn said.

A short time later, Quinn hustled upstairs to Gary's bathroom where the orb sat. The apartment was tiny with red brick walls. There was a bed, a computer, a TV, and a weight bench. Quinn's apartment was a mansion by comparison. In this tiny place, the orb was waiting for him to learn its secrets.

Quinn's mouth fell open. The orb transfixed his eyes, but he averted them long enough to pull extra cash from his wallet and hand it over to the gamers.

"Here's your prize money *if* you want it now. *Or* I could keep the money and double it if you can learn what the device is supposed to do and how it works."

"How do you expect us to do that?" Gary asked.

"That's for you to find out," Quinn replied.

"I know someone," one of Gary's crew members, Sam, said as he adjusted his oversized Ultima Online T-shirt and ran his fingers through the brown bowl cut on the top of his head.

"I'm Sam. My pronouns are they, them, or their," Sam said, right hand extended which Quinn promptly shook.

"You think you can get him here in time and figure this out before the end of the day?" Quinn asked.

"How late are we talking? My mother's expecting me home before curfew," Sam said.

"That's eight p.m. for Sam. I don't have a curfew," Gary added.

"I need it done by eleven," Quinn replied.

Sam made the call. Fifteen minutes later, a car screeched around the corner from Gary's residential building. Sam pushed up the window glass with their scrawny arms and peeked their head out the window. Gary and Quinn stood over Sam's shoulders from behind.

A tall woman with long, auburn hair and full lips kicked open the car door. The female figure had on a long, black skirt with white trim and flats. She had a rustic look and a natural beauty. Quinn recognized her immediately.

"Cameron?" Quinn whispered.

She was unmistakable. Cameron carted up two small boxes with expensive-looking electronics that filled the top and hung over the edges. She maneuvered up the steps, using her knees to keep the boxes from falling, then pushed the call button to announce her presence.

"It's Cameron. Let me in."

"How do you know her?" Quinn asked Sam after they had buzzed Cameron in the building.

"She's my cousin. She's brilliant, and she works at a physics lab, a few blocks down the street. It used to be part of Columbia—before the director of the lab decided they needed more privacy. At least that's what she told me," Sam said.

"Does she work with her dad?"

"Yes. You know her?"

"Yeah. We went to the same high school," Quinn replied.

Gary and Sam squinted their eyes.

"That's an odd coincidence," Gary said.

"I don't believe in coincidences," Sam added.

"I think you're right. And you're about to find out what's really going on," Quinn said.

"Cameron," Quinn said in greeting.

She dropped her boxes on the floor and gave Quinn a once-over.

"You look familiar… Wait… We went to school together, didn't we?" Cameron asked.

"Yeah, that's it. I remember you."

"You look older, but I remember you, too. It's Quinn, right?"

"Yes. Now I'm going to ask you a stupid question, so don't laugh. I think I already know the answer to this since you're the one that confirmed what I thought about the branching timelines. Do you remember a conversation I had with you about time travel? And do you happen to remember a day, the first week in ninth grade, when I took you to an underground Chinese gambling house, and you won a couple grand?"

Sam's eyes contorted. Cameron took a deep breath and pondered the question.

"Sorry. Doesn't ring a bell," Cameron replied.

"You guys are going to think I'm full of it, and I'm not going to be able to prove it to you either, at least not in this loop," Quinn said.

"What do you mean this loop?" Gary asked.

"At precisely eleven thirty-three p.m., a bomb is going to explode."

"You're joking, right?" Gary said before Sam interrupted. "You mean that thing in the bathtub?"

"That would be my guess. I can't say for sure, because I wasn't at the exact location of the blast when it went off the first time," Quinn said.

"You're saying you've done this before? That's what you meant when you said in this loop."

"Yes. I'm on loop forty-seven. I wake up at exactly seven thirty-two a.m., and then the day resets a little after eleven thirty p.m."

"You've done this forty-seven times? Like in *Groundhog Day*?" Cameron asked.

"I've done today forty-seven times, but today's not the only day that's been looping. You may not believe me, but I went back to the day we first met in 1999."

"The day at the lake?" Cameron asked.

"That's right. Each night before I started the loop over, at least the first few times, I was tired and exhausted. I wanted to learn what was going on, and so I kept replaying the day's events in my head until I passed out," Quinn explained, pausing. "On one of those days, I thought about my best friend, Jeremy, and what he would've done in my situation. And the funny thing is, I dreamed about you the day at the lake just before my first time loop. The two things kind of went together. Just before I went back to 1999, I ended up in the hospital at the end of the night, and *The Price is Right* was on television. It brought all those memories back from the summer that year. Then I fell asleep and woke up in 1999."

"You're saying that all you had to do was think about the previous day you had lived right before you fell asleep, and you woke up that day?" Cameron asked.

"Exactly."

"Did you try waking up on any other day?"

"No. Not yet. Just the last day I was in from 1999 in the updated timeline whenever I returned to the present. When I was in the past, I didn't think about any day at all if I wanted to wake up a day later, but that only worked in 1999. I haven't tried not thinking about anything this year. I'm afraid to. I'm not sure if I'll die forever or just start the loop over again," Quinn replied.

Cameron paused. She tied her hair into a ponytail, which

she always did when she was theorizing and using her mind to its fullest potential.

"What you're saying could be possible under the right circumstances," Cameron said.

"You mean like a dark-matter explosion just as I'm about to fall asleep?" Quinn asked.

"Maybe, but there's something else that's happening tonight," Cameron replied.

"What do you mean?" Gary asked.

"Over the past few days, we noticed an increase in cosmic rays emitting from one sector of the galaxy—thirty-thousand light-years away. A supermassive binary black hole system prevented us from seeing it. It went supernova, and the readings are just coming in," Cameron explained. "The last report was that the exploding star was at a far enough distance that most of the cosmic rays will be either deflected or absorbed by the black hole system. It shouldn't be a cause for concern, but it's going to make for one heck of a light show."

"When will the light start?" Quinn asked.

"Hard to say exactly, but it should increase over the coming weeks and should be large enough to view in the day-time. A similar event happened a few hundred years ago and gave the world a fantastic display in 1604," Cameron replied.

"In 1604? Wow. People must've thought it was the second coming of Christ," Quinn said.

"Or Satan," Sam added.

"You think the cosmic rays from the event, combined with a dark matter explosion, would be enough to trigger a time loop?" Quinn asked Cameron.

"We're treading in uncharted waters. The possibility of the holographic mind is something I've been researching for a while. It's different from retrocausality, where the present state of events can influence the past," Cameron said.

"I don't pretend to understand half of what you're talking about," Quinn added.

"It just means that I think there's truth to what you are saying. I don't fully understand the complexity of it all, either. What I do know is that Einstein was wrong. God does play dice. And he plays it in multiple universes."

"This is all just a bit peachy, but do you have the slightest idea how to defuse this thing? We are talking about a bomb, aren't we? And not just any bomb. If I understand what you guys are saying, it's that this thing is going to blow up the world, and we're all royally screwed," Gary said, interrupting.

"That about sums it up," Cameron said as she inspected the device and attempted to flip it over.

"There's nothing you can do to stop it?" Gary asked.

"I'm not a bomb expert, but this design looks suspiciously like an old-style atom bomb—only condensed. This sphere and the hollow tube look as if they're intended to cause an implosion, which would start a nuclear reaction. But the design isn't completely accurate."

"What's making the water disappear, and what's that glow?" Gary asked.

"I honestly have no clue. I don't see any reason to doubt that it's made of dark matter. But if the Russians, or whoever built this, discovered how to create or locate and capture dark matter *and* harness its power, it's a massive leap in our understanding of the universe."

"And you forgot to mention the part where we're all royally screwed," Gary said.

"That, too," Cameron replied.

"Aren't we forgetting something?" Quinn asked.

"You mean the fact that you can loop time and do this, over and over again, until we get it right and discover how to unravel this thing?"

"Exactly."

"No. I haven't. It just doesn't do us any good now. We're still all going to die."

"All I have to do is fall asleep before eleven thirty-three p.m., and this won't happen."

"I hope you're right. Am I correct in assuming this is the first time we've had this conversation?" Cameron asked.

"Yeah, this is the first time."

"Then let's make the most of it. I need to teach you everything I know about my current understanding of dark matter and temporal causality before then."

"I might end up falling asleep before then."

"What about the bomb?" Gary asked.

"There's nothing we can do about that now," Cameron replied.

"I don't think we should give up so easily," Quinn said.

Cameron smiled. "Give it your best shot. Maybe you'll stumble upon the answer after fooling around with the device over the next few hundred time loops."

"Or maybe you'll just end up blowing us up," Gary said.

"I don't think it matters. This is clearly not a conventional bomb. It's either a dummy and Quinn has the world's coolest live version of a beta game for gamers, or he's telling the truth. If it's the latter, it won't matter. His death will just reset the clock," Cameron said.

"How do you know that?" Quinn asked.

"I don't exactly, but the math points in that direction. If I had to venture a guess, I'd say it wouldn't just reset the time loop today but your 1999 loop as well."

"It's already happened once. I got shot and died before the end of the day. I woke up again this morning after I died, and when I thought back to a few days later in 1999, I woke up on the first day of the new timeline."

"I knew it," Cameron said as she cracked a half smile and jolted up.

"It was really irritating because I had to explain everything all over again. It was fun the first time, but it gets old quickly. But I did have one question."

"Let me guess. You want to know what will happen if you forget to think about the day's events before you fall asleep in the present?"

"Yes. In the past, I just wake up the next day of the new current timeline if I don't think of anything."

"That's right. It makes sense because the universe already branched off, but if you die in the present, at the point of the explosion, that's when retrocausality would get involved. You'd repeat the day over in the present, but if you went back into the past, you'd sever the link to the branched universe or any branched universe you visited since your time loop began. But I don't think it would prevent you from visiting a date before."

"Brilliant." Quinn sighed.

"You guys are nuts. Do you actually believe what you're saying?" Gary asked.

"I think it's awesome. I'd love to be a time traveler. You're so lucky," Sam said.

"I'm not so sure about that just yet. I *am* having fun when I'm not getting shot and killed, but it sucks reliving trauma in an endless loop. I hope I don't get a super gnarly case of post-traumatic stress disorder."

"Think on the bright side. At least you'll have an eternity to work out your issues in therapy," Cameron said.

"I was never that into therapy."

"I haven't met many guys who are. It's a shame. Therapy can be very helpful. Especially if you're caught up in a different kind of loop."

"Gee, thanks," Quinn replied.

"Don't mention it," Cameron said.

"I'm going to defuse this bomb," Sam added.

CHAPTER 17

August 17th, 1999
Day 4.
7:00 a.m.

"IS TODAY YOUR first day in this timeline?" Jeremy asked.

"The second, technically, but it's the fourth day I've been here today, not including my time growing up," Quinn replied.

Jeremy looked up and wrinkled his brow. "So, today's going to be a boring day."

"You don't know that."

"Didn't you say you didn't repeat days that were important when you went to the future, then came back? You said you went only when you found a boring one since you would have to repeat that day. You said if you didn't think about that particular day the night before, you would wake up the next day, but *only* if you were in the past. You haven't tried it yet in the future."

"Yes, but I didn't say why I repeated today. You could be right, but it could also mean something failed miserably last time, so I'm doing it over. Or, I learned something, but

I need to keep learning. I never said my last day was in the future," Quinn said.

"Was it?"

"Yes. It was, and you're not going to believe who I just met."

"The president?"

"No, Cameron."

"So what? Big deal."

"I keep forgetting I haven't told you all the details in this time loop. I thought my memory was bad before, but I can't keep my timelines straight. I'm thinking I should start keeping a journal."

"Wouldn't it just be erased each time you repeated your time loop?"

"Only if it reset all the way back to the beginning like it did recently. But even if it did, I should keep a log of the number of days, or at least what I remember. Of course, each day I repeat it would get erased for that day, but I'll write as much as I remember, so when I do move forward, at least I have some idea of what I did and who I talked with about big things."

"Sounds too complicated. I say just keep doing what you're doing. But back to what you said. What was the big deal about meeting Cameron?" Jeremy asked.

"I lost track of her in the future. She's not on Facebook or anything."

"What's a Facebook?"

"We had this conversation before."

"No, we didn't."

"I know we didn't in this timeline, but we did in the other one. All you need to know is that we lost track of each other. She dated Scott Channing throughout high school, and then we never heard from her again. I forgot how much that kind of thing happens all the time, or at least that's what my parents told me. Kind of sad, really."

"Enough with the mushy stuff. What's the big deal?"

"The big deal is that she's awesome."

Jeremy rolled his eyes. "I'm going to hurl."

"No, that's not what I meant. But she's amazing in that way, too."

Jeremy shook his head. "See, I told you this was a stupid day."

"It *was* awesome. I followed your advice about setting up a fake beta game. It took a few tries, but I found some hard-core gamers. One of them, Sam, happened to be Cameron's younger cousin."

"Did Sam learn how the device worked?"

"Not exactly, but Sam did open it. I thought it looked like something the Asgard from *Stargate SG-1* would make, but when they opened it, it was something else—a futuristic bomb."

"Well, that would make sense since you're from the future."

"No. I mean, it looked like tech that hadn't been developed yet in 2021. Anyway, Cameron's a physicist. I only spoke with her once in the future, so I didn't get all the details, but she's been working on time travel as a theory and agrees with this past version of herself that dark matter might be involved."

"That makes perfect sense, the part about her agreeing with herself—not the dark matter part."

"I still find it hard to believe the Russians are behind it. The US *has* lost a lot of its balls in the future, but I still find it hard to believe the Russians figured out dark matter all on their own."

"Why? Don't you have futuristic computer phones and all kinds of cool stuff there? I don't think it's too hard to believe any smart person who has a computer and an internet connection would be able to use some kind of program to help them discover almost anything." Jeremy went on. "Here's a thought. Maybe you're not the only person who can travel through time. There could be others. Maybe someone from the future is inventing tech from the future and improving it until they can make it do whatever they want it to do."

"Wouldn't that be a paradox?" Quinn asked.

"This is why you need me. Even if you are from the future, you still miss the obvious. No, it's not a paradox. The universe splits off each time someone makes a new decision. If this person is from the future, then he would be creating a new branch when his mind returned to a point in his past. We just happened to be in that past."

"It still doesn't make sense. I'm still not sure how I started looping in the first place. Cameron thinks the bomb, especially if it's a dark matter bomb, could be part of the reason. The other part is a cosmic event that's meant to occur later that evening, a supernova explosion hidden by a binary black hole system."

"Aren't supernovas giant explosions when a star explodes?"

"Yeah, and normally we'd see it well ahead of time. Scientists could flag a star that's expected to go off. They just didn't see it because of the other stuff in the way."

"So how does this explain your time-jumping?" Jeremy asked.

"Something about the intersection of dark matter,

cosmic rays from the explosion, and the holographic mind, plus the fact I was thinking about what I would have done differently just before I fell asleep."

"I'll have to take your word for it."

"I don't pretend to understand it all, either, but my point is that if it's the explosion that's responsible for my time-looping, I would be alone in this timeline since it's *my* timeline. It couldn't exist without the explosion."

"It sounds like what you're saying is that only *one* time traveler could exist in each universe or timeline—or whatever you want to call it."

"I don't know if that's exactly true, either, but I think I'm the only one that could go back into my past because that would create a new branch. I can't change the past, so I'm just surfing from one point to the next when I fall asleep. If I return to a prior point, that point is fixed. I can only make changes in the present, so no traveler could jump back with me," Quinn said.

"I guess that makes sense."

"Which brings me back to my original point. I'm not sure if it's possible that a time traveler could have started the looping."

Jeremy paused. "I think that's where you're wrong. Didn't you say you can only change your present? If that's true, then another traveler could change your present. At least the one in the future, because for you it hadn't happened yet."

"I see what you mean. I think I should clarify—the explosion couldn't have been caused by someone who was already traveling through time *to start* their time loop. But I guess *anyone* could've caused the explosion, and anyone who underwent similar conditions as me could be living in their own loop."

"How would that work exactly?" Jeremy asked.

"No traveler could ever meet *before* the explosion, because each visit to the past by each traveler creates a new timeline and a new universe. So, none of them would ever meet. But if I stop the explosion, or find a way to stop the time loop and move forward in time again after the explosion, then it's possible for everyone who did start looping in that timeline to interact. That's assuming there's anyone else who can."

"At least you don't have to worry about Biff screwing up the future."

"That's not exactly true. Anyone could change the current timeline. That's already happened."

"What do you mean?"

"The first time we went to Ling's she found my list of stats in my pocket. Remember that gun I told you about? You won a little too much money the first time we played, and the smelly guy sitting next to us was threatening you. Ling had to calm him down, and she ended up searching us to see if we had cards up our sleeves. She found my stats and kept them."

"Let me guess. You went back and reset the day."

"Exactly. That timeline never continued beyond that point, at least with us in it, since I reset the day and started a new timeline. Each time I go back into the past, regardless of my starting point, I'm creating a new timeline. One theory is they don't continue if I restart the loop. But it may be more likely they continue on without me. It's hard to know for sure. All I know is in the timeline I'm currently living, they always reset unless I live them out."

"This is getting confusing," Jeremy said.

"It is, but all you need to know is that from my

perspective, whatever's already happened can't change. I can always go back to the morning of my last day in each timeline, or any day before that, and pick up where I left off. All the other timelines I created, at least since my last death, still exist, and I can visit them, too."

"That's amazing. You get to have all the fun with none of the downsides."

"There still is one huge downside."

"Which is what exactly?"

"I'm still stuck in a time loop. If I want to survive, I have to stop the explosion, or I won't be able to move past 2021. No one I know from my timeline will, at least in New York City."

"You think you'll still be able to surf different timelines if you stop the explosion?"

"I have no clue."

"Then why bother trying to fix it? You could live forever."

"That would be awfully inconsiderate of me. I'd be condemning everyone from my timeline to death just so I could live in the endless loop. I'd be stealing time—like a time thief," Quinn replied.

"Wait. That's stupid. It's also not true. Didn't you say each new day in your loop creates a new timeline, which is just another branch within the multiverse? You're creating a new universe or finding a branch that already existed. Those people would die, no matter what. If there's an infinite number of universes, then there's an infinite number of people. Some of them die, and some of them don't. You can't change that. The only thing you can change is which universe or timeline you're on, based on what actions you take."

Quinn stopped to think about the implications of what Jeremy had just said. It made perfect sense. There *were* an infinite number of universes. There had to be. It was the only thing that fit. He'd have to confirm that with Cameron. Still, the only question remaining was whether his actions were creating a new universe or simply allowing him to surf the current universe and timeline he was on.

Quinn didn't think he was actually creating new universes. That would violate the law of conservation of matter and energy. Technically, that law applied only to his universe, but he was almost certain it applied to the multiverse as well. Not that it mattered, since the multiverse was infinite.

"I think you might be right, Jeremy. I think I am just able to surf different universes and in essence different timelines, just the ones I've already visited or the new ones I create with my own actions."

"There you go. You can feel free to do whatever you like without any consequence," Jeremy said.

"There are always consequences."

"What consequences could there be?"

"The only one that matters. Since my actions determine my fate, every choice I make steers the course on the final timeline that I'll end up living. The only thing I can truly control is my present and the current timeline."

Quinn's words brought to memory a famous poet's words: *If you don't like something, change it. If you can't change it, change your attitude.*

At that moment, he realized he wasn't responsible for what happened in every world in the multiverse he intersected, only the one he currently occupied. All others would branch off on their own into infinite possibilities—none of which Quinn could influence.

"Yeah, but you don't have to worry about anyone else. You can still do what you want," Jeremy replied.

"And what about me?"

"So, you're saying that the only reason you want to help people is because you're selfish and you just want them to live."

"I guess that's one way of looking at it. I do want everyone to live, especially the people I love, so from that perspective, it *is* selfish. And I'm fine with that. But I think the bigger picture is that if I'm going to live with myself in this infinite time I have, I need a purpose. I can't think of anything more miserable than wandering through time directionless."

Quinn stung himself with those words. The truth was, he didn't feel he had a purpose until he *had become* a time traveler. Before then, he *had* been lost. His last bit of direction died when he buried Jeremy.

For the first time in a while, Quinn felt he had a reason to keep on living. He just knew that he had to find a way to stop that explosion so that his timeline could move forward.

"I feel like you're dropping the ball. We used to have such great ideas when we talked about what we would do if we could time travel, and you got the souped-up version. Feels like a big letdown. Like you're afraid or something," Jeremy said.

"I *am* afraid. It's easier to pretend to be afraid of death when you're not staring down its throat. But believe me, it's scary. It's not just me who I'm scared for. It's for everyone else who's going to die if I don't stop that explosion. If I can stop it, I should. If I can save them, I should."

"You can't save everyone. No one can. Even Superman couldn't save everyone in Metropolis. You shouldn't feel like you have to save the whole world. You can probably save anyone, but you can't save everyone, at least not all the time."

"Maybe I can't save everyone, but I can save *some* people,

and isn't that better than no one? I guess the more important question is if I don't save them, who will?"

"You always were too good of a person, Quinn."

"I don't know how good of a person I am, but I *do* want to do the right thing."

"Like I said, a good person. But think about it like you're the parent on the plane. If the oxygen masks fall during an emergency, you better put your mask on first, otherwise, your kids might die if you pass out while you're trying to save them."

Jeremy *did* have a point. It had been a wasted day, and Quinn had been on a mission to save the future. He didn't like having wasted days. The more he tried to fix things, the harder he realized it was. They made things look so easy in the movies, but in the real world, solving problems took time and effort. At least Quinn had plenty of time.

After school, Quinn talked with Cameron as they walked away from the schoolyard.

"You're not going to believe who I met in the future," Quinn said.

"Who is that?"

"I met you."

"Well, that's not very interesting."

"It is if you knew the circumstances. In the future, I lost contact with you after high school. I tried looking you up later—you just kind of vanished. Then I ran this beta game contest and you showed up out of nowhere."

"How did you find me?"

"You had a cousin named Sam."

"You don't know much about me at all. The only Sam I know is Samantha, and she's just a baby."

"Then Sam's the one."

"What happened?"

"Sam called you for help. You worked at a lab that used to be run by Columbia."

"That's my dad's lab."

"So, you know it, then?"

"He talks about it all the time. I've visited the lab a few times myself. He started working there after something happened at his old job and he couldn't work there anymore."

"You were amazing. You worked as a physicist or something similar, and you were working on your own theory of time travel."

"I guess this is the point where I should ask you if you should be telling me all this stuff, and maybe the reason is because of this conversation, but I know better than that."

"Yep. I asked you if you remembered our conversation the other day, just to see if you remembered. You said no, so your idea about the branching universe must be the right one."

"Did you discover what was in the bomb?"

"We didn't get that far. You thought it was probably some kind of exotic matter or dark matter. It looked futuristic. Water disappeared whenever it came close to it. It was shaped like a small sphere with something that looked like a handle. There was a tube in the center that spun and glowed. I heard two kinds of ticking."

"Interesting. Maybe there are two bombs. What happened?" Cameron asked.

CHAPTER 18

"DON'T DO ANYTHING stupid," Gary said.

"We can't sit here forever, staring at the thing. We might as well try to stop it," Sam replied.

"Couldn't you set it off if you touch the wrong cord or something?" Quinn asked.

"I don't see any cords, except for the timer on the outside. I haven't seen anything like this. If it's a bomb, I have no idea what we need to do to stop it."

Just then, Sam yanked off the timer, threw it on the ground, and stomped on it.

"There. No explosion."

"That was reckless and stupid," Gary said.

"Sometimes you need to be a little reckless," Sam replied.

"I'm not sure where to start. If dark matter is inside this thing, it wouldn't give off any electromagnetic radiation, but there is still a way we might be able to detect it. Dark matter still has mass," Cameron said.

"What about the encasing? That sphere looks like it's impossible to open. Do you think we could drill into it?" Quinn asked.

Cameron took off her ring, which had a small arrangement of diamonds. She rubbed the surface of the ends of the tube that held the chrome sphere, careful not to get too close to the center that appeared to vaporize whatever touched it.

"It didn't scratch—whatever alloy this is made from is stronger than diamonds. We won't be able to drill into it, and the sphere has some kind of cloaking device—that or maybe a transporter of some kind," Cameron said.

"This is pointless. We're never going to be able to figure this thing out. We're dead already," Gary said.

"We're going to figure this thing out. I just know it," Sam said.

The sphere spun and gleamed. Sam flipped it over, careful not to touch the center.

"Where do you think all the water that flowed to it went to?" Gary asked.

"My guess is another dimension. But I don't know what that thing is, what's inside of it, or how it works, so your guess is as good as mine," Cameron said.

"I think another dimension sounds good to me," Gary added.

The birds stopped chirping, and the few cars they heard from the outside quieted. A deafening silence grew.

"Do you hear that?" Quinn asked.

"No. I don't hear anything," Gary replied.

"That's my point exactly," Quinn said. "It's too quiet. This is Manhattan. There's always noise outside."

Cameron opened the curtain a crack and peered below, careful not to make the room visible from the outside.

At first glance, nothing was out of place. There were several cars motionless at the street level, but no one was walking on the sidewalks. She tilted her head to peer at the sky, which was scattered with a few clouds and the overhead sun.

"I don't see anything."

Quinn walked over. As he did, a large thud shook the building . Vibrations rattled their bones.

"What was that?" Gary asked.

The scent of the air changed. An odor hung in the air, and each breath brought in a stale, dry taste.

This time, Quinn dashed to the window and looked down. He squinted his eyes, half expecting an army of Russians to storm the building, but the streets were clear. The entrance was empty, and the sky was a deep blue, more profound than he remembered.

"I don't see anything, either, but that felt close, and it felt big."

In that time, they never bothered to check if Sam had made progress on the device. When Cameron glanced over, her mouth opened. Immediately, she rushed over to help Sam.

"What is it?" Quinn asked.

"I don't know," Cameron replied as she stopped just a few feet from Sam, who was frozen in place.

"Sam," Gary called.

Sam didn't move, but their hand hovered over the center of the chrome sphere. Sam's eyes were immobile, catatonic.

"Sam looks like they're in a state of suspended animation. What happened?" Quinn asked.

"I'm not…"

Now the device had captured both Sam and Cameron.

Cameron's pose was unnatural. Sam's form had a fluid pose that made their state less noticeable.

"It's the device," Quinn said. "Sam must have triggered it."

"What do we do? How can we save them?" Gary asked.

"I don't know that we can, at least not in this time loop. I think we have to save ourselves for the moment. We'll have to find a way to save them later."

Gary was a few feet closer to the device than Quinn, who was still near the window. Gary grabbed his box. "Let's go," he said. But it was too late. Those were his last words before he stood silent like a statue, a prisoner of the orb.

Quinn flung the door open and ran down the stairwell. He jumped several steps in a mad dash to make it out of the building before whatever had seized the others captured him, too.

He escaped to the outside, but it was quiet. The streets were solemn, empty of wildlife, and the bustle of the city. The clouds stopped moving. Only *he* roamed the streets, as if he were the last man on Earth, or at least on the block.

Quinn ran faster and turned the corner. The disturbing scene melted away into a typical city block filled with fast-paced walkers and normal urban fare.

Quinn hailed a taxi, then returned to his apartment half an hour later, just before noon.

He worried that whatever Sam had done to the device had accelerated the explosion, only there was no explosion, just a loud boom. Was it the same thing that had happened in the other time loop? Quinn couldn't be sure, but the device did something terrible as if it had broken time.

Quinn took one last look outside before he sprawled out on his bed. He wasn't sure if the device would engulf the entire city or if it was confined to a single city block. If it kept expanding, he wasn't sure if he would fall asleep fast enough, or become a prisoner like the others.

Quinn closed his eyes.

August 17th, 1999
Day 4.
7:05 a.m.

"It didn't turn out the way we planned," Quinn said.

"What does that mean?" Jeremy replied.

"We made things worse. Cameron's cousin Sam tried to figure it out, but Sam had no idea what to do. None of us did, even Cameron. Sam got too close to the center of the device and must have triggered it."

Quinn continued. "The next thing we knew, Sam froze like a statue. Cameron went over to help, but the same thing happened to her without her even touching the device or Sam. A half minute later, Sam's friend, Gary, stopped moving. I ran outside to escape whatever was happening. I think I made it out just in time."

"That sounds like a time bubble, like the one in that episode of *Star Trek: The Next Generation* when Captain Picard traveled through a pocket of shattered time. Different sections of the ship moved at different rates of speed," Jeremy replied.

"Yeah, I remember that episode. There was a life form living inside a black hole. Alien eggs caused a rupture in space-time."

"That must be it, then. You think there's an alien ship hovering over the Earth in your future? With some alien eggs in a warp drive causing ruptures in space?"

"Yeah, that makes total sense. All I have to do is steal a transporter or shuttle-craft up to the ship."

Jeremy smiled. "At least you know you were right about the bomb or orb, or whatever that thing is. It's connected somehow."

"*Somehow* is the key word. We can touch the edges of it, but the center of the orb sucks whatever is near it into nothingness or maybe into another dimension. If we try to open it, we trigger some kind of pocket in space-time."

"Why don't you take the device and dump it into the East River, then drive away as far as you can?"

"That's a big gamble. I have no idea what will happen if I do that—if the water would do anything. For all I know, it could suck up the entire river and create a massive sinkhole, then still explode. If I don't fall back asleep, I could end up permanently dead or frozen in space-time."

"I still think the easiest way to stop it is to stay in the past and live the timeline over. It might be the only way."

"I'm not ready to give up just yet."

Quinn thought about the time he had stolen by reliving the past, and he felt guilty for not spending more time with his sister and parents. He wrestled with emotions he thought were usually reserved for parents.

He knew he shouldn't feel that way. He had enough time. Impatience was the issue. It kept him from seriously considering what Jeremy said. Or at least accepting the notion as a realistic possibility.

For all Quinn's lip service about stopping 9/11, he felt he had abandoned the idea in favor of an easier yet impossible choice, stopping the Russians from breaking time. But he knew if he kept playing God in the future, he might get frozen and never get another chance, or get killed and have the 1999 timeline erased again.

"What happened to stopping nine-one-one?"

"You mean 9/11, and I haven't forgotten it. It's just a while from now, and I've been focused on—"

"On something that won't happen for another twenty-two years?" Jeremy interrupted.

Quinn took a deep breath. Jeremy was right. It was twenty-two years in the future, but it was also yesterday. It was a reality no one should have to think about, but Quinn had no right to complain. He was in a position to stop one of the greatest horrors of all time. All he had to do was some initial planning and then wait.

"That's not fair," Quinn said.

"What's not fair? You mean asking you to stop something you know is going to hurt a lot of people—something that's within your power? Not only that, but it most likely solves your problem in the future, too," Jeremy said. "Think about it. If you stop something that big, the ripples in time and changes from that one act will be significant—the world would be completely different. I don't think whatever caused the problem would have happened."

Quinn wanted to scream. He knew every possible choice likely existed in some universe, and all choices branched off into infinite versions, almost as if it didn't matter to anyone but himself.

Then Quinn remembered what Cameron had told him, about the supernova and cosmic rays. It wasn't just the bomb that could be the sole culprit of the time loop—it might also be the explosion.

"I just remembered something we should check out," Quinn said.

Quinn spent the next few minutes explaining what Cameron had said in the future about cosmic rays and how the interaction with the dark matter explosion might have triggered the time-looping. With what had happened with the orb, he was more convinced than ever that might be the reason.

Several hours later, Quinn and Jeremy met up after school with Cameron to discuss the issue.

"If I could speak with your dad…."

"I'm not sure that's such a good idea."

"You mean because of what happened?" Quinn asked.

"You know what happened to my dad?"

"I read about it in the future. Something about how a member of the team your dad worked with, had ties to the ninety-three World Trade Center attack, and the project was shut down."

Cameron took a deep breath and averted her eyes. Quinn touched her hand, then quickly pulled it back when he realized what he was doing.

"I'm sorry. It just makes me think about the bad times when my parents fought the most. They never fought. They never yelled, except for one night. My mother started it right after my dad told her the news. He fell apart right in front of us. I couldn't believe it. He was always so calm and emotionless. But not that night."

"What happened?" Jeremy asked as he noticed Quinn's hand pull back from Cameron's.

"After he told Mom he lost the grant, she screamed at him. She told him he just threw away their entire marriage and our future. She said she had wanted to leave him for the longest time, that he was cold and didn't know how to behave around his own family," Cameron explained. "That hurt him more than anything. Not that she wanted to leave, but that for all that time, she thought he didn't or couldn't love us enough. He knew what she meant. She didn't say it, but she meant it."

"You mean because of his autism?" Jeremy asked.

"Yeah. My dad's the smartest person I've ever met, but he *can* be cold sometimes. But it's not his fault. He loves us in his own way, and when she told him that, I could see his face transform like she had sucked the life out of him. He broke down. He *never* did that, at least not in front of me. She really hurt him."

"I'm sorry," Quinn said.

Cameron's eyes welled up. Quinn could see she was holding back emotion, but there *was* a resolve in her face that struggled with sadness.

"Do you get along with your mother?" Jeremy asked.

"I still talk to her, but I spend most of my time with my dad."

"I still don't understand. Is it because of your dad's autism that you don't want to talk with him about this?" Quinn asked.

"No. I just don't want to bring up that whole thing again. It hurts him every time I do."

"I hope I don't sound like a complete jerk when I say this, but I think he may be stronger than you think. It's clear to me you're strong yourself, but one thing I've learned as an adult," Quinn said as Jeremy's eyebrows lifted, "is that things don't matter so much when you get older. The things that used to bother us seem meaningless in comparison to everything else in the world. At least they have for most people."

Cameron exhaled and gave Quinn a disapproving look. "You don't think what my dad went through was important?"

"Of course I do. What I mean is that despite his autism or the circumstances, I bet he's more resilient than you think. That, and when he learns the fate of the world is at stake, his personal pride and emotion over any event will be small by comparison."

"Fine. I'll talk to him about it. What do you want me to say exactly? Other than the fact that you're traveling through time."

"Everything I've already told you about the orb, and there's something else. In the last loop, I spoke to you in the future. And you're awesome, by the way. Anyway, you said there was a star that went supernova. It was close, but we didn't know it was there because it was obscured by a binary black hole system." "You mentioned that the explosion should become visible that night, right around the time of the explosion. You said it wasn't expected to have a harmful impact despite its distance because most of the energy would be absorbed or deflected by the black hole system, but it would put on a light show and shower us with harmless neutrinos, which you had wanted to study after the confirmation of gravitational waves a couple of years earlier."

"You think the supernova is important to the time-looping?" Cameron asked.

"I don't know, but I get the feeling it's important. It's just a huge coincidence that something of that magnitude occurs at the same time as the other explosion. And the thing is, I don't even know for sure if the device caused the explosion."

"Fine. I'll talk with him and see if he has any ideas."

"Will you tell him about the time-traveling part?" Jeremy asked.

"I haven't decided. I want him to take me seriously. He doesn't have any reason not to trust what I'm saying. We don't have a typical father-daughter relationship, and I rarely joke around with him, but I don't want him to think I'm teasing him," Cameron replied.

Dr. Green flung the door open and tossed his bag onto the couch.

"You're not going to believe this."

"What is it, Dad?"

"That star you mentioned, the one you think might go supernova soon."

"Yeah?"

"I ran the numbers, *a dozen* times. There *is* a binary system that's hiding the star *most* of the time. But there's a period with the rotation of the two black holes where the star becomes visible."

"So, you found it?"

"Yeah, but if what you're saying is true, the black hole system wouldn't deflect the energy for the entire time. In fact, for one short period, it would amplify the explosion by concentrating the energy and funneling it into a narrow range."

Cameron's face dropped. "What are you saying?"

"I'm saying that in precisely twenty-two years from now, our planet is toast."

CHAPTER 19

"OH MY GOD. I can't believe it," Jeremy said.

Quinn exhaled. "I guess that answers one question. I *am* going to have to live this timeline over for the duration. It's all we can do to find a way to save the world from the supernova explosion," Quinn said.

"That's not something you can do. A supernova explosion of that type won't just wipe us out. It will rip apart the atmosphere, boil the ocean, and incinerate the planet," Cameron replied.

"I told you, you shouldn't have worried about your boss, Logan," Jeremy said.

"If I had never tried to save Logan, I would have never known about the bomb. And if I had never known about the bomb, I would have never known about the supernova."

"I don't get it," Jeremy said.

"Get what?" Cameron asked.

"If your dad can figure that out now, how come they couldn't figure it out in the future?"

"They only discovered the supernova a few days before most of the light was reaching us. There's a time delay. Even though the system went supernova thousands of years ago, it's taken the light that long to reach us."

As she spoke, her father arrived. Dr. Green had dark curly hair, the same comic book eyes as Cameron but in no way as beautiful. He wore a brown cardigan sweater that hung like a lab coat, just below his waistline. Jeremy thought he looked a little like Data from *Star Trek: The Next Generation* mixed with Doc Brown from *Back to the Future*.

"There's something we haven't told you, Dr. Green. You're going to call me crazy, but I already know about the supernova, and I don't even have a telescope. I'm hoping you hear me out," Quinn said.

"How *do* you know about the supernova?"

"The first evidence was from the neutrinos. That's how we learned about it—they pass through ordinary matter unobstructed."

"*We*? Who's *we* in this conversation?"

"The short version is I sent my consciousness back through time using a principle of physics known as the holographic mind—that combined with M-theory and a few other things that are above my head. At precisely eleven thirty-three on August seventh, 2021, an explosion will occur. Except that in my mind, it has already occurred. I started living a time loop," Quinn explained. "I lived weeks in the same day. At first, I just tried to save my boss from an accident that I later learned was connected to a Russian terrorist attack. Then I learned that I could send my mind back through any point in my life as long as I thought about it before I fell asleep." He went on talking.

"I think a dark matter bomb caused the explosion. It goes off at the same time the height of the supernova reaches Earth. The working theory is that they're connected. I've confirmed a few things, but I'm still learning as I go."

As much as he could, Quinn explained over the next few minutes what had happened in the prior weeks. He gave detailed accounts of what happened with the orb, and what he tried to do in the past.

Dr. Green showed no emotion on his face. Quinn thought he would make the perfect poker player.

"If what you're saying is true…"

"It is true. And if you need proof, he can give it," Cameron said.

"Then, I'm going to agree with your assumptions. I don't know about the dark matter bomb since you've given me very little other than it's a bomb and you think it has dark matter. But assuming that's the case, it could interact with a supernova explosion."

Dr. Green explained. "The neutrinos are incidental. They're more of a curiosity, but the energy that's being funneled by the binary system could create a flashpoint if they interacted with dark matter—much the same way that normal matter becomes plasma, the fourth state of matter, in nuclear fusion within our sun. It would be the sheer energy from a hyperenergetic supernova with a narrow but precise focus."

"What would happen with this different state of matter?" Quinn asked.

"As you said, one theory suggests the universe is a hologram. Not just the universe but the multiverse, an infinite number of universes where each possibility that could exist *does* exist. This flashpoint would allow anyone who happened to be thinking about a specific set of events to move back and forth in time."

"That's so cool," Jeremy said.

"It's possible the light pulses traveling in your head could interact with neurons, creating their own holographic image, which exists outside of space-time as we know it. If you came in contact with some exotic matter, due to a cosmic explosion from a primordial black hole with dark matter, for example, it could trigger something like this."

"Wouldn't it be happening with other people, too? What about the fact that I went back into the future, and it was the same as before? Should my actions now have changed it?"

"You mentioned before the idea of a fork in the multiverse. At an elementary level, you are correct. The math is a little more complicated, but in essence, you should theoretically be able to return to any point in the multiverse where you've ever existed. The only thing is, for that to happen, another factor must come into play."

"Which is what?" Quinn asked.

"Radioactive decay. Theoretically, the nexus of your holographic mind, dark matter, and the decay of radioactive isotopes would allow you not only to repeat days you've lived in the past but also to return to any point in the future when you've ever existed, just by thinking about it."

"Wait, what?" Quinn asked.

"This is all new science. I have been working on a new theory of time I came across by accident before I was shut down," Dr. Green said.

"I don't think any of this is an accident. I read about what happened in the future, how one of your colleagues was connected to the ninety-three attack on the World Trade Center."

Dr. Green's face dropped. His chest expanded, and he took focused breaths to calm his mind. "I had nothing to do with that attack."

"I know, but that's not what I meant. I'm trying to say that the person responsible may be connected to the Russian bombing in the future. And I know from what I've learned in the time loops that they were part of a cell that goes on to finish the job and destroy both towers in the worst terrorist attack in American history," Quinn said.

"You mean 9/11?" Jeremy asked.

"That's right, 9/11. It was a coordinated attack on Washington DC and New York by bin Laden. Your colleague also connects bin Laden and Ayman al-Zawahri to the Russians. Beyond that, I don't know much else. Just take my word for it. This is no coincidence."

"If these connections exist, there is one way to stop them."

"Kill them?" Jeremy asks.

"No. Tell the world about the supernova. It won't be hard, either. It's not like the movies where there's some secret government entity trying to keep everything from the public. Once we put it out on a few internet threads of an enthused astronomer, news will spread quickly."

"What if they come to the same conclusion the scientists in the future did?" Quinn asked.

"The scientists in the future didn't have the benefit of seeing the position of the stars we do now. If they had more time, they would figure it out quickly. My guess is that it will be a curiosity at first, but in a few weeks, reality will settle in. Shortly after that, people will start coming up with options."

"What kinds of options?" Cameron asked.

"You know, the usual. Underground caves to house the select few, unworkable deflection devices the size of the Earth, or desperate attempts to change the position of the planets."

"The underground cave won't work?" Jeremy asked.

Quinn smirked.

"Not unless you have an exoskeleton that can survive several thousand degrees or lungs that can breathe in the new modified atmosphere, whatever's left of it," Quinn replied.

The severity of the probability sunk in and showed on Jeremy's face.

"So, you're saying we only have twenty-two years left before the world ends?" Jeremy asked.

"As of now, yes. But the good news is I don't think those radical terrorist connections you mentioned will care so much anymore about building that dark matter bomb or blowing up a couple of buildings in New York. The world will go into survival mode. And honestly, despite the potential of mankind, I'm doubtful they will succeed in finding a solution in the short time we have left."

Quinn exhaled slowly, wondering if he'd been completely honest with himself, or if it was just wishful thinking to assume the terrorists would give up. But he didn't want to convey that doubt to them, at least not at that moment.

"It's a good thing the world has a new hero, a time traveler from the future who can save us all," Cameron said.

"That's not funny. I'm not a hero."

"But you are," Dr. Green added. "And you have the benefit of looping time. You are the only one who can save the planet and the species. I don't know how long it will take you to get the basics of complex math, physics, and engineering, but I think it's time you set your sights on a new college major."

Quinn exhaled. "I don't know if I can do this."

"You'll never know unless you try, but I think after a few tries, you'll do just fine."

CHAPTER 20

"DON'T DO ANYTHING stupid," Gary said.

"We can't sit here forever, staring at the thing. We might as well try to stop it," Sam replied.

The floor trembled as a series of loud thuds reverberated through the hallways. Quinn stuck his head out through the window. Several large trucks had blocked the entrance and half a dozen heavily armed men in military gear had stormed up the stairwell.

"Holy crap. This didn't happen last time. We must have done something different," Quinn said.

"What should we do?" Sam asked.

"When they enter the door, grab the center of the orb. It will trigger a pocket of warped time."

"And why should Sam do that?" Gary asked.

"To keep from getting shot. The bubble will protect us until the supernova irradiates the planet and I restart the time loop. Did any of you guys by chance drop a wallet or something that could have led the Russians to our location?" Quinn asked.

"That would be me," Gary said, raising his hand.

"I'll have to warn you in the next time loop. Don't lose your wallet, or the Russians will kill you."

"What are we waiting for?" Sam asked as they slammed their hand on the center of the orb.

A sharp pain needled Sam's arm. Then all sensation stopped. Cameron stepped forward. Quinn and Gary rushed toward the orb just as the Russians made their way to the door and knocked it down.

Automatic machine gun fire exploded into the room, but before the bullet shells landed, the time bubble enveloped them, and the bullets heading toward the orb froze right where they were.

The bubble expanded, demarcated by the slugs that stood frozen in midair. The men stopped firing, standing motionless as the time bubble ballooned throughout the city.

AUGUST 7TH, 2021

DAY 49.

9:58 A.M.

Quinn peered out the window. He had warned Gary about the wallet ahead of time, and there were no vans parked outside and no men storming the building.

Cameron knocked on the door, and Sam let her in.

Over the next hour, Quinn explained what Dr. Green had said about the supernova. Gary and Sam were still in disbelief and waited to hear what Cameron had to say.

"If what you're saying is true, it does sound like we're screwed. At least in this timeline."

"So, you believe me?" Quinn asked.

"There's no way you could know about the coordinates of the star unless you were part of a select few scientists who discovered it."

"I hate to interrupt, but I thought I should let you know the last time we were here, Russians stormed the building. If it happens again, press down on the shiny button in the center of the orb to hit reset. It'll prevent a bloody mess on the floor, and I'll come out the other end in the morning."

"That's comforting," Sam replied.

"So, what are we supposed to do with this? If you're stuck in the loop and we screw up everything, how the heck are we going to beat this thing?" Gary asked.

"Today, we're not. At eleven thirty-three, this world is going to get toasted by a big shiny diamond in the sky, and I'll be sent back to the morning, just like I always am. But now, I have a mission and a plan. I need to discover how to save the world from the supernova. I have exactly twenty-two years to do it, but I can take those twenty-two years as many times as I need. I figure it's best to learn as much as I can in 2021 about physics and engineering and take that knowledge into the past. And while I'm here, I might as well start with this dark matter orb."

"Are we sure that's what this is now?" Gary asked.

"Not a clue. But everyone says it makes the most sense—Cameron in both timelines and Cameron's dad. So, who am I to argue? The only thing is if we get too close, it creates a time bubble that increases in size and envelopes the city," Quinn said.

The ground shook. Soot filtered into the room through a crack in the window. Quinn ran to the window to check to see if the Russians were at the base of the building. No one was there.

Adrenaline flooded Quinn's veins, and he held his body upright. At that moment, the realization of how long he'd been in the time loop hit him. It was over two months, and he hadn't seen Logan or Valentino in weeks. The world he knew began slipping the moment he fell into the loop, but it wasn't until that moment when his body seized him and forced him to throw up on the floor.

"You okay, Quinn?" Cameron asked as she walked toward him, tucking her auburn hair behind her ears and then pulling it into a ponytail.

"Be careful. You don't want to get your shoes dirty from all the vomit," Sam said.

"Oops. Too late," Gary added.

Cameron put her arms around Quinn. He let out a gasp of air, then steadied his breathing.

"It's going to be fine. I can't imagine what you've been going through these past couple of months, but I know it must be taking its toll," Cameron said.

Quinn wiped the bile from his lips. Gary cringed.

"I'm doing my best, but I'd be lying if I said I thought this was going to be easy. Bill Murray made looping in time look like a cakewalk. I'm not sure how long it took him to learn how to carve that ice sculpture of Rita's face, but figuring out how to keep the planet from getting incinerated by a supernova explosion is a tad bit trickier."

Quinn's heart pounded. His face warmed. Cameron put her hand on Quinn's shoulders.

"You'll figure it out. I know it's not fair, but nothing ever is. It wasn't fair when my dad died five years ago. It wasn't fair when thousands of people died during 9/11, and it's not fair that millions of people starved to death after last year's pandemic. But the world keeps chugging along, anyway. It has no choice. We have no choice," Cameron said.

"Yeah, I know," Quinn said as he took another deep breath. "I guess I just need to know where to start."

"Looks like you have already started," Sam said.

"I don't know you, but Cameron's right. You got us all here. Just keep on moving. You'll figure it out. You have to, and you have eternity to do it," Gary said.

Eternity was a long time, but that word comforted Quinn. He hated the idea of doing everything alone, but he wasn't alone. He had Cameron and his own family in 1999. He would have to get creative with how he would hang out with Logan and Valentino, but he did have eternity.

The banging on the door interrupted Quinn's brief reflection. Sam hit the reset button.

CHAPTER 21

SIX WEEKS INTO watching every episode of *Star Trek*, *Battlestar Galactica*, and *Stargate SG-1*, and every time-travel movie he'd ever seen, Quinn created a short list of ideas to stop the supernova. Cameron provided most of the help, culling a longer version of ideas Quinn scribbled on paper.

They were all implausible. The physics worked, but there was only one that might just be doable…with a couple hundred years of practice.

Quinn worked out a few things he needed to consider about the supernova: the biggest problem was the concentrated gamma rays that would funnel directly toward the Earth. The other issue was that while the neutrinos were supposedly harmless, it was still possible they interacted with the dark matter device to start the time loop.

Aside from time travel, Quinn thought the distance of the device and the limited span of the concentrated gamma and neutrino bursts might give him an advantage in finding a solution.

In some martial arts practices, the philosophy behind the movements involved using an opponent's weight against them. Quinn thought it would be most effective if he could not only save the Earth from the supernova but use its harmful effects to mankind's advantage by harnessing its power.

That notion gave Quinn what he thought was the first idea he should try out—an array in space that served many functions. Quinn would have to learn the engineering behind the array, fund it, and either convince the government to allow him to launch the array or go around them.

His idea was that the array would act as a giant rechargeable battery in space. It would be powered by both the sun and the gamma rays from the supernova. He hadn't worked out all the details, but he thought if he could turn the array into a beacon of hope instead of a last-ditch plan to save humanity, it could have the most impact.

Quinn's idea was to use the energy stored in the array for space travel. When the array detected an elevated level of gamma rays, a series of ultrathin, but durable panels spanning thousands of miles, would unfold. The panels would shield the Earth and absorb the energy from the gamma rays. Batteries would hold the energy, which humans could use for space travel within the solar system. It could be the foundation for a permanent foothold and expansion into space.

Quinn would need a team, but he also needed dozens of iterations on his own mini test projects before he could hire the team. He would learn everything he could about lightweight materials, solar power, batteries, and the engineering needed to get those materials into space. He also needed to review current space laws.

For the rest of the evening, Quinn researched online everything available on each area of focus. He jotted down notes on what technology existed and what was still in the planning stages.

He studied breakthroughs in the last five to ten years, in the hopes of jumpstarting those ideas a decade earlier, to buy the time needed to advance past technology fast enough to build the array and save the planet.

Thursday, August 19th, 1999
Day 3.
7:30 a.m.

"I finally found a use for these wasted days I've needed to use to loop between the future and the past," Quinn told Jeremy.

"What's that?"

"You had the right idea all along. I need to invent technology from the future and improve it to save the planet."

"See, I told you there was value in the Jeremy-meister. What are you making first?"

"I need to learn how to build a giant solar array in space to channel the supernova's energy. I'm hoping I can use it to power a ship or interplanetary transporters for research and space tourism, maybe even our first colony on the moon."

"What's our first step?"

"*Our* first step?" Quinn said.

"You don't think you're doing this all by yourself, do you? I'm not going to let you have all the fun. I want a piece of the action, too," Jeremy replied.

"And don't forget about me," Cameron said as she walked through the door.

Quinn's mom walked in from the hallway. "Oh,

Cameron. It's so nice to finally meet you. Quinn's been going on and on about how smart you are, just like your father," Quinn's mom said.

Quinn gave his mom a look that expressed his irritation with her embarrassing statement. It was all true, but it made him feel like a dolt.

"It's nice to meet you, too, Mrs. Black," Cameron replied with a smile.

In the time Quinn had spent creating his plan, he realized he needed to change himself. He needed new habits, and he needed to like them. He needed a routine to develop them, so he spent the better part of the evening after school working out the details with his new crew: Jeremy, Cameron, and her dad.

The biggest change was learning. He was an above-average student but not exceptional. He was invisible to most teachers and did just enough to go to college and graduate with decent job prospects.

Now, Quinn understood he had to master physics, become an expert engineer, and think like an inventor. He wasn't convinced he could do it in one lifetime, even with the advantage of shifting back and forth twenty-two years in the future, an advantage that would decrease as he progressed on the new timeline. He figured he'd master one subject each timeline, with added time loops as needed.

Dr. Green spent the afternoon calling a few former colleagues and several astronomers across the country.

At MIT, a renowned astrophysicist, Lionel Shaw, opened a war room at one of the conference centers. He switched venues three times after the number of participants increased exponentially once the news of the supernova had unfurled within academic circles.

The room filled with brilliant thinkers—the background chatter grew deafening as the scheduled meeting time approached.

Lionel stepped up on the podium. He wore a flamboyant pink Prada shirt matched with sculpted salon hair and manicured nails, including one long pinky nail painted black.

"I would like to thank you all for being here, but under the circumstances, let's just get started."

The room quieted to dead silence.

"I've triple-checked the numbers, as I'm sure all of you have as well. The evidence is irrefutable, and by ten p.m. tonight, the world will know what we know. That brings me to the point of this discussion. I'm not sure it's possible to find a solution in the limited time we have, but if we dispense with the pleasantries and cheat the rules, I'm sure we can at least make some progress," Lionel said.

The room was filled with academics, mostly PhDs in theoretical physics. A couple of engineers were sprinkled across the hall. There was one reporter. She had long black hair, designer glasses, and worked for the *Boston Herald*. She raised her hand.

"Can I ask you a question, Mr. Shaw?" she asked,

pausing briefly. "Can you tell me why a star that's over thirty thousand light-years away will have so much power when most scientists agree that a supernova would need to be much closer to have the impact that's rumored to destroy the planet. And why are we only finding out about this now?" she asked.

"Well, that's two questions, Ms.….?"

"Young. Kim Young."

"You're right, Ms. Young. Most supernovas would need to be about thirty light-years away or closer to be planet killers, but this is no ordinary supernova. It's a hypernova that will yield a concentrated gamma-ray burst, the rarest and most energetic of all the explosions that happen in the universe," he explained. "It's coming from a supermassive star that exploded just under thirty thousand years ago, but we know that it's already gone supernova by a leading set of neutrinos from the star."

He continued. "The problem is we've detected a resonance or frequency within the star. It suggests massive tidal forces are ripping the star apart and will result in a gamma-ray burst in precisely twenty-two years. It will last for only a few seconds. That energy will be funneled so precisely towards our planet that it will heat up the surface a thousand degrees and blow off our atmosphere."

"What are your plans to stop it?" she asked.

Lionel squirmed where he was standing, coughed, and swallowed.

"Stop it? There is no stopping it. It's already happened. We're just waiting for it to arrive. Nothing on this planet will survive. That's why I'm here. That's why we're all here."

"So, you're giving up?" she asked.

Quinn sat a couple of rows behind Kim and interrupted.

"What about a Dyson sphere—an inverted Dyson sphere—one that doesn't harness the energy of our sun, but of the gamma-ray burst that's heading towards us?" Quinn asked.

"That's an interesting suggestion, and it sounds like a great idea, but the devil's in the details. I'm sure that would be a fine idea if we had a hundred years to work on it, but we don't," Lionel said.

"That's true, but we're the human race. Our back is up against the wall. We can either throw up our hands and do nothing, or we can come up with the best possible solution and make it happen," Quinn said.

A few scientists in the audience chuckled. Quinn had grown sick of the level of cynicism across the country even in 1999. Pessimists trying to pass themselves off as realists had long taken over most aspects of government and academic circles. It was time for a change.

Dr. Green sat next to Quinn, and the expression on his face shared the anger that boiled inside him.

"Excuse me, but what exactly about what Quinn said is funny? Are you going to resign yourselves to the end of the human race, or are *you* going to take action? Surely something would be better than nothing. You're guaranteed to fail if you don't try," Dr. Green said as he drew the ire of the scientists who laughed off Quinn's suggestion.

Six-thousand three-hundred miles away in an Arabian palace, Osama bin Laden met with several dozen Arabian, Russians, and American followers of The Way.

"*Allah* has smiled on us today," bin Laden said in fluent English, a language he knew but had hidden from the world until that moment. "The oppressive American regime and Western governments will finally fall to their knees."

Several of the Arabian followers cried out, "*Allahu akbar. Allahu akbar.*"

"Yes, indeed. God *is* great. And he is surely smiling on us today. With this fire from the sky, he's signaling to us that it's time to usher in the new Caliphate and the Final Empire," bin Laden said.

Shouts of "*Allahu akbar. Allahu akbar,*" spread in the room. A couple of the Americans in the back laughed.

"What do you find so funny?" bin Laden asked.

"Won't you drop the pretense? You don't believe in *Allah* any more than I do," said a figure hidden in the shadows in the back row behind several men in white robes.

"How dare you—"

The man cut him off, "There is no God. There is no *Allah.* There is only the universe. And the universe just gave the world and all of us a great big middle finger."

"What do you mean with all this madness?" bin Laden asked.

"Why waste our time with this plan? The world will die on its own. It doesn't need our help anymore. I've been a follower of The Way from the beginning, but with the news of the supernova, The Way serves no purpose."

"But that's where you're wrong. It's more important than ever. We will let the Americans and the world get complacent, and then we'll strike. We'll strike at the heart of Babylon, New York City, and Washington, and demoralize their spirit even more."

"Why continue? Our purpose was to save the universe, save the world from pollution, and the greed of the unnatural human race. The universe is doing that for us. What's the point in playing this game if we've already won?" he asked.

"We can't take for granted that the greed of the Americans will inspire a solution to their quest to control even more riches and spread across the vast expanse of space. They are like Babel, and I have no doubt they will build their tower. There is nothing more frightening than whacking a hornet's nest, and this news has done that.

"We can't take for granted the possibility they will find a solution, however remote. We must help the world along the path to destruction to save the universe from mankind. The Final Caliphate is upon us, and we must ensure that we do everything we can to hasten it along," bin Laden replied.

Two of the robed men in front of the Americans stood up and shouted, "*Allahu akbar. Allahu akbar.*" They turned, aimed, and fired their fully automatic machine guns into the chest of the Americans, who fell back and landed on the dirt floor with a thud.

"Indeed, brothers. God is great."

CHAPTER 22

AMY SAT HUNCHED over the kitchen table in pajamas she had worn since last night. Tears streamed down her face, wetting her tangled hair. All the progress Quinn had made consoling her over their grandmother's death the past summer had vanished. Her hands trembled.

"Talk to your sister, Quinn. She won't listen to us," Quinn's mom said.

Frank looked on, quiet. He had tried moments earlier but had given up. He'd seen the same persistence in Amy when she had mourned her grandmother, and he didn't want to invite more trouble.

Quinn's mom was the enforcer in the household, but Amy ignored her pleas.

"I think you should let her stay home," Quinn said.

"That's not what I was hoping you would say," his mom replied.

"I get it. You want things to go back to normal. The

problem is they're not normal. I get that we can't give up our lives and quit doing stuff, but the world just got a sucker punch in the gut. Everyone's still trying to process it," Quinn said.

"I'm going to school. I have things to do, but let Amy stay home. Let her deal with things in her own way."

"I think he's right," his dad said.

"I don't like it," his mom replied.

"I love you, Mom, but considering all that happened, I'm surprised you care so much."

Quinn's mom grabbed a glass from the kitchen cabinet and hesitated. She planned on filling it up but paused. Instead, she smashed it on the floor.

"It's not fair. It's not right!" his mom said.

Quinn and his dad rushed over and threw their arms around her.

"You're right, Mom. It's not fair. But we're not giving up, either. The world isn't giving up. Maybe some people, maybe even most. But I'm not giving up. Other people won't give up, and we'll find a way through this," Quinn said.

"I think the same thing. We still have a lot of life left in us," his dad added.

"I'm sorry, Mom. I didn't mean to upset you. I'm sorry. I'll go to school. I will. I'll get dressed right now," Amy said.

Quinn's mom wiped away the tears that streamed down her face, straightened the strands of hair that dropped in front of her face during the episode, and then stood erect.

"I'm sorry. I didn't mean to…" she said as she continued wiping away her tears.

"That won't happen again. And like I was saying. You *will* go to school, Amy. You'll go to school, too, Quinn. And you'll go to work," she said, staring at Frank.

The room fell silent.

A few moments later, Jeremy arrived and walked with Quinn to school.

"You're going to stop this thing, right? You can loop time, so if anyone can do it, you can."

"Yeah. I'm going to stop it. I have to. It's just going to be crazy during the next four years in this timeline. At least I don't have to worry about 9/11," Quinn said.

"Well, that's some good news at least. So, when do you start inventing cool stuff from the future?" Jeremy asked.

"It'll be awhile. I'm going to have to actually pay attention in school this time and make an attempt to learn advanced math and science. I was just an okay student in my last life, enough to get to college. The closest I came to becoming an actual scientist was binge-watching Discovery documentaries on Netflix."

"What's Netflix?" Jeremy asked.

"You'll find out next month, assuming they still launch their subscription service. Who knows? Maybe they'll make a killing—it's happened before."

Quinn's thoughts moved to his sister. He worried about her. If the morning was any sign, she was going to take things a lot worse as time went on. He'd seen it before.

Quinn hoped he could strike a balance between consoling her and transforming his mind into a sponge for the next twenty-two years. He didn't think he could get it done the first go-round, but he knew if he didn't do his best, he wouldn't make enough progress. If he didn't think like everyone else, that there were no do-overs, he wouldn't put in the needed effort.

Usually, Fridays were crazy enough, but the day the world learned it might soon end, school was even crazier.

"What the…" Jeremy said as they arrived at the school. Several cars were blaring loud music. Half a dozen students were drinking various forms of alcohol in and around the cars. Closer to the entrance, several couples were kissing and making out in varying degrees.

"Why are we even here?" shouted one of the students. He gestured wildly, disheveled, and threw his hands in the air. "What's the point?" he said, adding a few obscenities.

One of the students who'd been drinking tossed an empty bottle against the school's brick exterior. Glass shattered and peppered Quinn and Jeremy in the face. A larger piece nicked Quinn's neck. A trickle of blood began to flow. Quinn put his hand on his neck and pressed tightly.

"Oh my god!" Jeremy said. "Are you okay?"

"Do I look okay? Take off your shirt."

"What?"

"I said, take off your shirt. I'd take off mine, but I'm a little busy right now," Quinn replied.

Jeremy pulled the cloth above his head. "Now what?"

"Rip it in half. I need something to cover this gash until I can get to the hospital."

The world around Quinn spun, the air cooled, and he began shivering.

"You all right, Quinn?"

"Definitely not all right, but it would suck to lose this timeline over a stupid piece of glass, so I'll do my best to…."

Quinn's eyelids drooped, and he keeled over sideways.

"Quinn! Quinn!" Jeremy cried out bare-chested, holding the makeshift bandage over Quinn's neck.

Five hours later, Quinn opened his eyes. He was lying in a hospital bed connected to an IV drip.

A female doctor stood over him. "Good, you're awake.

You gave us a big scare there for a while, but the surgeons were able to close the nicked artery and stop the bleeding. We had to give you a blood transfusion, but you're going to be okay."

Quinn's family and Jeremy were by his side. *It wasn't fair to them*, Quinn thought. He already knew that his death meant the timeline would be reset and that he'd be off in another branch of the multiverse doing it over again, and they might be stuck in this one, though he couldn't be sure.

It took all the resolve he had not to break down. The muscles in his cheeks loosened, just like they did every time when he was about to lose his composure. The lump in his throat grew and made it tough to swallow in his already dry throat.

"You scared us there, buddy," Frank said.

"Quit doing that," Jeremy said, smiling.

Amy held back tears, and Quinn's mom's face softened from her typical stoic appearance.

"I'm glad you're okay," she said.

Quinn spent the evening and the next day in the hospital. The food wasn't up to 2021 standards, but it wasn't as bad as he remembered as a kid. Quinn's parents spent the entire weekend there until the doctor discharged him.

The entire country went through the five stages of grief. Over the next few weeks, school attendance plummeted, and then slowly regained some sense of normalcy. Students acted out in the beginning, trying to process and cope with what had just happened. But as the days and weeks passed, people resolved themselves to accept the reality of the situation.

The usual agitators kept up their work, which surprised Quinn. Conspiracy theorists dominated the airwaves and the internet. Politically funded activist groups stepped up the tactics to elicit social change, both good and bad. It gave Quinn both worry and hope.

A few months later, there were three camps of people. It was the new social order that all schools, including his own, adopted. The first was the people who pretended nothing had changed.

The second group was those who gave up any pretense of effort and decided to do whatever they wanted.

The third group of people were those like Quinn, who decided to be as productive as possible. That took different forms. For some, it was art or writing. For others, it was making a mark in some other way.

Most people fell into group two. It was easier to do nothing. Some people fell between one of the three camps, but the distinction between the three groups was clear at all institutions across the country and the world.

Over the next year, Quinn streamlined his effort. While it may have made sense to focus on grades and acceptance into the best university, Quinn thought a better approach would be to focus on the effectiveness of time. He still brought his GPA up from 3.2 in the original timeline to 3.8 for his freshman year, with English being the sole B on his school records.

Quinn wondered how news of the apocalypse would alter the college acceptance practices of most universities. He expected the engineering and hard sciences would become more competitive, with many more people trying to do precisely what Quinn was doing.

Quinn's first step was to focus on learning the basic foundational principles of engineering. During the following year in 1999 and 2000, he spent a third of his free time engrossed in advanced math and physics, which he discovered were essential subjects *before* he could gain a true understanding of engineering.

Another third he spent with family, which his parents demanded. Quinn understood why his parents wanted to spend more time with him. His parents were also in camp three, but for different reasons. Their life was family, and they were going to make the most of it.

Quinn used the remainder of his time to study the stock market and legally increase his family's wealth. He decided it was better to do it gradually the first year then ramp up growth soon after—to fund his inverted Dyson sphere.

The time requirements divided Quinn's time, but he didn't mind so much. It kept him grounded and from feeling lonely and detached, which he worried might happen if he got caught up in an endless feedback loop. Quinn handled the time divide by living most days four times, and occasionally, more if needed.

Quinn dedicated day one to learning, day two to family, and day three to investments. Day four, he combined the best of the previous days, since it would be the only day that mattered—he only relived a fifth when things didn't go as planned on the fourth day.

Augustus 16th, 2000
Day 1.
3:15 p.m.

"I have to admit, I'm not making as much progress as I'd hoped. I'm barely ahead of my class in Algebra II. I've skipped ahead, and sort of understand the basics of simple calculus, but if I'm being honest, I'm getting discouraged," Quinn said.

Cameron smiled. Over the last year, he had spent nearly every hour of the day with her. He usually kept his mental struggles to himself to avoid looking weak, and he convinced himself he could pull it off. It worked most of the time, but between the past and 2021, he had lived another five years and wasn't seeing the progress he'd hoped for.

Cameron placed her hand on Quinn's shoulder. "You're going to do fine. You said it would take longer than one lifetime. Now it's my job to cheer you up. You're going to feel like this sometimes. No one stays upbeat forever. But don't worry. I know you can do this."

Quinn took a deep breath. The lump that had been growing in his throat vanished, and his chest relaxed.

Cameron had grown a couple more inches over the last year and was even more beautiful. He spent five years in actual time obsessing over her and feeling bad about it. He felt it was wrong to act on his feelings toward her due to their age difference, and he forced himself to keep their relationship platonic.

Maybe it was possible in another timeline, but not this one, at least not for a while. Still, her presence relaxed him. Her words calmed his mind, and in the insanity of all that was happening, she understood him and always knew exactly what to say. He wondered what she had ever seen in Scott Channing.

Scott observed the building's tall, sleek frame. The shiny exterior glass complemented its stoic foundation and contrasted the bustle of people around it.

Cameron stroked his shoulders and flattened his collared shirt.

"Your mother works there. You have tons of experience. I think you're a shoo-in. And if by some chance he doesn't hire you, I have no doubt you'll be able to find another job just as good."

Scott's chest tightened. In one sentence, she both inspired and frightened him.

He didn't want to look for another job. This was the last good job he could find. They had already discussed his backup option, which she didn't like, not after what had happened to her uncle. Scott worried if this didn't work, everything would fall apart. He would have no choice but to enter the police academy, which his father had prodded him to do since high school.

"You're so tense. Take a breath. Here, have a sip of this latte," Cameron said.

Scott's clunky arms tilted the cup in the wrong direction and spilled a dribble onto his white shirt.

Scott sighed. "Look at me. I should just quit right now and avoid the humiliation."

Cameron's eyes told Scott he had said the wrong thing. It was a constant discussion they had. He didn't believe in himself. She was the one who prodded him to take chances and believed he could compete with everyone else.

She tried to overlook his persistent hesitation. She knew why he believed it and how he had bought into the words his father had told him nightly growing up.

Scott's father was a lifer. He had worked for the NYPD for thirty years as a beat cop. He saw the worst in people. He heard the hard stories about how life had cheated them. He believed life was tough, and people had to punch back twice as hard. He tried to instill that way of thinking in his son. It was his job. And if he didn't do it, he knew Scott would be just like every other punk he picked up off the street.

He drank a lot, and when he did, he beat into Scott the lessons he wanted to teach him.

Cameron discovered that about Scott's father when she was fourteen, right after Quinn Black had found himself unable to speak in her presence.

CHAPTER 23

CAMERON TURNED THE corner on the way home.

Scott fled from his front door. He dashed toward the street as his father shouted at him in a drunken stupor, "You get back here, boy. I'm not finished with you yet."

Blood trickled from the side of Scott's lip where his father had struck him. He ran a few blocks away from his house, then kneeled on the ground, crouched up to the side of his neighbor's brick home. He turned on their garden hose.

Water streamed from his face and loosened the blood that had already started to congeal at the corner of his mouth.

"You okay?" Cameron asked.

"Do I look okay?" Scott replied.

"I'm sorry, it's just that…"

"It's just what? There's nothing you can do for me."

"What happened? Should we call somebody?"

Scott chuckled. "No one can do anything for me. My

dad's a cop. He's the one that did this. He thinks he's teaching me a lesson—how to be a man."

"I'm sorry."

Cameron approached him. She didn't usually talk to strangers, but today, she'd already talked to two.

A cold hand touched Cameron's shoulder from behind.

"What do you want with my boy?" Scott's dad said.

"I'm not your boy," Scott replied.

Scott grimaced, shifted in his place, then attempted to hoist himself up from the ground.

"Don't speak to your old man that way," his dad replied.

"You have the old man part right. Now leave me alone. I'm not going with you. Not now."

Scott's father lifted the police-issue semi-automatic from his holster and aimed it squarely at his son.

"You're coming with me… now."

"I already told you, I'm not going anywhere with you. What are you going to do? Shoot me? Go ahead. I dare you."

Cameron took a deep breath. The fine hairs on the back of her neck and arms stood up.

"Maybe you should just let things cool off first," Cameron said to Scott's father.

"Shut your mouth, you little whore. I know what you're here for. You find someone you like, someone you think might have something you want, and then you try to trap them."

"I don't know what you're talking about. I don't even know your son. I just saw him run out of his house away from you, bleeding. I'm on my way home. He just happens to be here."

"Liar! You are a little whore, and I'm not going to let you trap my son like—"

He stopped himself.

"Like who? What were you going to say?" Scott asked.

"Like your whore of a mother," he replied.

Cameron's eyes widened as she gasped.

"You're the liar. You have no right to talk about Mom that way," Scott said.

Scott's father lifted his hand back. "You little…" Before he realized it, his hand struck Cameron in the face and knocked her down. Scott rushed forward and punched his father in the face.

"You leave her alone. And don't ever talk about Mom that way again, or I'll kill you. I swear. Don't ever say anything about her. Do what you want to me. I don't care, but leave her alone."

Cameron brushed herself off, and Scott helped her to stand up.

"What's going on?" a voice said behind Scott.

Cameron turned to see her dad.

"This guy's drunk. He hit his son. He hit me in the face and called me a whore when I tried to help. Then he pulled a gun on us."

"That's not what happened, you little tramp."

Dr. Green walked forward and drew in a lungful of air. "You're leaving, and I'm calling the police right now."

"I am the police—NYPD," he said as he pulled his badge from his wallet.

"I'm sure the NYPD will want to know that Officer 732," he said as he reached over and inspected the badge number, "beat his own son and pulled a gun on him and my daughter. Now, unless you want to shoot me, I suggest you walk away and never lay a hand on my daughter or say another word to her again."

In his drunken stupor, Scott's dad thought about shooting Dr. Green but then backed down. "I better not ever see you again," he said.

"Or what?" Scott asked. "Are you going to pull a gun on him, too? Is that your answer to everything?"

Dr. Green signaled for Cameron to follow him. They started walking away.

"I'm sorry," Scott said to Cameron.

"It's all right. It's not your fault."

Cameron hesitated. Dr. Green tugged on her hand and continued to walk away.

"I'll see you at school," Scott replied before they turned and walked off.

"This isn't over, boy," Scott's father said to him.

The next time they met was a couple days later in English class. They clung together for the rest of the day. Scott told her how his father came home drunk every night and beat the crap out of him as part of some "lesson" so he didn't end up like the criminals he had picked up on the streets.

He explained how their parents argued all the time and how it had gotten worse in the past year. He feared his dad was going to kill his mom. It always got worse later in the evening until he passed out and woke up the next day.

Each morning, Scott's father apologized for taking things too far and explained he was just trying to save him from a life of crime—tough love, he called it.

For the rest of high school, Cameron and Scott were inseparable. For the next eight years, Cameron had three men in her life: her dad, Scott Channing, and Albert Einstein—but that all changed in 2007 when Scott applied to work for Logan at Robert's & Son's.

CHAPTER 24

THE SUBURBAN MANSION cast a decadent silhouette on the surrounding homes. Quinn had insisted his father build it after the first fifty million they had made from the stock market.

In any other timeline, his neighbors would've feigned jealousy, but his father was the opposite of arrogant, elite, and privileged. He did his part to alleviate the suffering of the lost and homeless. It was his new project after Quinn convinced his parents to quit working. It didn't take much convincing. Yet his mother and his father were still humble, still wearing the same clothes as they had before the money poured in.

The world was ending, and Quinn explained how he needed the mansion for the lab housed on the second floor because he needed it to plan with community leaders on how best to help those in the neighborhoods that surrounded them.

"I'm amazed at how much you've actually done," his dad said.

"You didn't think we were going to take this lying down, did you?" Quinn replied.

"I don't know what to say, other than I'm proud of you for taking the initiative in all of this. You've really applied yourself…y'know…the differential calculus and physics lessons with an actual physicist, the lab, investments—all of it."

"Thanks, Dad, but thank me after we find a way to stop the supernova."

"I'm saying thank you now because we don't know what's going to happen tomorrow."

Quinn smiled. If only his dad knew the truth, but he didn't want to tell him. He didn't want to rupture the image his dad had of his son. Quinn was a good kid, but he was no genius. And he certainly wasn't an investment expert. That much he had proved to himself after trying his hand at day-trading weeks after Jeremy quit college to start his own business.

But what Quinn learned in the ten years shuttling back and forth and looping through time was that Malcolm Gladwell was right.

When Quinn undertook the plan to build the inverted Dyson sphere, he lacked the self-confidence that he could do it. His reality may have made for a great TV series or movie, but the only way he was going to succeed was if he found a way to believe in himself.

No amount of looping through time was going to magically build the inverse Dyson sphere. He was going to have to learn the nuts and bolts of that on his own. But before he could make any progress, he had to admit that Jeremy was right. Quinn lacked self-confidence and needed to develop it.

Quinn started with a few books he'd seen online on personal development. He read all the greats from Napoleon Hill to Zig Ziglar and Tony Robbins. His plan was a hundred books in thirty days. Then, he came across *Mindset* by Carol Dweck and *Outliers* by Malcolm Gladwell.

Gladwell's book explained how the world sees highly successful people as outliers, but when he looked closer, they all shared something in common. They all experienced a confluence of events that provided a base of support to earn ten-thousand hours of work in their particular field.

IQ, innate talent, and other factors mattered little. What separated the greats from everyone else was the fact that everything in their lives led to gaining that time, which was something Quinn had in abundance.

Quinn convinced himself he just needed the experience. The hardships, pain, and struggle would be expected in the first ten years of work. The thirty days Quinn spent reading those books had a profound impact on his life and the fate of the planet. They gave him the needed one-two punch to get the ball rolling and codify a daily routine until it became habitual.

The routine was the magic Quinn needed to push forward. When his efforts produced nothing, when experiments failed, and when his spirits declined, his routine propelled him to keep going on his very specific, but nebulous plan to build an array to save the world.

It was hard—monumentally hard. But Quinn knew what he needed most was focused, deliberate practice. Time would amplify his progress until he developed the required habits into a system that would create his desired result.

A while later, Quinn hit ten-thousand hours of focus planning and studying for one clear goal: to build the array.

Quinn stared at the computer and squinted his eyes. He double-checked the numbers and hit Enter.

The computer spat out the sequence of images he'd hoped for.

"Dr. Green, take a look at this."

Dr. Green inspected the results of Quinn's latest model. The array was sound as far as he could tell. It honored all the laws of physics and structural mechanics. He could manufacture the materials with current technology. In theory, the array would shield the Earth and the moon from the blast.

Three pieces of the puzzle could cause a problem. Cost was the biggest issue—over one hundred and fifty trillion dollars was the estimate. The second issue was the size. Based on the computer estimates, it would take fifteen years of orbital launches to get the required materials to space, plus all the logistics that went along with it.

The last potential stumbling point was the guts of the array. A double-sided coating—sandwiched together with nanopolymers—needed to be constructed and applied throughout the panel. The application was easy. But the coating was wholly Quinn and Dr. Green's creation. They needed to find and equip a manufacturer, and that could take some time.

The coating also relied on a subnetwork of non-lithium batteries with a dual-response system to overcome overload. If the system exceeded a certain carrying capacity, a secondary channel network would direct the excess energy into necessary subnodes to reflect the energy back out into space.

Quinn didn't want to have to use the overload system. The plan was to keep the batteries charged and to use it for several decades for launches to various bodies in the solar system. But if the supernova overtaxed any one of the panels, the nearest subnode would kick in and keep the overload from reaching the batteries and spreading to the rest of the channel network.

The last component relied on their inventions working flawlessly. They had to simulate and model each prototype before they built it, then render a model, which would take even longer. But after enough time and effort, they completed a tiny, yet hopefully, working prototype.

"This is it. We did it," Quinn said.

"Let's not get ahead of ourselves just yet, but I do agree it's progress," Cameron's dad said.

"Progress? All the numbers are in the green zone. That last tweak should more than hold a full charge. It won't even need to redirect any of the energy. We did it. All I need to do now is make a few changes within our in-house channel network to prototypes."

"No. Wait!" But it was too late. Quinn had already hit the button that directed a surge of power to the miniature channel network and the prototypes housed within the lab.

CHAPTER 25

QUINN FORGOT DR. Green had recently decoupled the channel network from the storage units to test each system separately. The program directed a surge of electricity to end units that couldn't hold the charge.

Sparks lit up the lab and engulfed the section of the room Dr. Green occupied. Seconds later, four concurrent bangs shook the lab and the surrounding mansion.

The explosion incinerated Dr. Green in an instant. The smell sickened Quinn, and his skin was sweltering. Severe burns covered the right side of his body, closest to where Dr. Green had stood.

Safety measures implemented in the lab shortened the duration of the fire, but not fast enough. Quinn hobbled over to Dr. Green, but it was pointless. His body lay limp and charred. The putrid smell of singed hair and flesh forced Quinn to vomit his breakfast onto the floor.

Quinn wiped his mouth, then inspected the computer

screen to see if it still worked. He took a deep breath, then coughed. His eyes glazed over. His mind went blank. It was a do-over day.

It wasn't the first time he'd seen someone die. Each time it got a little easier. The shock wore off faster. The importance of the event diminished within him, and he felt he lost a little bit more of his soul. But each time, he still did everything he could—within reason—to prevent it.

Quinn worried that the power from his abilities might eventually deaden him to the world. He loved hiking, walks in the park, and doing small things. He hoped traveling through time wouldn't numb him to life's simple pleasures.

It was a grand contradiction. Every action was important, and yet nothing mattered if it could be repeated over and over again. The problem vexed him.

In that moment of realization, Quinn vowed to himself to make sure everything mattered. He decided every day would have purpose. Every death would have meaning. Every mistake would be a teachable moment, and every simple pleasure would be appreciated.

He thought for a moment, then decided that a daily journal would be ideal. He had started one earlier, then had stopped after the incident with Ling. After that, he only occasionally wrote down important facts and figures in case he needed them.

This time, he would be careful what he wrote. He would use a code for names and dates and any information that would be out of place for each time. He would write it even on loop days when it would be written and rewritten by time's tapestry. In each entry, he would include someone who made an impression, something he learned, and a place or event that should be remembered or appreciated.

Quinn ran the simulation of the array's response to the supernova. It gave the same results. All levels were in the green. It should work.

"It's a fantastic result. I'd like to test it out on the prototype. Can you recouple the channel network and see if it will hold the charge?" Quinn asked.

Dr. Green spent the next several minutes recoupling the device. Quinn double-checked the network. He didn't want to tell Dr. Green he had died in an earlier version of the day. It would be too distracting. Instead, he found a fire blanket from the other room and brought in a glass of water as if he was thirsty.

"Will this hold it?" Quinn asked.

Dr. Green inspected the data and reexamined the prototype. Every connector was in place. Every equation worked out perfectly.

"I don't see why not."

"On three, then."

Quinn inhaled. His pulsed increased, and the temperature of his skin shot up. His heart pounded against his rib cage.

Quinn hit Start. A charging sound indicated the computer had initiated the test, and electricity began flowing through the channel network. As the network increased the charge, the nodes luminesced with growing intensity.

The electricity hummed in the background. The

computer screen flashed green, yellow, and then red. The hum increased in pitch, followed by an alarm.

"Shut it down!" Dr. Green yelled.

Before Quinn had time to react, four nodes exploded. This time, the force of the blast blew Dr. Green out of the room and knocked Quinn against the wall, slamming his forehead against the concrete.

Quinn fell to the floor. The light dimmed. His eyelids shut tightly.

Several hours later, Quinn awoke. A familiar haze clouded his mind. A morphine drip fed his veins. Both his parents stood over him.

Quinn forced his mouth open. "What happened?"

"An accident in the lab. Dr. Green didn't make it."

It didn't make sense. Even in Quinn's drug-addled haze, he had fixed the mistake. He even dialed back the charge in case he had missed something, and planned on running it on higher power in the next test.

SEPTEMBER 12TH, 2000
DAY 3.
4:25 P.M.

Quinn tripled-checked the nodes, the network, and the program. All levels were green. This time he decided to use half the power.

Quinn wondered how much longer he should keep up the pretense before telling Dr. Green the situation.

Dr. Green's face exuded disappointment as he walked in from the other room.

"When were you going to tell me?"

"Tell you what?" Quinn asked.

Dr. Green held up Quinn's journal.

"It says here I died twice from running this experiment. Last time, you were badly injured. Why are we rerunning this experiment if it didn't work these last two times?"

"I was hoping to discover why it didn't work. I dropped the power to half. I triple- checked the connectors. It should work."

"If it didn't work at eighty percent power, why do you think it would work at fifty?"

"I'm not sure. I was just hoping—"

Dr. Green cut him off. "That's shoddy science. You know better than that. *You* might have the luxury of looping time, but most of us don't. We need to understand why it didn't work before we move forward. Otherwise, we risk the accident happening again."

Quinn exhaled. "I'm sorry. I just wanted to figure this out on my own."

"I get it. I usually feel the same way, but don't let time travel make you sloppy. Do it right every time, or don't do it at all."

Quinn felt guilty. He knew Dr. Green was right. Quinn was being impatient and arrogant. He needed to rely more on others and give everything his full effort. But it was more than just this incident. Quinn worried again that the power might consume him if he cut corners.

"You're right. What should we do?"

Dr. Green went through a checklist of all the components and subroutines. They analyzed and reanalyzed each piece of the puzzle until they were certain it worked correctly. By the time they'd finished, the outside light was dim and the air cool.

"I couldn't find anything wrong. Everything checks out."

"Should we run it again?" Quinn asked.

"Not until we find out the problem."

"Can we run a simulation of a simulation?"

Dr. Green stroked his lips.

"There should be a way to see how much current would flow through the channel network without actually doing it. We'll have to create a new subroutine embedded below the top-level code. But it will have to wait until tomorrow. I'm exhausted, but still alive, thankfully."

Quinn frowned. Dr. Green had a right to be angry, but it still hurt. Quinn reflected on what Dr. Green had said. He didn't have to do it all alone.

CHAPTER 26

IT FELT LIKE forever since Quinn had seen Gary, Sam, and Cameron. He used the same pretext of the beta version of a game to lure them to the apartment, then filled them in on the situation.

After Gary unloaded the equipment and the orb, Quinn told them about the supernova and how everyone in the current 1999 timeline knew about it. In between sentences, he paced across the room and watched for men with guns.

"You look nervous," Sam said.

"Why do you keep doing that?" Gary asked as Quinn inspected the window from the crack of visible light that gleamed from the outside.

"Each time I come here, it's not the same. Sometimes we're alone. Other times they track us down and storm the building."

"You're just telling us this now?" Cameron asked.

"I know I have all day, but I still have to be efficient with my time."

As he paced, Quinn continued to explain his idea about a modified Dyson sphere and the explosion in the lab.

"I would have run the test a few more times, but then your dad found my journal and said we should stop running experiments until we figured out what went wrong. I had planned on running it at half power, and if that didn't work, running it at ten percent to see if it changed anything."

Cameron squinted her eyes. She swallowed as the skin on her cheeks and forehead warmed.

"Wait. Are you saying you killed my father, *twice*?"

Quinn coughed, then paused before speaking. "I'm sorry, I didn't… I…"

"I'm totally messing with you. I probably would have done the same thing if I could loop time. And it's not like those universes don't exist somewhere else. You're just finding the most ideal one. Knowing Dad, I'm assuming he made you run all the extra protocols until late at night."

"Too late, and yes. I couldn't find anything. I'm not sure what I'm missing. I'm tempted to go back and just run it at ten percent power to see what happens."

"I think you should. If everything you're saying is true…"

"It is, but that reminds me. This is kind of a personal question, and it's been bugging me ever since Scott said it in the interrogation room during my first few loops."

Cameron's eyes widened. Gary and Sam stopped fiddling with the components they were tinkering with to turn to Quinn as he continued.

"Scott said he tried to apply for my sales position in 2007. It was at the same time I got hired. His mom works as an executive assistant at the company. He blamed me for not getting hired and then got angry. He insinuated I had something to do with you guys breaking up."

Sam's mouth opened as they waited for Cameron to speak.

"Oh. That *is* personal, and I really don't want to talk about it," Cameron replied.

September 15th, 2007
5:42 a.m.

Scott slammed the door behind him after he entered. He took a deep breath and exhaled.

"That bad?" Cameron asked.

"Do you know a Quinn Black?" Scott asked.

Cameron looked confused. "The name sounds vaguely familiar, but I'm not sure from where. Why do you ask?"

"Are you sure?"

"Like I said, it sounds familiar but I—"

"Cut the crap already. It's too much of a coincidence. You had something to do with it, didn't you?"

Cameron wrinkled her brow.

"Something to do with what? What happened?" she asked as she approached him and put her hand on Scott's arm.

Scott pulled away.

"How long have you been seeing him?"

Cameron's expression changed. She looked hurt, crushed.

"What are you saying? Where is this coming from? I haven't been seeing anyone."

"My mother knew who he was, recognized him right away. I recognized him, too. I got a lot of beatings because of that kid when I was in ninth grade. I'll never forget him or that face."

"I still have no idea what you're talking about."

"Quinn got the job. I didn't. Are you happy now?"

Cameron still looked confused, not sure where all the accusations were coming from.

"I'm really sorry about the job. I am. You'll find something else. You're a smart man. You just have to…"

Cameron tried to ignore the accusations and move forward. It was too hard to think about confronting the accusation at that moment, not with her uncle, who had just died, and her father, who was ill. There was enough loss for one year.

"No. I'm not. I should have done what I said I was going to do before. The job's there waiting for me. I should just go and take it."

Cameron's expression changed again, this time to deep concern. She was the one who had prodded him to apply for the sales job after he had hesitated to accept the offer from the precinct. She saw how uncomfortable he was in the academy.

"I don't think that job is right for you. You know what happened with my uncle, and you saw how it changed your dad."

"My dad was a drunk and a prick. A job is just a job."

"You know that's not true. Remember what you told me when we first met. You said the job changed your dad. Seeing the worst in everyone made him cynical and dark. He took his hate out on the world and on you. And did you know the average cop dies at age fifty-seven? The number-one cause of death is suicide, and the second is murder. Is that what you want, to die from suicide or murder?"

"I'm not my father."

"Not yet."

"It doesn't matter, anyway. How long have you been screwing Quinn?"

"That's enough. I haven't been screwing anyone but you. You know that."

"I *don't* know that. But that's all done with now. I'm done. I'm going to go to the precinct tomorrow and take the job. I have nothing else—not anymore."

"Stop this. I've been with you all this time. Don't throw everything away. You're not thinking clearly."

"You're lucky I'm not my dad."

Cameron's mouth dropped open. "And why is that exactly?" She squinted her eyes. Her pulse jumped, and she eyed the exits.

"I could never see how a man could hit a woman, but now I understand."

"Have you lost your mind? What happened to you? All this because you didn't get the job?"

"Don't sit there and pretend you're not the one who did something wrong. This is *your* fault. My dad was right. I should have listened to him. You are a whore."

Cameron walked around him toward the front door.

"Don't leave me when I'm speaking to you."

Scott blocked the exit and grabbed her arms to hold her in place. She gritted her teeth, then kneed him in the groin. Cameron's cheeks lost their color, yet blood raged throughout her body. She stepped outside to the sounds of the city, but they only clouded her thoughts more.

An hour later, Cameron arrived at her dad's home.

"I hope you don't mind, Dad. I need to stay here a while. Scott's being a real dick. How are you, by the way?"

Her own situation kept her from seeing what was in the room until she finished her sentence and looked up. A male doctor stood over her dad and held a glass of liquid to his lips. Dr. Green sipped.

"He's a little weak right now, Miss…?"

"I'm his daughter. What happened? I know he's been sick, but what's going on?"

"Shut the door."

Cameron's heart jumped again. She forgot about her own situation, then looked at her dad as if for the first time. She hadn't seen him in a few days, but during that time he'd lost weight. She could see the life draining out of his jaundiced face.

"A couple of days ago, I suspected radiation poisoning. I ran a test, and it confirmed my suspicions."

"What? Radiation? Where'd he get exposed to radiation?"

"The kind of radiation that's affecting your dad, Polonium-210, is rare. Companies used it in small amounts in certain watches. Now it's almost always related to one thing."

"Which is?"

"Russian spies."

"You think my dad's a Russian spy?"

"I think Russian spies are trying to kill your dad. And right now, he could go either way. What I'd be more concerned about is whoever's trying to kill your dad is still out there. If they don't finish the job now, they could try again. And they're probably watching us right now."

CHAPTER 27

QUINN SPENT THE better part of the day inspecting each line of code and each step of the process. He also made sure to hide his journal in a place where Dr. Green couldn't find it.

He thought it would be easier after repeating the process a few times, but his pulse raced throughout the day. He felt as if he had a fever, and he was an outside observer possessing his own body. He couldn't shake the feeling that what he was about to do was wrong.

Dr. Green told him he should find out what was wrong first before he ran the test, but Cameron was right. He needed to run the test, anyway. He couldn't always count on finding out what the problem was. Science didn't always work that way. He needed to do the test. What use was time travel if he couldn't go back and change things if he screwed up?

Quinn ran the first preliminary test.

"Everything looks good," Dr. Green said.

"Looks that way," Quinn said as he exhaled.

He was careful with the settings and dropped the power to ten percent, the lowest setting that would give him any reliable data from the experiment.

Dr. Green glanced over Quinn's shoulder at the screen.

"Why are you running the charge at only ten percent?"

"Just being overly cautious. If it works, I'll run the experiment at full power later. But if we need to fix anything, it would be useful to run the reduced-power test first."

Dr. Green looked perplexed.

"I don't disagree, but I'm a little surprised you didn't go over this before. It's a nice safeguard, but it slows down the process."

Quinn's actions weren't part of the protocol, which was the first thing Dr. Green taught Quinn when he started working with him in the lab. If you didn't follow protocol, people got injured, and experiments failed or couldn't be replicated.

"I hope you're right."

Quinn pressed Enter. The computer gave green lights for every section of the run. The program emitted a sound as the run progressed. The bars on the computer went from green to yellow, then red. The sound increased in pitch.

An explosion shook the room. Sparks flew as the energy flowed from the mock channel network to the model nodes. The program stopped. Wisps of opaque smoke tinged with a burnt-rubber aroma wafted above the model array segment that connected the channel network to the nodes.

Quinn was relieved he had escaped injury and that Dr. Green was still alive after the experiment. He took a deep breath and exhaled.

"I'm glad you made that call. If the energy output had

been any higher, we would have been in serious trouble," Dr. Green said.

They inspected every section of the model and double-checked the output from the program.

"This is odd," Quinn said.

"I see it," Dr. Green replied, looking at the energy output of the program when they replayed the signal feedback.

"The nodes are giving off excess energy, more than should be available by an order of magnitude," Quinn added.

"How is this possible?" Dr. Green asked as he held up the nodes and rotated them.

The nodes were intricate devices, composed of several layers and shielded on the outside with carbon fiber polymer panels and a patchwork of small nanoparticle grids. They were designed to convert the supernova's direct energy into a field.

The specially designed embedded batteries would then absorb the energy from the field. Any extra output would be fed back into the channel array and dispersed to neighboring nodes. If the overload increased further, a central section would direct the excess energy outward in directed bursts.

In the model, they designed an extra panel on the outside of the central section to absorb any excess blast, since focused beams of energy flying off into various sections of the lab would have been catastrophic.

In the prior loops, those panels had peeled off and created a cascading failure in the process. That time, the panels held.

"Look at the readings at the moment—the panel's fried," Quinn said as he pointed to the screen.

"I think I've seen something similar before," Quinn said.

After Quinn filled in the crew on what had happened and with the latest test, he resumed his work inspecting the orb.

"Careful with that," Gary said as Quinn drew closer.

"You don't have to tell me. I've seen what this thing can do."

Quinn wasn't sure where to begin. The last time Sam had gotten too close to the central components, a massive time bubble had engulfed the city.

"Help me flip it over," Quinn told Gary. He realized he'd never inspected the back of the orb after it was opened.

"What is that?" Quinn asked as he squinted his eyes.

"Do you have a magnifying glass in that bag of tools of yours?"

Gary nodded and pulled out a set of scopes he used for computer work.

"Do you have a paper clip?" Quinn asked as he tilted the orb.

"I have a bobby pin," Sam replied, handing one over to Quinn.

Quinn raised his eyebrows. His heart jumped. Then he needled the pin into a suspicious groove at the bottom.

The Geiger counters started crackling.

"What's happening?" Gary asked.

A seamless panel popped off the bottom next to the groove. Then the Geiger counters blared loudly.

A blue glow intensified.

"I think that's…" Cameron said before her body drew still.

The room fell silent. The bubble expanded outside the room and into the city.

Quinn remained frozen in time inside the bubble. At 11:32 p.m., time stopped.

August 7th, 2021
Day 535.
7:32 a.m.

Quinn stumbled off his mattress.

He strutted into a section of his closet he rarely visited. It contained stylish clothes he never wore from a phase in his early twenties when he was experimenting with who he was as a person. A girl was involved.

Quinn put on a thin leather jacket and biker gloves to match his skinny black jeans and gleaming white sneakers. Designer shades completed the ensemble.

"Valentino, I need to meet you at the coffee shop across from the office. You know that day off you keep promising we're going to take someday? Today we're going to take it."

"Now?" Valentino asked.

"Right after I speak to Logan."

"Don't do it, Quinn. If you talk to Logan, it'll never happen."

"Don't worry, Valentino. I got this."

Quinn called Logan.

"I have something big to tell you—something huge that's going to change everything. I need to speak with you this morning. Do you have a meeting?"

"In fifteen minutes."

"I'll be there in ten."

Quinn tilted the motorcycle he'd stolen a couple blocks down, turned the keys in the ignition, and sped off.

After the time bubble, Quinn wasn't sure if his adventures as a time traveler would soon end. Limited time deprived him of needed reflection and sleep. Whatever happened at the end of the evening, it sent him back to morning. He didn't know if it was *his* last day, the *planet's* last day, or if he could go back to 2000 or even 1999.

Eight minutes later, Quinn rested the motorcycle on its kickstand and strutted into the office. He turned heads when he walked the corridors. Meredith's eyes widened, and her mouth dropped as Quinn approached Logan's office. The few people who were present gawked at Quinn's sudden transformation.

"Logan, cancel the meeting. I've been working on something for a while, but this morning I had an epiphany. Whatever you had planned, it doesn't matter anymore. Let's walk to the coffee shop across the street."

The expression on Logan's face was impossible to read. He wasn't fazed by Quinn's new outfit or the request to cancel the meeting. He called off his scheduled meeting and walked with Quinn across the street.

"There's one thing I've been meaning to ask you. Why'd you hire Meredith?"

Logan stared Quinn in the eye. "For one, she's good at her job. Actually, she's amazing at it. I know her Jersey charm takes a bit of getting used to."

"You know that *now*, but why did you *hire* her? What's the real reason?"

Logan paused. Quinn could tell Logan was debating whether to tell him the answer.

"Sometimes when you meet somebody, you can tell right away the kind of person they are on the inside. The wall they put around themselves isn't quite as thick. With other people, it takes longer.

"Meredith came into my office just like you did. She was hungry, but there was something else. I could see it in her eyes. Something had beaten her down, but she had fought back. That's the Jersey in her. She wouldn't tell me what it was, only that she spent her entire life protecting her son and it was time for her to do something for herself. She had no experience, no degree, but she could type, and she could learn everything else. That was good enough," Logan said.

Logan ordered their coffee and sat at a table with Quinn by the window.

"Then why didn't you hire her son? We applied for the job at the same time."

"Whatever it was she'd been fighting in the past, it had already destroyed him. I didn't see that drive or passion. All I saw was someone lost—someone angry at the world. Then you came along and put things into perspective." He changed the subject. "Now, what's this big thing you have to tell me?"

Valentino sat next to them. Logan nodded. Valentino nodded back. For the next several minutes, Quinn explained the time loop, the supernova, and everything else. They stared expressionless until a crash occurred at the precise time Quinn told them it would happen.

Rubber and metal squeaked like nails on a chalkboard. People scattered near the intersection. A speeding truck slowed, but not fast enough. It hit the curb. Inertia carried the trailer forward. Several pedestrians sprinted ahead, but the truck rolled, flipped, and took turns smashing everything on the sidewalk before it finally launched into the air.

The massive steel rectangle raced forward. It crashed in the intersection, then shuddered. The ground trembled, followed by a moment of silence.

"Holy crap. I can't believe it," Valentino said.

"Shouldn't we do something? Go out and help those people?" Logan asked.

"Like I said, this already happened. I tried everything I could think of, but this day is just going to repeat itself unless I can stop the supernova, or I should say, protect Earth from the supernova, because nothing is going to stop it."

"I wouldn't have believed it if I hadn't seen it with my own eyes. I still don't," Logan said.

"We need to get out of here. There's a bomb in that truck. A crazy dark matter device or exotic matter or some futuristic thing made by Russians, I think. It goes off later this evening around the same time as the supernova, but I haven't quite figured that part out yet."

"You want to leave and walk out of here, just like that?" Logan asked, his New York accent bleeding through.

"You heard the man. Clear your schedule, and let's enjoy the evening," Valentino said.

The shock made it easy. They blocked out the accident and went to their favorite hangouts. Quinn knew from the last loop that he didn't need to fall asleep to get thrown back. It would happen automatically if he survived the day. The only time he needed to think about another day in his life was if he wanted to wake up there. So, they took their time.

Valentino was his usual extroverted self. Logan was more modest, but his inner child slipped through. It was as if they were in a dream. The cloud of what had happened hung over them, but they spent the day like it was the last opportunity they might have.

The evening grew late, and they found themselves at Lucky Strike after a fun-filled yet horrible game of bowling. The three men, all dressed in black suits, didn't really fit in there.

"How does this happen? We just sit here and get fried?" Logan asked.

"I'll have another beer, then," Valentino said.

Quinn explained how he needed to learn if the time bubble would keep him from returning to the past. He plugged in his earphones and stretched out on a plush sofa in the lounge area, thinking back on the accident in the lab.

Valentino sipped on his beer until time stopped at 11:31 p.m.

CHAPTER 28

AFTER SCHOOL, QUINN'S expression told Cameron he was deep in thought.

"I don't know how long this power I have will last, and I still don't completely understand why it's happening."

Cameron turned toward Quinn. "Maybe you should go back and spend time with someone important while you still can."

Quinn *had* been doing that. Ever since the news of the supernova had broken, he'd been spending more time with his parents than he thought was possible even with the extra time at the lab. But he realized he hadn't gone back to an earlier day in his life in all this time.

That was partly because there were only a few days in his life he actually remembered. Most days just bled into one another, but he did remember a few—the special and the most frightening days.

That day was impossible to forget. It was that feeling of antic-
ipation when one had wanted something for so long and had
been counting down the hours for the past month. That time
had arrived. Quinn's face beamed and his eyes widened as he
hurried with Amy and their family to Disney World.

At eight years old, Quinn was tall enough to ride nearly
all the rides, but Amy was limited and stayed back with her
grandparents half the time. She didn't mind because she got
extra helpings of ice cream and sweets. They could peruse
the rides and watch the live-action characters in costumes
who populated the walkways on their way through the long
queues leading to the different rides and exhibits.

Once they arrived at the Magic Kingdom, Quinn's parents purchased the required C-tickets, then helped them
onto the thirty-five-foot Davy Crockett Explorer Canoes
ride that ferried them across to Tom Sawyer Island.

Quinn's little sister looked adorable with her mouse
ears on her head. Quinn felt smaller than usual. His knock-
off Nikes were huge, like clown shoes. But it didn't matter
because he could see his family member's faces, and they
were smiling—and together.

Much like the first time, the day went too fast. The
cotton candy, chocolate-covered everything, and stomach-
ache that came along with it were only half the reason Quinn
had returned to this particular day.

It was his grandparents, Marty and Edna, that Quinn
remembered the most. In '93, they were both healthy and
fun. His grandfather wore a zany yellow Hawaiian shirt

with speeding trains on it. His grandmother was a little too formal, dressed in white with a parasol to protect her fair skin from the sun.

When Quinn was eight, he missed all the adult references in both grandparents' speech, but what surprised him the most was the expert wit they both expressed. It blossomed throughout the conversation and laughter that peppered the day.

"I need sunscreen," Quinn said.

Quinn looked like a giant red berry after the trip, and his pink arms and cheeks reminded him of how badly it had hurt afterward in his original timeline. It was already too late to avoid getting burned, but it would take the edge off the pain he felt later in the evening.

Edna held Quinn's hand as they walked into the shop to grab sunscreen and a few trinkets to bring back to New York after the trip.

The perspective of an eight-year-old boy makes any store look huge. Plush characters of every Disney animated movie in the last half century covered giant pinwheel shelves. The idea of hoarding all the items and hawking them on eBay a few years later tickled Quinn, but he was only there for the day. One day.

He should have done this sooner—visited earlier versions of his life. They were the happiest, the purest. Quinn thought about how life had jaded his perspective when he grew older, polluted by the cynicism of those around him. That day was perfect—burns, bellyaches, and all. And then, it was over. But reliving it wasn't the same. The mind is like the apple in the Garden of Eden. You can never truly go back.

Quinn and Dr. Green could not have appeared more serious in matching white lab coats.

"Here we go," Quinn said, pressing Enter.

He lowered the energy output to five percent. All indicators stayed green. For a brief second, one of the lights flashed yellow. Quinn stopped the test just in time. He checked the parameters indicated by the light.

Four corner nodes emitted too much energy. It wouldn't have been picked up at higher energy levels, only below ten percent. Quinn had to rewrite much of the computer code to do that since lower levels didn't tell him anything about how robustly the array would work in space. Still, after several loops, it was the only option he could think of to find the source of the problem.

"It's right here," Dr. Green said.

Quinn inspected the panel, screwed off the casing, and removed the inner covering that housed the absorption unit.

The center nodule emitted a blue glow.

"I've seen this before," Quinn said.

"That's impossible," Dr. Green said.

"What? What is it?"

"We need to get out of here. Now."

Dr. Green tugged on Quinn's hand and rushed through the exits, but not before shutting off all the breakers and grabbing the data log from the table.

They ran. Quinn's heart pounded with a force so loud he could hear it. Dr. Green hustled along with him until they were well clear of the lab and Quinn's mansion that housed it.

"I saw the same blue glow in the orb from the future. It was at the bottom of the device covered by a panel of some kind. I discovered it just before I accidentally triggered a time bubble. What is it?"

"Time bubble? Why didn't you tell me this before?"

"I guess I was trying to figure it out on my own first."

"The blue glow is Polonium-210. It occurs naturally in the ground and is mildly radioactive because it's usually in trace amounts. But it can be weaponized. The Russians like to use is to murder people. If it's ingested in the right amounts, it can kill you like a poison."

"So, someone's trying to kill us?"

"It's more than that. If the Polonium-210 is on both the orb and nodule, then someone that's connected to that orb and the Russians who tried to kill you has been in our lab."

"That doesn't make any sense. I don't know any Russians, and my future self hasn't done anything to get that kind of attention."

"But I have. And it's not just the Russians who are involved. This goes back to when I lost the grant at my old job. I had a colleague who had ties to the ninety-three World Trade Center bombing. I don't know how or why they were involved, but the investigation proved they were also in close contact with the Russians."

"What are you saying? And what's the point of Polonium-210?"

"I'm saying someone's trying to kill us. The way the Polonium-210 was packaged suggested it would aerosolize in an explosion. That's why we needed to leave the building."

"You think it has something to do with my time-looping?"

"It's impossible to say. Up until this point, I'd assumed your travels through time was a result of your unique set of circumstances and the supernova. That included falling asleep at the right time, the explosion, and the supernova itself. Once the initial trigger was set, your hologram mind became tethered to your existing timelines."

The explanation continued. "It's possible the Russians and whoever else is involved with the Polonium inadvertently triggered your time-looping. The presence of the Polonium in the two timelines could have created fixed points that allowed your holographic mind to branch off in the first place."

"But I never came in contact with Polonium-210 before in any timeline."

"Are you so sure about that? You know my daughter. And I've been exposed. And in the future, it sounds like you were close enough to the blast to be exposed as well. The packet you found at the bottom of the orb sounds like it was intended as a weapon, but a low-range targeted weapon."

"And what about the other bomb that was attached to it? Why did they need two bombs?"

"That's hard to say, but two bombs going off at two different times might be used to kill a few people in close range and allow for others outside a certain radius to escape before the second explosion."

For the first time, the events started to make sense. A plausible reason started to emerge about why the Russians would launch the truck remotely. But there were still several unanswered questions, such as how did the other bomb work, and why did anyone in the current timeline want to kill Quinn and Dr. Green, and what, if anything, did the Polonium-210 have to do with Quinn's time-looping?

As Quinn removed his lab coat, he knew he needed to get another look at the orb.

CHAPTER 29

QUINN CAUGHT GARY, Sam, and Cameron up on everything until that point. Sam stood watch by the window, in case anyone decided to storm the building, and Gary waited next to his bag of techno tools in case his expertise was needed.

"So, do you have any idea how the Polonium-210 is related to the time-looping or what it might be doing attached to our beta model in the other timeline?" Quinn asked.

"I can tell you what I do know. At least in this timeline, my dad died from Polonium-210 poisoning. It was in 2007, right after I broke up with Scott," Cameron replied.

"You think Scott had something to do with it?"

"Not a chance. The poisoning had been happening for a long time. There are different methods of delivery. I know he was exposed earlier when my parents were still together. My guess is that he was a loose end that needed to be tied up. Whoever was involved with the ninety-three bombing thought he knew something that needed to be dealt with."

"What about the time-looping?"

"I think Dad was right. You just happened to be at the right place at the right time doing the right thing. Polonium has a half-life of a little over a hundred days. If you had enough exposure in the past and the Polonium came from the same source, it might explain how you were the only one who began traveling through time."

"The only one we know of," Gary added.

"That's a good point," Quinn said, glancing at the dueling dragons on Gary's shirt.

"Well, right now, you're the only one we *do* know of, and the supernova explosion, your proximity to my dad in the original timeline, and to the bomb in this one is enough to explain things within the realm of possibility. It could take decades, of course, to confirm it, but I think your travels through time are proof enough."

"I guess I'm back to finding a way to save Earth from the supernova."

"And stop the Russians," Sam said.

"Why is it that if I die before the supernova explosion, I lose connection to any timeline that started after I returned to 1999, but when I die or time stops because of the supernova, I don't?" Quinn asked.

"That, I don't know, but I assume in death your holographic mind is cut off from the multiverse," Cameron replied.

Quinn inspected the device one more time for several more hours, then continued his studies with Cameron on advanced theoretical physics.

By this time in his loops, there was little he could learn

that would be the same in his own timeline except for what Jeremy had told him about natural disasters, specifically large earthquakes and volcanic eruptions.

This time, Quinn didn't fall asleep. He waited until the explosion and the supernova. At precisely 11:29 p.m., time reset.

OCTOBER 12TH, 2000:
DAY 1.
10:30 A.M. LOCAL TIME, ADEN HARBOR, YEMEN.

The hills in the distance accentuated the white-and-brown. low-rise stucco buildings harborside. The sky was clear, except for a few clouds that clung to the low mountains in the distance. A few boats moved slowly in the water.

The *USS Cole's* gray exterior contrasted with the harbor. Her Arleigh Burke-class hull with five-inch, 54-caliber mounted guns commanded attention as she waited near the dock.

Commander Lippold checked over all her communications to assess her refueling progress.

Just under an hour later, seamen and crew lined up on the ship's deck for chow.

OCTOBER 12TH, 2000:
DAY 1.
6:28 A.M. NEW YORK.

"Looks like we stopped one attack, and we didn't have to do anything," Quinn said.

"How do you know we stopped it?" Jeremy asked.

"The *USS Cole* should have been bombed ten minutes ago. The first time it happened, I remembered that my Aunt

Lisa called Dad. He seemed upset. I could hear him talking loudly over the phone. Then he turned on the news, and they were talking about it. He hasn't gotten a call, so things have changed."

Quinn turned on the television, then flipped through the channels. Nothing was happening in the news. It either didn't happen, or they weren't reporting on it.

OCTOBER 12TH, 2000:
DAY 1.
11:38 A.M. LOCAL TIME, ADEN HARBOR, YEMEN.

"Commander, we have an unidentified bogey at nine o'clock," the seaman said.

"You sure it's not a friendly? Are they speaking over the comms?"

"Negative, Commander. There's no response, and it looks like they're floating dead in the water in our direction. I see two men on the port side staring straight at us, but there's radio silence."

The line grew longer on deck. The scent of eggs and bacon wafted across the packed line that stretched around the mess.

Within seconds, the small boat drifted closer. Before the seaman had time to signal alarms, a fireball flared, followed by a deafening roar. The explosion struck down dozens of sailors.

A massive hole opened up in the side of the ship. Shouts and screams echoed in every direction. The ship tilted. Whoever was responsible had struck down the mighty *Cole*.

Frank's demeanor darkened. His head drooped as Lisa shouted through the other end of the phone.

"Turn on the TV."

Quinn complied. The news displayed a breaking news banner: *The USS Cole attacked by an unknown ship—dozens of American soldiers injured and feared dead.*

"What happened?" Jeremy asked.

"It's worse than before."

"But you can change it, right? Just go back to yesterday and call someone."

"That's the plan, if they don't lock me up first and put me in a straitjacket. But I have a few tricks up my sleeve if that doesn't work."

Throughout the evening, the number of deceased inched higher. Instead of the seventeen dead and thirty-nine injured, it was twice that many.

CHAPTER 30

"I KNOW WHO did this," Quinn said over the phone to Lisa several hours later.

"What could you possibly know about what's happening?"

"I know there was a trial run that wasn't reported months earlier, but the ship sank because too many heavy explosives weighed it down. I know Khalid al-Mihdhar discussed it in Kuala Lumpur al-Qaeda. And as we speak, he is developing a close relationship in San Diego with Anwar al-Awlaki. Bin Laden's involved, too, and they have something bigger planned."

"How do you know all this?"

"It doesn't matter right now. We need to focus. There is something much…much worse coming down the pike. So, I strongly suggest you take my advice and do something about it."

Hours later, a commotion near the front door interrupted Quinn's thinking. A bang, then a series of thuds jolted Quinn from his desk.

Quinn turned the knob, then shut the door behind him.

"Get down on the ground. Now!" one of the men said in

full riot gear, completely covered in black. Other men rushed beside him and stormed the mansion. Quinn felt his hands twisting as they handcuffed his wrists and yanked him up from the floor.

"You're going in a deep hole, Mr. Black," the man behind the mask said.

"Leave him alone. Can't you see he's trying to save the world, you stupid idiots?" Frank shouted at the men, and they dragged Quinn through the hallway and out the door onto the outside steps.

"Don't worry, Dad. *I'll be back*," he said in his best Schwarzenegger impersonation, which wasn't great.

Kathy ran through the door and followed him. "We're going to figure this thing out. We're going to bring you home," she said.

They shoved Quinn in a black van, shut the door, then sped off.

Half an hour later, Quinn sat chained to an interrogation table. It reminded him of the one from 2021, but there were subtle differences. The room was white and longer. The mirror was wider, with a shorter table. The scent of fresh sanitizer made his nose tingle.

Quinn slowed his breathing. He expected this. One can't just go around telling military intelligence officers hidden details about a terrorist attack without attracting attention, even if that person was Aunt Lisa. Her response to him in the first few time loops convinced him she was the one who had said something.

A woman entered the room: tall, thin, sure, and attractive.

"My name is Melissa Reigns, FBI. Tell me everything you know about the *USS Cole*."

"I don't know much other than what I told Lisa."

"Your aunt?"

"You already know that."

"Humor me."

"Yeah, my aunt."

"What else do you know?"

"They're planning another attack. And it's going to be much worse. I honestly didn't think they were going to go through with it after the supernova. I thought it changed everything, but I guess I was wrong."

"So, you admit you've been working with terrorists? With al-Qaeda?"

"No. I'm not working with al-Qaeda. They don't even know who I am."

Quinn hesitated. "At least I think they don't. I'm not so sure about the Russians."

"Russians? How are the Russians involved?" Melissa asked.

"Hard to say. All I know is that they planted Polonium-210 in the array model we've been working on to save the Earth from the supernova."

"And by 'we,' you mean Dr. Green?"

"Exactly."

"So, you and Dr. Green have been working together for the last couple of years? Is he the one who turned you?"

"No one turned me. I'm not working for al-Qaeda or the Russians. The only thing I'm working on is trying to save the planet. You guys are just too dumb to see it. You can't even coordinate. That's why 9/11 happened in the first place. Your agencies don't talk to each other."

"You have intel inside the US government?"

"You could say that."

"*Classified* intel?" Melissa said before pausing, and added, "9/11?"

Quinn shook his head and exhaled. "I'm not sure how classified it is, and it doesn't even matter, really. The only reason I'm even talking to you is to find out exactly what you know so I can go back and stop it."

Melissa's face contorted. "What do you mean, 'go back'?"

"You wouldn't understand. I just need to make sure it happened the way it was supposed to, and if it didn't, why not."

"So, you admit it."

"I admit nothing. I told you, I need to find out if anything was different so I can go back and stop it. Why don't you start by telling me what *you* know?"

"*You're* the one being interrogated," Melissa replied.

"Humor me."

Over the next hour, Quinn continued the exchange, providing Melissa with information about the *USS Cole*. Some of it was similar—other bits were different. Throughout the exchange, Quinn pieced together names, dates, and places. He hoped it would be enough to stop the attack. He was about to find out.

Quinn's story progressed quickly, but not fast enough. Only Dr. Green, Jeremy, and Cameron knew about Quinn's abilities. That needed to change.

CHAPTER 31

QUINN CALLED HIS dad and Aunt Lisa.

"I'm going to tell you something big—something huge. You're going to have to trust me. It's going to sound crazy. You're going to think I'm nuts, but I hope that everything I've done over the last year will convince you that I'm not. You can talk to Dr. Green if you need more convincing."

"What is it, Quinn?" his dad asked.

"You need to sit down for this."

Lisa wasn't sure what to expect. She thought it might have something to do with the research Quinn was working on. Frank was less certain, but he had a feeling in the pit of his stomach, the kind he usually got just before something terrible happened. He had to consciously remind himself to breathe.

"You know all this money we've made over the last year?"

Frank's heart beat faster. It was bad enough that the world was going to end in the not-too-distant future, but now his son was about to tell him he was an international drug lord. He knew the luck from the last year was too good to be true. There was absolutely no way his son could have made all that money in the stock market. He could have done it only if he was at the heart of an international drug ring. It was the only explanation that made sense. Sweat beaded up on Frank's forehead. Aunt Lisa waited for the punch line.

"You know how I've been able to get right nine out of ten stock picks every week for the last however many weeks?" Quinn asked.

This was it. Frank was right—an international drug lord.

Of course, the only reason it wasn't ten out of ten was that Jeremy had told him that the authorities would get too suspicious if he made money on every single transaction. No one does. Still, nine out of ten drew attention. He had already been audited and investigated, but Quinn always made sure to find a reason to invest in a company before he actually did it. However, he always did his research in reverse after he knew which investment was a sure thing.

"Because I know exactly what the outcome is going to be before I invest," Quinn said.

There it was. Frank couldn't believe he was actually right. His own son had been a liar, a cheat, and a thief. He waited for the other shoe to drop—international drug lord.

"Yeah, right. How exactly do you know what's going to happen before it happens?" Lisa asked.

"You just hit on it right there. I know what's going to happen before it happens."

All Frank could think about was what they would do to Quinn in prison. He was an attractive young boy. He knew what they did to boys like Quinn in prison. He was certain they wouldn't even send him to juvie. He'd go straight to the adult prison with a bunch of men with neck tattoos.

Frank's heart raced. Sweat was streaming down his face and formed into ugly wet spots underneath his arms and the center of his chest.

"Are you saying you're psychic?" Aunt Lisa asked.

"Not exactly, but close."

The pressure lifted from Frank's chest. Maybe he wasn't an international drug lord who influenced the markets through back-channel deals. Maybe he was just crazy. Maybe he was a crazy genius. There was no way he could be psychic. He didn't believe in psychics.

Frank believed in God, and he was certain God wouldn't let people cheat the system. Quinn had to be a crazy savant, someone who could see patterns in the air. He didn't know how it all worked, but that was definitely the answer. Yet that must mean Quinn was a tortured soul.

Admittedly, being a tortured soul was better than being an international drug lord. Quinn might even have a chance at saving the world. Still, he felt pained by the suffering Quinn must be going through. What did it look like? Did he actually see shapes and letters flying through the air like he'd seen on TV with people who had similar issues?

"The reason that I can see the future is because I can travel through time."

Frank squinted his eyes.

"Shut up. What kind of game are you playing, Quinn?" Aunt Lisa said.

"I'm not playing a game. Not only can I travel through time, but I can loop time and move back and forwards through time. The only thing I can't do is slow time or stop time completely. Although I did get caught in a time bubble once or twice, and I'm pretty sure time stopped for me and everyone else in the bubble, but I couldn't walk around or anything."

Frank looked on, paralyzed, in silence. The temperature of his skin dropped as a cool breeze grazed the back of his neck.

"I'm actually a future version of myself from 2021. I started looping in time after the supernova, and a separate explosion happened at the same time. Dr. Green thinks something about both explosions—combined with what I was thinking about before I fell asleep allowed me to travel across the multiverse, or more specifically, allowed my holographic mind to travel across the multiverse and create new branches in time."

"I have no idea what you're talking about, and I don't really care. I have more important things to do. I realize you want to be important, respected. You've made a lot of money. I guess you've done some good things with research, at least from what I've heard from your dad, but I don't know what you're trying to pull here," Aunt Lisa said.

"Turn on the television."

"Why are we even entertaining this?" Aunt Lisa asked.

"Just turn on the TV. The market's going to close in exactly two minutes, and I'm going to tell you exactly what the market price will be of the three major indexes right after the closing bell. If I'm wrong, walk out. If I'm right, then you need to hear me out."

Frank still didn't know what to think. His heart was being pulled in three different directions, and he kept forgetting to breathe. If Quinn kept this up, he was sure he was going to pass out. Frank was no scientist, but time travel was sheer fantasy. It wasn't even science fiction—it was pure, unadulterated fantasy.

Quinn rattled off his prediction for the three indices. Aunt Lisa found the business channel and waited for the closing bell.

The numbers zeroed in on Quinn's predictions. After a few more seconds, the prices settled exactly where Quinn said they would be.

"This is a prank. Some kind of joke. A recording, maybe?" Aunt Lisa said.

"It's no joke. Are you ready to listen?"

Frank didn't know what to think, but he knew this was impossible.

"See, Dad? This is how I made all that money in the custodial account. At first, I could simply read the stock prices from the future, but once everyone found out about the supernova, things changed. My actions altered things. It's the butterfly effect. But I have the advantage of being able to repeat days and loop time, so I could just go one day forward and see what happened." Quinn continued with his explanation. "Unless I make some huge change that day, it rarely affects the market, and when it does, I can just go back one day and change my investments. I still occasionally get one wrong because of the butterfly effect, and I even intentionally get some wrong, so I don't draw too much attention from the Securities and Exchange Commission."

Frank chuckled and shook his head.

"I don't know what to think. I really don't. Lisa's right. There has to be some other explanation for what's going on."

"Then tell me how I could possibly know that. How could I know that all three market numbers would close at the exact price? It's the only explanation."

"No, it's not. Maybe this is a replay. I'm more likely to believe you hired someone to play an elaborate prank than to think you're traveling through time."

"Fine. I get it. You don't believe me. Think about something right now, and I'm going to go back and tell you what you were thinking."

"All right, so what am I thinking?" Frank asked.

"Tell me what you're thinking right now."

"Aren't you supposed to tell me what I'm thinking? You're the time traveler."

"But this is only my second loop today and the first one where we have had this conversation, so tell me something only you would know unless you told me just now and I traveled back through time to repeat it."

"Fine. One, nine, two, eight, three, seven, four, six, five. That's the number I was going to play for the lottery until your mother convinced me it was a waste of money."

"I didn't know you played the lottery."

"Used to play the lottery."

OCTOBER 9TH, 2000:
DAY 3.
4:05 P.M.

Quinn's heart raced. He had always wanted to do this. For that brief second, his mind was that same kid he was growing up—carefree, with no real worries. He forgot about the supernova, the terrorist attacks, and the weight of adulthood. And then it all came crashing back, like a torrent of water bursting through a dam after a once-in-a-generation flood.

"Fine. Think about something right now, and I'm going to tell you what you were thinking."

"All right, so what am I thinking?" Frank asked.

"One, nine, two, eight, three, seven, four, six, five. It's the number you were going to play for the lottery until Mom convinced you not to waste your money."

Frank's mouth opened. His ears started ringing. Quinn couldn't be telling the truth, or could he? Frank finally started thinking about the implications—the moral implications.

"So, you're cheating?" Frank asked.

Aunt Lisa interrupted. "I'm sorry, but I'm still not buying it. Both of you could be in this and playing a prank on me. I could be on some kind of hidden camera show. I'm going to need a little more convincing."

Quinn repeated the exercise with Aunt Lisa. He asked her about something specific, then looped time to tell her the answer. Each trip she was as skeptical as the last.

He started stacking questions, telling her events that would happen moments later. They went outside the mansion onto the edge of the lawn, and then Quinn pulled a Bill Murray.

For the next fifteen minutes in linear time, Quinn pointed out one thing after another—seconds before it happened. He predicted cars that passed by, people jogging, sounds of nature, airplanes, and everything else that stood out while they were there.

"This is just too crazy to believe," Aunt Lisa said, shaking her head.

"I know. It *is* crazy, but it's real, and it's happening."

"So, all this time, when I thought you were some super genius who figured out the market and then took it on yourself to stop the supernova, that was all because of time travel? Because you were cheating?" Frank said.

"It's not really cheating. No one's getting hurt. In fact, it's the opposite."

"Except yourself. It means you're not doing things the right way."

"If you want to call me a cheat, go ahead. But we're rewriting the rules about how things work. I'm not going out and killing anyone—at least no one who doesn't deserve it. I'm trying to stop bad things from happening."

"I think this is too much power for one person to have. Look what you've already done. Most people don't make millions of dollars in a few months as a teenager. It's got to have some kind of negative consequence in the long run."

"Call it a victimless crime, then. I don't care. You're missing the bigger picture, the reason we're having this conversation in the first place"—he hesitated—"and I'm not a teenager."

"Actually, no. Why are we having this conversation?" Aunt Lisa asked.

"It's not victimless if someone else loses," Frank said.

"This isn't a simple black or white. I'm not taking someone else's slice of the pie. I'm growing the pie. I'm doing this to stop the attack, and I'm doing this to save the world. What you need is perspective. And we think all the other possible timelines will exist anyway, with or without my help."

Frank couldn't believe he was having this conversation. "It just seems wrong to me."

"Whether you like it or not, it's happening. I didn't have control over this. I didn't ask for this. I didn't invent a time machine to go back and cheat people or hurt people. It just happened. I can either do nothing, or I can use this to make things better in *this* timeline in *this* universe. I can stick my head in the sand, or I can push my way through. Would you do nothing? Is that how you raised me, Dad, to do nothing while facing a crisis? What would you do in my position?"

Quinn continued talking. "And honestly, I don't care if this is moral or unethical. I'll let someone else figure that out. I don't have that luxury. And I haven't been this sure of something in a long time. I know two things. The first is that I'm the only one who's able to loop time—at least as far as I've seen. The other thing I know is that the world is going to end, or at least our world if I don't do something about it. So, we can have an endless conversation about ethics, but it won't do a damn thing to save the human race."

"It may not seem black and white now, son, but if you keep down this path, one decision leads to another. One moral compromise to the next, and before you know it, you're shooting up heroin and beating up some old lady to pay for it."

Quinn's heart jumped. His pulse raced. "Come on, Dad. Really? I know it may seem like I'm still the same fifteen-year-old son, but I've lived as long as you have. I get that this ability can be abused, but I think I should've earned some extra trust by now. And here's the thing: I can't be afraid—I can't be timid or shy."

"And who decides what has to get done? Who decides what moral line will and won't be crossed?"

"Right now, that person is me. I'm focused on saving the planet from being incinerated. If someone has a problem with me using my ability to time travel to do that, I don't really care. It's a luxury none of us will get to debate if we're all dead. I'll have to take on the burden. And it *is* a burden.

"Every person in the world makes those same decisions every single day, no time travel required. I can either live in fear or I can save the world, but I can't do both. I know you're worried and concerned and all of that, but you should be lucky that this happened to me and not someone else," Quinn added.

"You raised me well, Dad," Quinn said, "and I love you for it. Now you're just going to have to trust that I know the right thing to do or at least the general direction. I'm still going to screw up from time to time, but I'm going to figure this thing out. I have to."

Frank stopped himself from continuing. He realized Quinn was right. Quinn overanalyzed everything. It was a flaw that gave Quinn enough reticence to think through any big decisions that required a moral compass, making Quinn the Frodo in that situation. Quinn was growing with experience, and his dad needed to trust him.

"But you're right, Aunt Lisa. I didn't explain the full reason why I'm telling you this now. Saving the Earth from the supernova is my highest priority, but something else is going to happen a lot sooner, and I need your help to stop it."

Over the next several minutes, Quinn explained every detail about the attack on the *USS Cole* and how certain details deviated from the original timeline. He explained about the 9/11 attack, which still might be coming in eleven months.

"I have an idea," she said.

CHAPTER 32

"I SEE IT, Commander. It's at twelve o'clock."

Commander Lippold gave the order. The *Cole* fired a warning shot into the water at the small dinghy tied to the harbor. Four seamen surrounded the ship from behind the dock.

"Get out now," they shouted in English and Arabic. The seamen apprehended the men and took them back to the ship.

Quinn wore a black, Steve-Jobs turtleneck that highlighted his animated, jaundiced hands.

"We got 'em, Quinn. I gave my contacts your intel, and they put a team in place to stop them and apprehend them before they could get the boat off the dock. The ship is safe, and they just left Aden Harbor," Aunt Lisa said.

"What about bin Laden and Ayman al-Zawahiri?"

"I gave the Navy everything you told me. They're looking for both men, and I think it's safe to say they'll have protections in place to stop those men at the airport if they show up on 9/11."

Quinn exhaled. "Thank God. At least we're able to stop something."

"Quinn, you're going to discover how to save the Earth. I know I didn't believe you at first, but your dad told me more about what you've already done with the array or the Dyson sphere, or whatever you call it. Not to mention all the math and engineering you had to learn to make all that progress."

She continued. "I have no doubt you'll figure it out. It may not happen overnight or even in a few lifetimes, but I guess that's the luxury of being able to travel back and forth through time."

August 7th, 2021
Day 537.
10:30 a.m.

"So that's the story. So far, I've been able to stop the attack on the *Cole*. Now I have to stop 9/11," Quinn said to Cameron.

"The thing that sucks is that we're not even going to know if you succeeded. You get the luxury of having your consciousness swept back to whatever day you want, or at least the beginning of today if you don't think about any place at all. But we all die. We don't go back."

If that's how it worked, Cameron was right. She would die, and the infinite other versions of her in this branch of time would also die until Quinn perfected the inverse Dyson sphere and saved the Earth.

"How do you know the same thing isn't happening to you in another universe?"

"I'm sure it is. But this isn't that universe. I'm not, and Gary and Sam aren't the ones with the memory of the explosion or the Russians or any of it. Do you remember any of this, Sam?" Cameron asked, looking at Sam.

"Nope."

"What about you, Gary?"

"That's a negative."

"So, you see, we're all going to die. And it's just starting to sink in."

"I'm sorry, Cameron. I…"

"You don't have to say anything. It's not your fault. And I'm glad I can help. I'm glad we can help. I know we can't save this version of Earth, but we can save an infinite number of Earths that will survive once you figure this thing out."

"That's just messed up. Why are we even helping you if it doesn't matter to us? I thought how time travel works is you go back in time, and you change things. And you guys are saying that's not even what you're doing?" Gary asked.

"Yes and no," Cameron replied. "Quinn is changing the timeline, but only *his* timeline, and only if you think of it as a giant maze. More like a three-dimensional maze."

They had a similar conversation before, but last time Quinn wasn't thinking about all the other levels of the maze he was creating with each change and all the people that were dying. It was easy to block it out since for him, it wouldn't matter. He could jump along any point he could remember since his last death. But everyone else in this world and any new versions of this Earth being destroyed by the supernova were royally screwed.

Cameron waxed philosophical for the next couple of hours. It made Quinn's brain hurt. All Gary wanted to do was jump on screen and play the latest beta version of any one of the RPGs he'd been obsessing over for the past week. It was better than thinking about his own death.

Sam was somewhere in the middle, hoping Quinn could solve the problem so other versions of Sam could play even more RPGs.

"Oh crap," Gary said.

"What is it?" Cameron asked.

"It looks like those pesky Russians," Gary replied.

"Should I take one for the team?" Quinn asked.

"Don't be stupid. If you die before the supernova, you'll have to start all over again. Just think about all those infinite other Earths that will branch from the new timeline until you figure things out. It's not just about you, Quinn. It's about everyone else in the multiverse."

The only problem was those universes would branch off anyway because there was some other universe where Quinn did make that decision. Now Quinn's brain hurt even worse.

"Don't just stand there. Move," Cameron said as she shoved Quinn out the door.

"I'll try to reason with them. You take the emergency exit."

"Actually, we don't have to do any of this, Quinn," Cameron added.

The Russians grew closer. Gary stood paralyzed, not knowing what to do next.

"Sam, grab the center of the orb. Twist it. Now!" Quinn said.

The first thug to reach the door leveled a barrage of bullets that pierced Cameron's chest. She fell to the floor. He aimed the gun at Quinn. The Russian pulled the trigger. The bullet pierced Quinn's chest. The bubble expanded. Two more bullets entered Quinn's torso. The bubble expanded more.

Quinn stood immobile, eyes open, and tilted back. If the time bubble hadn't enveloped him when it did, he would have fallen to the floor, but not before the other bullets would've entered his body and killed him instantly.

The bubble expanded and engulfed the city. Quinn stood frozen in time until the loop reached 11:28 p.m. and reset.

AUGUST 7TH, 2021
DAY 538.
7:32 A.M.

Quinn spent the day reviewing and studying everything he could about the latest physics theories and engineering developments. He researched nanoparticles and manufacturing, battery storage, and semiconductors.

At 11:25 p.m., Quinn reflected on October 12th and stopping the attack on the *Cole*. He stared at the clock. A bright light covered Quinn's field of view, and at 11:27 p.m., the supernova incinerated the Earth, and Quinn woke up in a different time.

CHAPTER 33

"I JUST SAW something on my last visit to 2021. The supernova is reaching Earth faster. The event happened six minutes earlier this time. I haven't been watching the clock each loop, but I think it's been happening sooner with each loop."

Dr. Green pursed his lips and squinted his eyes. "Are you sure?"

"Positive. I saw the blinding light and time restarted at eleven twenty-seven p.m. That's six minutes earlier than it was before. It used to be eleven thirty-three p.m. What's happening? What does this mean?"

Quinn plugged in some calculations on the computer. The expression on his face suggested Quinn might be in trouble.

"I think I may know what's happening."

"How screwed am I?"

"We made the assumption you were jumping back into the same timeline, the same universe. But I think once the

Russians killed you, your holographic mind was no longer tethered to your timeline in your universe," Dr. Green said.

"Time doesn't change in any universe. You can only go back to a single point where you once were and then travel to another fork in the multiverse where events are different. I think what's happening is that your holographic mind is converging on a cluster of universes that are identical in every respect, except for the timing of the supernova," Dr. Green added. "Eventually, time will reset for you in a universe when the supernova reaches Earth at the precise moment when you wake up. When that happens, your journey will end."

"What does that mean? How does that change things?"

"The first thing is that if you die again before the supernova reaches you—I have no idea. The results are unpredictable. My guess is that you would start waking up in forks that diverge even more from your original timeline," Dr. Green said. "More importantly, even if you don't die, the timeline, or more accurately, your perception of the timeline is collapsing. Each loop, each time you return back to a prior point either in your past or your present, you'll have less time in 2021, until eventually, you'll be cut off completely. After that, I'm not sure."

"Are you saying I should reset time?"

"Not unless you have to. The more you do it, the closer you'll get to the critical event."

Quinn's heart jumped. Now he knew this madness wouldn't last forever, but his present, his real time, was forever lost to him.

He still struggled with the concept of it all and where he fit in the big scheme of things.

"In a recent visit in 2021, Cameron said that each time I loop, I'm creating an infinite number of universes, and

I'm responsible for the deaths of everyone in each one of those universes."

"That's not exactly correct. Those universes already exist. You're not creating matter out of thin air. The multiverse is like an infinite pot of boiling water. Each bubble within that water is its own universe. You're not creating those bubbles—they're a natural product of the universe. You've just been traveling a maze that already exists. Once an event happens, your holographic mind is free to travel along any road."

"That sounds like I have no control over what happens. Are you saying I have no free will?"

"No. You have free will. The road is already there. You're just deciding which road to travel with every choice you make. They diverge in an infinite number of paths, and your holographic mind just happens to have the ability to traverse them," Dr. Green said. "You're not responsible for what happens in every possible universe. Those universes will exist. Those timelines will exist, no matter what you do. Your choices are relevant because they will determine your final destination and the final outcome within that universe."

Quinn exhaled. It was starting to make sense, and Quinn didn't feel as guilty about the choices he'd made. Based on what Dr. Green said, everyone was responsible for their own choices. Where people ended up in their own universe, regardless of if they could time travel, was a result of the decisions and choices they made, or more precisely, how they responded to each situation in their own lives.

Quinn pondered Dr. Green's words and decided to focus on one thing—stopping the supernova. And he would do it without extra time loops or taking advantage of his ability to see the future. If he saw the project to the end, he would learn more. He would better understand what he could and couldn't do if the array failed to do its job. He would live out the timeline as much as possible and only loop back if he needed to improve the array or prevent something else catastrophic.

September 11th, 2001:
Day 2.
10:00 a.m.

During the past eleven months, the government had enacted major changes in education. A family sued the school system for forcing their daughter to attend school. They said it amounted to slavery.

Since their world would end with the supernova, they argued that she had a right to decide how to spend her remaining time on the planet, and forcing kids to go to school until they were eighteen was inhumane, impractical, unconstitutional, and generally insane.

The US Supreme Court agreed. The judges immediately released students from the requirements until Congress or the states came up with their own solution. The federal government enacted a policy that encouraged states to offer alternative schooling that focused on trades.

The government also offered students the ability to join one of the three federal projects to save mankind from the supernova. The first project was a massive hole in the ground covered by an alloy that would keep the interior cool. Almost no one expected it to work.

Only five thousand people would be permitted in the hole, and only the people who worked on the project could enter.

A second project was an intergenerational space station

that would hold a thousand people. It would be maneuvered to the far side of the Earth and have an extra deflector for background radiation during the supernova event.

The third project was an idea similar to Quinn's and Dr. Green's projects. The outcome was the same. The government wanted to shield the Earth from the energy of the blast. It was a behemoth of a project, but how it would work exactly was a mystery. It was the project the government touted in all their PSAs and marketing to encourage everyone to continue on as if nothing had changed.

Another option for those who didn't want to attend school was work. The legal working age was lowered to ten for those who didn't want to enter the trade school or work on one of the three projects.

The outcome of that legislation was transformative. Schools no longer felt obligated to keep students who refused to listen or follow the rules. In the first month of the new law, administrators dramatically increased the number of suspensions and expulsions. Many parents protested, and an expedited lawsuit resulted in the schools maintaining that power.

After that, the behavior problems that had plagued schools for the last forty years vanished. Students weren't forced to go to school. If they weren't respectful of the rules, they were kicked out and forced to choose one of the alternatives.

This also had the effect of improving morale in the school since students had the freedom to choose their own direction. Schools added more advanced courses, which allowed students greater flexibility. If students wanted to skip ahead and take more advanced courses, they were allowed to do so—if they met additional requirements within thirty days of the course.

Quinn and Cameron sat next to each other in Advanced Physics. An eerie silence crept into the room. The teacher turned on the TV.

Half the class gasped. The image on the screen showed Manhattan obscured by smoke. A couple of students walked out of the classroom to use their cell phones and call their parents to see if they were safe.

A banner flashed on the bottom of the screen: *Over 50,000 feared dead in Manhattan and in Washington, D.C., in an apparent terrorist attack.*

Commentators cut into the live coverage with periodic discussions on the attackers and those killed. They talked about their motivations and potential death toll.

Quinn's phone rang. He stepped out of class.

"I'm sorry, Quinn. I thought I stopped it. This shouldn't have happened." Background shrieks muffled the call. Crackling and thuds intermingled with Lisa's words.

"Where are you?"

"I had a meeting in one of the towers. This wasn't supposed to happen. I had assurances measures were taken on everything you told me. I informed on all players involved, the flight numbers, the landing times, even the activities and whereabouts of all the attackers. Either something changed, or someone dropped the ball."

"It's worse than before. It wasn't supposed to happen this way. And they're saying a dirty bomb was involved. It didn't happen this way before. Everything must have changed."

"Where are you right now?"

"I was on a lower floor and went two buildings down. I

remember what you said about the buildings, but it doesn't matter anymore."

"Why do you say that?"

"For one, this is a do-over day. You need to let the day play out so you can get as much information as you can. Maybe wait a couple extra days so you can get more information from the news. Otherwise, you won't be able to stop it."

Quinn hadn't repeated a single day or traveled back to the present since his conversation with Dr. Green eleven months prior. It was too risky. With each do-over, the supernova explosion inched toward the moment Quinn woke up.

The call disconnected just as Aunt Lisa was about to say something.

CHAPTER 34

LISA SAT IN front of the desk, waiting for the head of operations to return. Fifteen minutes earlier, he had begun fielding calls coming in across various defense networks. A few minutes earlier, he had stepped out and hadn't returned.

The South Tower housed the office building. An eerie thud rocked the building. Confetti- like paper filled the sky outside her window. Millions more pieces of various sizes covered the window.

Something was wrong. An emptiness in the pit of her stomach grew into a sharp pain. The timing was off. It couldn't be. It had to be something else.

Her colleague failed to return. A few minutes later, a portion of the window cleared. She walked up to the panes. A tiny uncovered sliver of glass revealed a person falling to their death. Aunt Lisa's heart jumped.

It couldn't be, but it was. Just like the *USS Cole*—it was the same but different. She tilted her head up to discover flames engulfing the adjacent tower and a gaping hole through the top part of the building.

She dialed her colleague. No answer.

She ran toward the door. It was jammed. She twisted the knob but made no progress.

Smoke started filtering in through the bottom.

She dialed her colleague again. The call didn't connect. A message that all the circuits were busy cut in before the click.

She tried the knob again, this time wrapping her shirt around the handle to gain more leverage. It was pointless.

She reflected on everything Quinn had told her but found no solace in the idea she would be brought back with Quinn's second chance. And then she realized she wouldn't be. It would be a different version of her in some alternate universe.

She twisted the handle again—nothing.

A thud shook the door.

"Lisa, are you still in there?"

"The door's jammed."

"Hold on. We're going to get you out of there."

Several men on the other side rammed the door in periodic bursts. She could tell they were coughing.

Smoke poured in from the bottom.

"Stand back from the door."

In three quick successions, the door shook. On the final time, the joints of the door ripped from the wall, creating an opening.

"Hold on," her colleague said.

The three men with him rammed the door. It gave. Aunt Lisa scurried out.

"We have to get out now," Aunt Lisa said.

"There's more people stuck. We should help them."

"The buildings won't hold. They're coming down."

"The firemen told us to stay put."

"They're wrong. The building's coming down, and if we want to survive, we have to leave now."

"I'm sorry, Lisa. I can't do that. I can't let the people stuck on this floor die."

Aunt Lisa would have done the same thing if she hadn't known what was coming next.

"Then you'll die with them."

His face revealed his shock at her statements.

Water from broken pipes covered the floor. She made her way down the stairwell, and despite her time in the Navy and having been warned about the atrocity of the attack, she was not prepared for what was happening.

The building creaked. By the time she made it to the first floor, hundreds of people lined the stairwell. It was chaotic. Water, debris, and bodies were everywhere.

Despite the warnings to stay in the building and wait for rescue personnel, people were now ignoring that order—the trickle of people leaving through the emergency exit transformed into a torrent.

People held other people—the maimed, injured, and elderly. Other people were jumping from the buildings. As she stepped outside, she looked up and saw the extent of the damage. At that moment, someone fell to her death and landed in front of her.

A gaping hole wrapped in a funnel of flames and smoke consumed both towers and several adjacent buildings.

In the distance, fire engulfed more buildings. An emergency siren blared. She escaped to a building farther down the block.

Aunt Lisa dialed Quinn. She was about to tell him what

she had learned. "Otherwise, you won't be able to stop it," she said after telling Quinn her location.

The phone cut off. The power died—the loss of power spread.

The school dismissed the students early. After Quinn returned home, his family glued themselves to the television and consumed every bit of information about what had happened.

It was different—worse. Five planes landed in New York, along with a dirty bomb that exploded in Times Square and contaminated a one-thousand-foot radius of Manhattan. Several transformers exploded from sabotage. The city was without power, and the death toll was estimated to be more than a hundred thousand people.

The attacks on Washington were also different. This time, the president was in the White House. The president ordered rocket launchers to shoot down the airplane headed for it. It was successful, but not with the second plane behind it. The second airplane landed, killing the president, vice president, and dozens more.

A plane hit the Pentagon, and another hit the Capitol building, killing over sixty senators and a hundred and forty congressmen in the attack.

It wasn't just New York and Washington. Los Angeles, Chicago, Houston, Miami, and Philadelphia all had separate attacks. In total, the attacks killed more than a million people, Lisa among them.

The attacks combined airplanes with ground operations—terrorists placed large trucks with radiological bombs in strategic centers for maximum damage.

Quinn waited a week. He learned everything he could, memorized every detail, and then he went back.

CHAPTER 35

QUINN EXPLAINED THE situation to his dad, then he called Dr. Green, Aunt Lisa, Jeremy, and Cameron.

Throughout the next half hour, Quinn laid out in detail what he had learned about how the attack had changed and the cities involved. He gave them the flight numbers, the location of the attacks, and all the different components.

"Can you stop it? What happened when you told them the first time?" Frank asked.

"It doesn't make any sense, I told them everything," Lisa said.

"There is one big thing that changed. The flight numbers. There were no flight numbers scheduled that matched any of the hijacked planes in the original timeline," Quinn said.

"That's the butterfly effect," Jeremy said.

"Yes. It's true. There've been so many changes to Quinn's timeline universe since he returned. Any number of things would have changed, considering how long he's been in the past.

"It's a completely different world than the original one Quinn lived in. Just the awareness of the supernova alone is enough to change, not just the flight numbers, but the flight times or even the airlines' flight routes. What's most surprising isn't the change of the flight numbers but the fact that the attack still happened at all," Dr. Green said.

"It didn't just happen. The attack was much worse," Quinn said. "This time, more planes just landed in New York. And it wasn't just New York and DC. There were several other cities involved, plus there was support from the ground, blown transformers, blackouts, truck bombs, and even a few dirty bombs. The death toll was more than a hundred times greater. It was a disaster. I don't know how I'm going to stop this thing."

"Do you think Lisa telling her contacts made things worse?" Frank asked Dr. Green.

"It's impossible to say. It's just as likely that the terrorists involved gained more recruits and were more willing to die because of the supernova. It's possible there were traitors in the military, and when they learned someone knew about the plans, they decided to make them bigger."

"What do you think I should do, then?" Quinn asked.

"There is a greater purpose you can't forget," Frank said.

"You can't think I should do nothing?"

"I think it won't matter if that supernova destroys the Earth," Dr. Green added.

"It won't," Quinn replied. His face displayed his confidence and determination.

"We're nowhere near stopping it. We've made progress.

That much is true. But then there's the other issue," Dr. Green said.

"What other issue?" Frank asked.

"The supernova is happening sooner each time Quinn returns to the future. The more he loops time, the sooner it gets. If it happens before he wakes up, he won't be able to return."

"What happens to us?" Aunt Lisa asked.

"That's a good question. It's unclear whether Quinn will still have the ability to return to prior points in his life or if that will stop completely. It's possible Quinn's consciousness will die, and he'll be separated from this timeline altogether," Dr. Green replied.

"Then what will happen to Quinn in this timeline? If his mind goes to the future, how does he continue in the past?" Aunt Lisa asked.

"Each time Quinn sends his consciousness to the past, all the other timeline universes his mind has touched continue, but since Quinn's holographic mind is driving those universes, they progress only when he is living them," Dr. Green said.

The explanation continued. "Like a particle of light, they will be frozen in time when Quinn leaves. My guess is that all the other possible universes will continue, but all the different outcomes that resulted from each loop Quinn created will collapse into Quinn's one reality because only one reality can exist for his holographic mind. We'll neither be aware of Quinn's failure nor be able to move forward in our reality if Quinn fails. But if Quinn succeeds, he'll likely continue with the ability to traverse his own personal multiverse."

"That just seems wrong," Frank said.

"It's neither moral nor immoral. It's neither wrong nor right. It simply is," Dr. Green said.

"Maybe you've changed too much already. Do you think you should try to stop this? It could get worse," Frank said.

"I'm sorry, Dad, but there's no way I'm not going to try. I can't let this happen. I have no idea what's going to happen because of this, but I refuse to do nothing," Quinn said.

"Sometimes doing nothing is the best thing," Frank said.

"I don't disagree with that, but I don't believe this is one of those times. I guess only time will tell. If you want to sit and talk about it, be my guest. But I can't do that. I don't know how many chances I have to stop this. I guess I figure that one out as I go, but you heard Dr. Green. What matters is the one universe that I'm currently living in."

Quinn went on. "I don't know why the attack changed the way it did, but I'm not sorry for trying to stop it. And I'm going to do everything I can to stop it now. I know I might not be able to change anything for all those other parallel universes. That sucks. It really does. But I can do something for my universe, so that's what I'm going to do. The only question is if you guys are with me."

"I'm with you," Jeremy said.

"You won't get any problems from me," Cameron added.

"If it's as bad as you say it is, we have to do something. I'm with you, too," Aunt Lisa added.

"I love you, Quinn. I just hope you know what you're doing," his dad said.

"No one ever does completely. We have to figure it out as we go along, but that's better than doing nothing in this case. Doing nothing is the only guarantee that we'll fail, and I can't let that happen."

Dr. Green interrupted and gave the short version of how

he thought the multiverse worked and how Quinn needed to navigate it to find the right outcome.

"Then tell us what we need to do," Aunt Lisa said.

Over the next few hours, Quinn listed, in detail, the location of every attack he had memorized. He wrote down the suspects, the flight numbers, and every other piece of information related to the attack.

By the time they were finished, they had agreed on notifying the FBI, NSA, and CIA, in addition to the Navy and the Air Force about the attack with the details of the participants.

Quinn would call the airlines, buildings, and power plants involved in the attacks. They would regroup after 9/11 and see what needed to be improved if they needed to do it again. They also agreed to keep everything else the same, except for Aunt Lisa staying in the city during the morning of the attack.

SEPTEMBER 11TH, 2001:
DAY 5.
10:00 A.M.

Quinn sat next to Cameron in Advanced Physics. An eerie silence crept into the room. The teacher turned on the TV.

Half the class gasped. The image on the screen showed Manhattan obscured by smoke. A couple of students walked out of the classroom to use their cell phones and call their parents to see if they were safe.

A banner flashed on the bottom of the screen: *Over 20,000 feared dead in Manhattan and Washington, D.C., in an apparent terrorist attack.*

Quinn's heart pounded. Conversations around him

faded. Thoughts flooded his mind about what went wrong and what he needed to change.

Later that evening, the crew met up at Quinn's place to discuss the attack.

"Can we even stop this thing?" Frank asked.

"Let's start by looking at what worked. Only half of the airplanes from the last attack were involved this time, and we stopped the truck bombs."

"We could double down on the planes that still crashed, maybe even hire a crew in each city to scope out the airport if we need to and keep those men from getting on the planes. We could do the same thing to the transformers targeted at the power stations, but the dirty bombs will be harder to stop," Aunt Lisa said.

"Don't forget, we don't know how many times Quinn can do this. It could be five times or five hundred," Dr. Green said.

"Is there a way for you to find out, Dad?" Cameron asked.

He thought for a moment. "It would be highly theoretical, but I suppose I could construct a formula based on Quinn's prior jumps and extrapolate how many more he has left until he hits the red line."

"How long will that take?" Quinn asked.

"Shouldn't be long—a few days maybe. I could do a preliminary estimate in a few hours, but I'd like to construct an algorithm to iron out the kinks."

"Then we have seventy-two hours," Aunt Lisa said.

Frank's expression revealed his concern. "Don't you think we should wait? If we don't know how many time loops Quinn has left, doesn't it make sense for him to use the time in this loop to work on the array as long as he can?"

"Frank has a valid point," Dr. Green said.

"What do you think I've been doing this entire time? We've made a lot of progress on the array. And didn't we already have this conversation?" Quinn said.

"I think Quinn's right," Cameron replied. "Dad's the expert, but I know enough to understand that the bigger the event, the harder it will be to change. This is one of those things. Let's wait to see what Dad says about how much time Quinn has. Then we can sort things out."

"That's right. I'm going back, no matter what. That's *my* call. I have that responsibility, for better or for worse. And if it weren't for the fact that all of you knew I could go back and change things, the attack would be hitting all of you much harder. I don't know how many people each of us lost today, but in the first timeline, we lost a lot. It was horrific. I can't let this happen again, and I certainly can't let it be worse than the first time."

Frank looked upset. Quinn could guess what he was thinking. Who died and made him God? He was just a kid, even if he did have an adult consciousness from the future stored in his body. It was already worse than the first time. Reducing the body count since the last loop wasn't much consolation, given how much worse it was than the original attack. Not to mention the fact that to everyone else, they couldn't do anything over. For them, if Quinn didn't stop the supernova in this timeline, their world would be over once the supernova arrived.

Frank shook his head and walked off. Quinn followed him.

"Dad, I'm not trying to be a dick here. I just want to do the right thing."

"I don't even know what the right thing is anymore."

"The right thing is to stop this attack and then stop the supernova."

"What if you can't do both?"

"I have to try. It's that simple."

"Is it? What if you can't? What if things keep getting worse?"

"They didn't get worse this time. We stopped some of it."

Frank exhaled. "But it's worse than the first time. And what if this keeps happening? You *try* to make a change with every big thing that happens, but it ends up being worse than before. You go back and make more changes. It's a little better than the second time but worse than the first. You end up screwing up the entire timeline and don't have enough juice left to stop the supernova. Then what happens?"

"Which one are you worried about? Me screwing up the timeline, or everyone dying in the supernova? And remember, I can't actually change the timeline. All I'm really doing is hopping universes. It just doesn't seem like that from my perspective. All of these realities already exist. I just need to build a new one. That's all I can do. I can either build a new one or fall into whichever one I'm in last and wait until I die. What would you do?"

"I didn't say do nothing. I just think it's not a good idea to keep trying to change things. It's like life—bad things happen. But you learn from those bad things and become a better person. Those mistakes teach you about yourself, and how you can overcome them," Frank replied.

"This isn't the same thing. You can't learn from something if you're dead."

"And who gets to decide who lives or dies?"

"Are we really having this conversation? If that supernova hits, all this discussion will be pointless. And I can say the same thing about the people that died in the attack. I'm not going to let that happen," Quinn replied.

"You keep saying that, but what makes you so sure?"

"If I've learned one thing from all this time travel business, it's that if you want something bad enough, you have to believe it first before you can have it. Call it faith. Call it a growth mindset. Call it whatever you want. The bottom line is that if I don't believe, I might as well give up—and not just on stopping the attack and the supernova, but on everything."

"It's clear you've already made up your mind, and I can't stop you. I just hope you're right because to me it doesn't feel right."

"That's called fear, Dad. That's how you know you're on the right track. It's what I felt all those other times when I never bothered to try and gave up. That's why I was so unhappy with myself, but I think you'd prefer this version of me."

Quinn continued. "If things ever get back to normal and I can't time travel, I'm going to take more chances, live more. I realize now the most reckless thing you can do is to do nothing at all. I can't live like that. Not anymore. There's no such thing as absolute safety. Most people can only see one side of risk. But there's usually just as much risk, if not more, in doing nothing."

Frank digested what Quinn said. He didn't agree with everything, but he saw a kernel of truth.

During the next three days, Dr. Green used the algorithm to check how many loops Quinn had remaining, gathering up as a team to hash out a new and improved plan. Quinn and his dad would hire a team of investigators in the locations where terrorists launched the dirty bombs. They would also station eyes outside airports, near transformer stations, and at major intersections where truck bombs initially exploded.

Quinn assigned everyone else specific agencies to call ahead of the attack, and they would put the PIs at critical points for backup in case one of the agencies failed to act.

On the final day, Dr. Green called in the team to the lab at the mansion.

"I've run the numbers, and I've double-checked and triple-checked with the perfected algorithm. Quinn has exactly fifty-seven loops left."

"That's a lot," Jeremy said.

"I hope you're right. I hope it's enough to stop 9/11 and then the supernova."

"Before you go back and stop 9/11, I think you should make an agreement with us," Frank said.

"What kind of agreement?"

"That you won't loop time again until you've stopped the supernova. Are there any more attacks you'd like to stop? Maybe a few wars you want to avoid, too? If so, now would be the time to tell us, because you've already looped so many times. Fifty-seven isn't that many when you think about it."

Quinn hadn't really thought about other things he'd like to change. He had the list of natural disasters burned in his head. He had his journal, which he now kept daily, with all the major events he wanted to stop. But aside from a few earthquakes, Quinn had no idea how the current timeline would unfold.

"That's the kind of promise you usually come to regret in the movies. Are you sure that's what you want?" Quinn asked.

"If you're serious about stopping 9/11 *and* the Earth

being wiped out by the supernova, I don't think you have much of a choice," Frank added.

"It is kind of a rigid promise that doesn't take into account any of the infinite numbers of variables in your unfolding multiverse, Quinn, but I think your dad's correct. We can't risk mankind, in this universe at least, being destroyed by something of lesser importance. Stop this attack, but then resolve yourself to find a way to save the Earth," Dr. Green said.

Over the course of the evening, Quinn reflected on what his dad and Dr. Green had said about the loops. He'd already gotten accustomed to using them to fix problems like getting out of interrogation rooms or away from Russian terrorists with machine guns. Still, he knew they were right. He wouldn't say absolutely no if the situation warranted it, but unless it was a matter of getting thrown in prison for a crime he didn't commit, it made sense to play out the timeline and fix everything else on the final loop.

Over the next decade, Quinn kept his list of things to do memorized. But it wasn't fair to let this world die if he could help it. He didn't know if he would need the extra time. So he lived out the timeline until the very last moment.

On the final day, it was clear they weren't ready. Not even close. So, Quinn chose to go back once more, this time a week prior to 9/11 in the most recent timeline. He closed his eyes and fell asleep.

CHAPTER 36

QUINN EXPLAINED THE updated events to the team. Frank exhaled. His frustration and concern were palpable. Jeremy smiled and munched on M&Ms. Cameron and Lisa took notes, and Dr. Green stared unflinchingly until Quinn finished.

"So, let me get this straight. In the original timeline, about three thousand people died. The second time, over a million people died, including a hundred thousand in New York. Then the third time around, tens of thousands of people died. So, between the first time and the last time, things are about ten times worse and you have one less time to jump to stop the Earth from getting pulverized by the supernova?" Frank asked.

"That about sums it up. But we did stop the *USS Cole* bombing after it got worse, and we are making progress on the array."

"That's true," Dr. Green added.

Frank sighed and shook his head. "I love you, son, but I really hope you know what you are doing."

After Quinn finished with the pleasantries, he kicked the plan and his team into high gear. Jeremy's role was to call in threats on an untraceable cell phone Lisa had procured as a private contractor for the military. Lisa went to work on her contacts in various government departments, and the rest of the team contacted the private companies and PIs.

Over the course of the next week, Quinn ran the scenarios over and over again in his head. He was sure he had backup plans for the next time around if they failed. Most of them involved hiring more PIs and making more calls. Some of the ideas were more exotic.

Quinn spent the remaining time in the lab with Dr. Green. He blew off school and focused on improving the array. Most of the work was still theoretical. He had good ideas on using nanoparticles to strengthen panels, but most of the plans were untestable until there was an industrial plant that could build the required parts.

SEPTEMBER 11TH, 2001:
DAY 7.
3:35 P.M.

The morning of, Quinn and the team made their final calls and then waited to hear back from their PIs on the ground.

Lisa's phone rang. "Hello," she said. Everyone in the room turned. Her face was impossible to read. "Okay. Anything else?" They looked at each other, and then they looked at the time. "Thanks. Call back if you have anything else."

"What was it?" Jeremy asked.

"So far, so good. None of the suspects showed up at the airport, and the FBI brought in several men for questioning."

"So, we did it, then?" Jeremy asked.

"There's a lot of moving pieces. It's still early," Dr. Green said.

Quinn turned on the TV to the local news station. His heart pounded.

"We interrupt this program for a special bulletin. Moments ago, several men with machine guns stormed the Empire State Building and the Sears Tower. There are also reports of large trucks being rammed into several major intersections in multiple cities," the newscast continued. "I don't want to say anything too early, but it appears the country is under a coordinated attack."

Quinn inhaled and cracked his neck.

During the rest of the day, reports came in from across the country. Most of them were clustered in Chicago, New York, and DC, with a few more in several other cities. The TV screen ran a rolling banner of estimated death tolls, which inched up by the minute and approached ten thousand by the end of the evening.

Over the next several days, Quinn and the team wrote down all the attacks, locations, and the people involved. Then Quinn wrote down the names, locations, and incidents from the attack the way it happened the second time.

The names and details were different, except for one transformer that blew. Quinn discussed the events with Lisa and found more connections between the new events and what her contacts in the military had found before the attacks.

The number of terror cells they uncovered was massive. Once they brought in the suspects for questioning, they found several more cells connected to each of them. But in true movie fashion, the information had been compartmentalized.

The men involved in the current attack were activated when the other men were captured or didn't follow through on a specific set of procedures, which kicked in the second cell, and in a few instances a third cell.

September 6th, 2001:
Day 40.
3:35 p.m.

Quinn summarized what happened in the prior time loops on 9/11. Frank exhaled. "So how many more times do you think this is going to take?" Jeremy asked.

"At this rate, too many," Quinn replied.

"I think you're going to have to come to terms with the possibility that you might not be able to stop this thing," Dr. Green said.

"I can't give up, not yet. We've got more than a dozen more tries, so I'll keep doing this until the second to last one. If I can't stop it then, I'll let events play out on their own except for the array," Quinn said before pausing. "I have an idea, and it just occurred to me. I don't know if it will work, but I think we've tried a lot of things, and if we keep taking the same approach, I'm not sure anything's going to change."

"What's your idea?" Frank asked.

"The biggest changes are from the original timeline which have occurred outside New York and DC, but we've been able to stop nearly all the other attacks. In this last jump, the only other successful attack was in Chicago. That means our focus should be on New York."

"That's kind of stating the obvious, isn't it?" Aunt Lisa asked.

"But I know someone who might just be able to help."

"Are you talking about Scott Channing?" Cameron asked.

Quinn smiled. "Not Scott Channing—Captain Mark Channing, Scott's dad."

"How is a douche like Scott's dad going to help?" Jeremy asked.

"He's NYPD. And not just any officer. He's highly ranked in the agency, so if we convince him we're on the level, he could put a strategic plan in place and convince more officers to stand guard and join in the fight."

"Isn't that what you've been doing this whole time, minus his involvement?"

"It hasn't been enough. We haven't told anyone about my ability to travel through time, so they haven't given us everything we've needed to stop all the attacks and keep the other backup terror cells from replacing the ones we're able to stop." Quinn went on with his explanation. "New York's always been the focus of those attacks. If we can convince him, he can put patrols on all the corners with substations or key intersections—all the areas previously attacked."

"Don't you think it would be better to convince someone like Mayor Giuliani?" Frank asked.

"We wouldn't get close to him, and it's too risky. Captain Channing would actually work better because his men trust him. The day before the attack, they'll have some intel anyway from the FBI, but just like the first time, the agencies are too archaic to even communicate well enough together. That's where we keep dropping the ball. So, we have to do it for them."

"Think he'll buy it?" Cameron asked.

"Not a clue. We'll keep doing what we've been doing and see if we can pull him in. I'm not sure what else to do."

"And you'll have to do it fast. You only have seventeen loops left before it's all over," Frank said.

Over the next few days, Lisa contacted the military with the new information and all the agencies involved. Quinn called the PIs, and the rest of them took care of the private companies. Two days before the attack, Dr. Green called Captain Channing into the lab.

"There's something important we have to tell you. You're going to think we're crazy at first, that we're pulling your leg, but I need you to resist the urge to think we're completely nuts and just listen," Dr. Green said.

Dr. Green summarized everything they knew about the attack and the supernova and how they knew it. Captain Channing's face lost color the longer the conversation dragged on.

"You expect me to believe this load of crap?" he said, followed by a string of profanity. "I'm a busy person, and dragging me in to give me this kind of bogus report is likely to get you thrown in jail."

Frank walked in the door with Cameron and Jeremy. "He's not lying," Frank said.

"What's with you guys? Are you all in on this joke together?"

"This isn't a joke. I know it sounds ridiculous, but how do you think I've been able to make all this progress with the array?" Dr. Green asked.

"I don't know anything about your little science project, and I don't really care. I've had a long week, and it's not even Friday yet. You interrupted my private time with my sofa and a bottle of Scotch. I'm pissed."

"I can give you the exact locations of where the attacks will take place. I've tried to put people on the ground as much as I can, hire private investigators, get government agencies involved where we have valid intel that we can claim came from somewhere else. But it's not enough. We need someone on the ground to run interference for us, to see what we can't see and stop the new cells when we block the old ones."

"You're right. I *do* think you guys are nuts."

"Wait, don't leave," Quinn said as he pulled on Captain Channing's arm.

A second later, Captain Channing's fist landed on Quinn's face.

"You keep your hands off my son," Frank said as he landed a blow of his own.

Quinn's time-traveling abilities had begun to rub off on him without even realizing it. Then Frank realized, that's not how it worked. Frank couldn't take the blow back. For all the talk about who had the ethical right to change the past and decide who lives or dies, technically, Quinn wasn't changing any of that.

Quinn just happened to be able to have his consciousness hop on any version of his body in the multiverse that would give him the outcome he wanted. This branch would still exist, which means Frank just struck a New York cop in the face.

"You're going to regret that."

"I already do."

Captain Channing struck back. The sound of knuckles thumping against his dad's face was painful.

He wasn't sure what hurt worse—his dad's face, or how he felt about the situation.

Captain Channing stepped back, then lunged forward.

Frank grappled Captain Channing to the ground. The glass table shattered.

"Are we going to stop this or what?" Jeremy said.

Quinn nodded to Jeremy and Dr. Green. They each took one arm from Captain Channing and pulled him back. Captain Channing elbowed Jeremy in the chin. Jeremy gritted his teeth. Jeremy took the opportunity to land a blow of his own.

"How do you like me now?" Jeremy said, after landing a couple of slaps on Captain Channing's face.

Dr. Green frowned in disapproval.

"I can't change this. Can I?" Frank asked.

"No. But I can."

"But only for you, right? From our perspective, nothing's going to change."

Captain Channing interrupted. "You guys are nuts. What's wrong with you people? All of you are going to jail."

"You have to help us. If you don't, it'll be your fault what happens with 9/11," Jeremy said.

By that time, Quinn maneuvered behind Captain Channing with rope and tied his wrists together behind his back.

"This really is some amateur hour. You know I'm a cop, right? I mean, you don't think I'm going to sit around and do nothing about being kidnapped and tied up? And if you were really smart, you would have just used the handcuffs."

"We can change this, right?" Jeremy asked.

"Afraid not—Dad's right. For you guys, time keeps moving forward. I'm the only one that will branch off if I go back and change things. This timeline will still exist. I just won't be in it."

"That's messed up. So, you're saying in this universe,

we've only got one chance to stop the attack and one chance to stop the supernova?"

"Yeah. That's right."

"So why are we even helping you? If you can't change things, what's the point?" Jeremy asked.

"Think about it this way. You've already benefited from all the other universes that helped me get here. It's because of those universes I've made as much progress as I have in figuring out how to save the Earth from the supernova. We still have a shot at this."

"I'm confused. So, what exactly happens in that brain of yours if you loop back in time and wake up on the same day as before?"

"Cameron's dad can explain it better than I can, but it's basic physics. Every possibility that exists does exist in an infinite number of worlds. It's an infinite number of branches that keep branching off with an infinite number of more possibilities. How it branches off, I have no idea. My physics isn't that good yet, but there would be an infinite number of versions of me regardless. I just happen to be in a position to benefit from the knowledge of worlds that are close enough to our own, so everyone else in this universe benefits, too."

"I don't know what you guys are smoking, but if you still think I'm going to help you, you're crazy," Captain Channing said.

"Yeah, I figured as much," Frank said.

"But I'm still confused," Jeremy said. "When you fall asleep and go back in time, or whatever you call it, finding a branching point, who's going to be in that body of yours the next day?"

Quinn thought for a moment, and he realized that

Jeremy had a novel question. Who would be driving the ship after he went back in time?

"I guess it will be some version of myself that decided not to go or couldn't go."

"But then we won't know whether you actually decided not to go, or if you did go and this is just another you," Jeremy replied.

"Technically, they're all me, and I think the answer is that it will be both. All possibilities that exist, exist. It still doesn't change what we need to do."

"You nutbags need to let me go," Captain Channing said.

"If you've been listening to what I've been saying, you should be very concerned about what we're doing here."

"Who do you think you are? You're a seventeen-year-old punk who just kidnapped me, told me you're a time traveler from the future, and there's going to be some giant attack by Arabs or Russians or someone in New York next week, and you expect me to take you seriously?"

"He does have a point. And I'm guessing you're down to nine loops left now because this one doesn't seem to be going so well," Jeremy said.

"Please stop talking, Jeremy. You're making things worse," Quinn said.

Over the next few hours, Dr. Green and Quinn did their best to convince Captain Channing they were telling the truth—they failed miserably.

Once they released him, the local NYPD gathered all parties involved and held them for questioning. But they focused the bulk of their efforts on Quinn.

Captain Channing strutted in the interrogation room with two fellow officers.

"So, tell us again about who you are and what you have planned for New York," Captain Channing asked.

"You know who I am, and it's not me who's planning anything. I'm the one who's trying to stop it."

"And for the record, how is it that you know of these details about this supposed attack?"

"The details change each time."

"And by each time you mean…"

"I mean each time I go back and try to stop it."

"Back through time?"

"That's right. And I realize that being locked up in this interrogation room will keep me from doing what I need to do to stop it, so let me ask you this. If you knew I was telling the truth, what would you do?"

"I'm the one asking the questions here, Quinn," Captain Channing said.

The room hadn't changed since Quinn's visit to the room in the future, and seeing Captain Channing's interrogation reminded him of Scott. It was uncanny how similar they were, everything down to their speech and mannerisms.

After the end of the seventy-two-hour hold, they charged them with kidnapping, assault, and a slew of other crimes.

Quinn learned everything he could about Captain Channing, his fellow officers, and changes that occurred on 9/11. And then he went back.

CHAPTER 37

CAMERON DID THE dirty work of getting Scott to the coffee shop.

"What? Why did you really bring me here?" Scott said as the rest of Quinn's crew ambushed him.

"I tried your dad the first several times, but that didn't go over so well. And we need someone with connections in the NYPD."

"You're still not making any sense."

"There's going to be an attack, the biggest attack that's ever happened in the country. New York's going to take the biggest hit. We've been able to stop most of it, but we still need more help in New York. We need the NYPD. And Scott, you're our only hope to do that."

For the next half hour, Quinn pulled a *Groundhog Day*. A patron walked in the door. A waitress walked over to take someone's order, and several more events in a row occurred just as Quinn had said they would. Then they turned to the live game playing on the television. Quinn gave detailed play-by-play information before it happened.

"Okay, fine. I believe you. What do you need from me exactly?"

Dr. Green and Aunt Lisa pulled out a sheet of paper with a list of the attacks.

"We've been able to stop all the attacks in the last few loops except for these three, and they're big," Aunt Lisa said.

Dr. Green jumped in. "What we need you to do is convince the NYPD to set up a team here and here," he said, pointing to the locations of a substation near Central Park and another at the heart of Broadway.

"But there's one more location. They'll target the Twin Towers again. We've stopped the planes, but they still placed a suitcase nuke somewhere in the building, and we haven't been able to find it. It's the one piece that's been consistent."

Scott's face dropped. "So, you think I can do something about this?"

Quinn exhaled. "We need you to. Everything else hasn't gotten us anywhere."

Scott thought for a moment. "There might be one person who can help us, but you're going to have to trust me."

Cameron looked at Quinn. He knew that look. It was the look that said, "I know you shouldn't trust him, but you have to because we have no other option." It was the same look his sister gave him when she wanted something, and he knew she didn't deserve it.

"Why the heck not? We've tried everything else." Not entirely true, but true enough.

Scott called someone using the pay phone. Twenty minutes later, a car arrived in the driveway carrying Scott's mom, Meredith, and a familiar face Quinn had not expected to see.

"What are you doing here?" Quinn said.

"Do I know you?" Logan's dad, Robert, asked.

"I know your son, Logan," Quinn replied.

"My son always has interesting friends."

The confrontation jolted Quinn's mind. Everything made sense now, why Logan hired Meredith—how Scott got the interview.

Quinn's stomach sank. After Jeremy had died, he couldn't get his head back in the game. His fire for the job vanished. For all Logan did for Quinn, it was nothing compared to what Robert had done for Meredith and her son. And Quinn took that all away from them.

"There's no way I'm going to let some terrorists destroy this city," Robert said.

"This is what we're going to do."

Robert waxed poetic about how the city saved him when he was a kid—how the toughness of the city and its people made him who he was and his company what it was. He told stories about hanging out with the city commissioner and Giuliani before they had political aspirations.

He named a dozen officers he knew who had his back, no matter what. He said the loyalty and respect they had for each other was what made the city what it was.

"I'll ask Joe or Bill or Tony or any number of three dozen cops I grew up with—they'll be there on a dime. They're family—the city's family."

"How many cops do you think you can get to help us?"

"I can do you one better. I'll get you all the cops you need, and I'll raise you a mayor."

"You can convince Mayor Giuliani to help us?"

"We go way back. He'll come through. No question."

Over the next week, they put everything in place. They

contacted the PIs, government agencies, and with the help of Giuliani, they even coordinated with the FBI to stake out the locations they could have never cracked in the prior timelines. And then the day finally arrived.

Quinn wasn't sure what to expect after they told the world about the supernova. And he was pleasantly surprised the city and country hadn't lost its heart. There were a few pockets of crazies, but those were the exception.

Government officials made a few key changes, but most daily activities continued as they had for the last few decades. It was in moments like those that Quinn felt it most.

At four thirty, Giuliani had cops on every corner within four blocks of the hot spots. FBI hunkered down near the buildings. The city placed undercover SWAT trucks in pairs at the locations of the blasts. Quinn, Cameron, and Frank stayed at Quinn's place.

"You think we did it this time? Is this it?" Jeremy asked.

"We're about to find out," Quinn said.

Streets were quiet at Ground Zero—at least quiet for New York. The night air nipped at the few late summer stragglers who crept along the sidewalks.

Darkness shrouded the Twin Towers, but eyes watched from a distance from all directions. Officers waited for the slightest hint of impropriety.

An hour later, a van crept forward a few blocks from the towers.

"I think we might have something here," an officer told the mayor over a walkie-talkie.

The officer's partner ran the plates as they waited for a reply.

"This is it. The van's got bogus plates. Get the team down here now," the officer added.

More stragglers started walking along the streets.

"Block it off," the mayor said from the other end.

Within seconds, four SWAT teams had cordoned off the area. A special team measured the van's radioactivity with Geiger counters.

The counter crackled louder as they approached the van.

"We've got a hit," the team member holding a Geiger counter said.

Within seconds, they inspected the van and instructed the men in the front to step out of the vehicle.

They used a full array of police-issued heavy arms.

"Step out of the vehicle."

The driver smiled. "You can't stop this. None of you can."

The team carefully pried open the back doors, revealing a sophisticated contraption attached to a metal cylinder encased in hard glass.

"Captain, you're gonna want to take a look at this."

Two of the officers from the team dragged the men away from the van.

"This is nothing. You can't stop us. There's more of us," the driver shouted at the team attempting to defuse the device.

Seconds later, the mayor shut down the city. Giuliani issued a state of emergency and ordered teams to turn away anyone within the cordoned-off sections.

Giuliani issued a statement explaining the situation and the discovery of a dirty nuke in the van. He went on to explain that they had received reports of a massive coordinated attack against the city as part of a larger attack on the country and they had been working with law enforcement over the past week to prevent the attacks.

He advised residents in all boroughs to stay indoors for

the rest of the day, with an additional ten p.m. curfew for the next seventy-two hours. He explained how it was possible that there was still more nuclear material within the city limits and that they were going to root it out as they continued with the investigation.

Most people followed the recommendations and stayed indoors, but enough people ventured outside to form a crowd just beyond the taped-off areas.

At nine thirty, a jumper crossed the tape.

"Stand down!" Captain Channing said, guns pointed.

The man kept running. He held a suitcase handcuffed to his wrist and ran toward the direction of the towers.

Captain Channing fired the gun. The man fell to the ground. A ringing in Captain Channing's ears shut everything else out. The SWAT team rushed the man lying on the ground and clipped off the briefcase handcuffed to his wrist.

They scanned the suitcase, which revealed a small bomb—nuclear.

"Can you defuse it?" the mayor asked over the phone.

"It'll be touch and go. There's a forty-minute timer, with a secondary conventional bomb attached and a GPS trigger to prevent aerial removal."

"Do what you need to do."

Seconds later, sirens blared through Manhattan. Mayor Giuliani cut into the local broadcast.

"Fellow residents of New York and visitors alike, moments ago I learned that a small nuclear device is currently active and is being defused near the World Trade Center. As of this minute, the bomb is set to go off in thirty-seven minutes," Mayor Giuliani said. "Based on statements from my experts, if we are unable to defuse it, it will contaminate a five-block radius of the city. I'm still trusting we can defuse the bomb, but for the safety of the residents of this city, I'm ordering an immediate but orderly evacuation within five blocks of the area. This includes everyone between Thames and Chambers Street, including City Hall Park, and between Centre Street, Nassau Street all the way to the Hudson," Mayor Giuliani said pausing. "I can't stress enough that you move in a quick but orderly fashion, and I'm trusting that we'll all get through this crisis unscathed. Godspeed."

The feed cut out.

A safe distance from the city in Quinn's home, he waited with the crew.

"What do you think? Is this a do-over?" Jeremy asked.

"I'm out of do-over's, at least for 9/11. I need to save those for the supernova. And this is the closest we've gotten to stopping it. In all the other loops, multiple suitcase nukes exploded. As of now, no one's died yet, so whatever happens, we're stuck with it. At least for now, anyway."

"My dad's in there. I mean, right there," Scott said.

"He's not the only one. Aunt Lisa's there, too," Frank replied.

Quinn jerked his neck to face his dad. "Why is Aunt Lisa there?"

"She said it was the best way to work with the FBI and agencies that were dragging their feet. She said they needed someone with a military background to give them a sense of urgency."

"But she knew this was the last loop. Why did she have to go and do that?"

"I think you answered your own question. Because it was the last loop. Whatever happens, happens. She didn't want any more people to die, even if it meant that she had to."

Frank put his hand on Quinn's shoulder. "She's going to

be okay. But either way, she did what she thought was the right thing. That's how life's supposed to be. You can't run from your battles. You have to face them head-on. In everyone else's life, they have to live with the consequences even after do-overs."

Back at Ground Zero, the timer counted three minutes. Two minutes before that, an expert, Lance, choppered in and went to work on defusing the nuke.

Lance scooted aside a three-by-five-inch panel below the timer. It revealed a maze of tiny wires connected to a smaller cube.

"How are we looking on that bomb?" the mayor whispered over the walkie-talkie.

"Turn that thing off," Lance said.

A member of the squad turned the knob to silent as Lance inspected the wires' path to the cube. Armed with tweezers and a Swiss Army knife, Lance made a cut, then exhaled.

"Well, that wasn't it," Lance said. His upbeat expression made the men around him squirm. "Don't worry. It's definitely one of these wires."

The timer ticked toward the two-minute mark. The whispers from the team around him quieted.

Lance took a few seconds from defusing the bomb to take out his phone and turn on the wireless feed for his earphones to AC/DC's "Back in Black."

The seconds ticked. Lance inspected. The team waited.

At the temporary headquarters of the operation the mayor had set up, Giuliani stared at the second hand on the wall clock.

"Any word back from the team?"

"Nothing yet, Mayor."

"How are we with the evacuation?"

"The first three blocks are clear, but there's still people streaming out from the zone."

"What are the latest potential casualty estimates if this thing goes off?" the mayor asked one of his experts in the bunker.

"Given the number of people that are still within the blast radius and their current distance, up to fifty thousand could die from direct radiation exposure within the year, and another one hundred fifty thousand from cancer caused by the radiation within another three to five years."

The timer ticked down from thirty seconds. Twenty-nine. Twenty-eight.

Lance bobbed his head as he rocked to the music.

Twenty seconds.

Lance finagled out one of the wires with a pair of tweezers.

Ten seconds.

Five.

Three.

Two. Lance clipped the wire.

CHAPTER 38

QUINN WOKE TO the sound of AC/DC's "Back in Black."

He stumbled off the mattress and banged against the cold metallic bed frame before he found his footing.

His room was immaculate. The eighty-nine-million-dollar Versailles-inspired mansion he lived in, even more so. Quinn wished he could have taken credit for the beautiful art on the wall that hung over his bed. He had no idea who the artist was. On the far wall next to his study, a painting of himself and Jeremy hung in an ornate golden frame. It was the same picture he had in his apartment, only bigger and painted in lavish oils by another famous artist whose name he also couldn't remember.

Cameron rolled over and planted a huge kiss on his lips.

"What time are we going to the lab, honey?" she asked.

"Nine. Scott's flying in with Logan from New York in an hour."

"I can't believe the day's almost here."

"I know. It seems like yesterday they defused that suitcase nuke in Manhattan."

"Is Lance going to be there?" she asked.

"Said he wouldn't miss it for the world."

"How's Sam doing?"

"Sam's my star pupil, almost as smart as you are."

Cameron smiled.

"You don't have to butter me up. We're already married."

Quinn brushed her cheek with his thumb before kissing her back.

"You know it's the truth. Sam's amazing, but you inspired them."

"You had more to do with that than I did. I mean, seriously, a tenured professor of Material Science at MIT?"

"Exactly. You're the physics professor. I had to cheat to get my job. You did it the hard way."

Cameron chuckled, then planted a huge hug around Quinn's shoulders.

Two hours later, Quinn met up with the old crew in the new pimped-out MIT lab. Even his lab coat was a gift from a notable designer and cost more than his childhood home. The school had outfitted the lab a few years back, once Quinn had secured tenure and made building the array the pride of the school. It helped that Quinn was the second-richest man in the world, worth over seven hundred and fifty billion dollars.

He would have been the richest, but that honor went to Jeremy. Of course, Quinn had spent most of his money building the array, over one hundred and fifty trillion in the last five years. Governments pitched in only another ten.

"Quinn, it's good to see you again," Logan said.

"Where's Scott?"

"Taking his time, as usual, bringing the bags from the car."

"So, what's it like working for the richest developer in New York?"

"You'll have to ask Scott, but I have done well for myself. We'll see if that matters after the big day tomorrow. That array of yours better work. I've staked my entire future on it."

"Is that why you didn't get one of the tickets onto the ship?"

"I don't think I could live on a ship flying out into space in the middle of nowhere. I figured that out the hard way after I caught island fever in Hawaii when I stayed in Kauai for the winter. A beautiful place, but I'm a city boy. If the supernova takes us out tomorrow, I'll be happy with what I've been fortunate enough to do for New York. It's been a great ride," Logan said.

"That new Civic Center of yours is amazing. You really have helped out a lot of people," Quinn said.

"And thank you for all your generous donations. We've been able to save a lot of people from the streets," Logan replied.

Scott placed the large suitcases down and extended his hand to Quinn.

"Good to see you again. It's been too long."

"I hear you're doing good work for Logan at the center."

Scott smiled. "I have too much to thank you for, Quinn, that is, unless your array crashes and burns tomorrow."

"That is the one-hundred-and-fifty-trillion-dollar question," Dr. Green said as he walked up behind them. "What are we waiting for out here in the hot sun? Come on inside. Everyone's waiting."

The lab was expansive. The cozy mission control center

connected to an adjacent auditorium where they could run intricate tests with tons of space. They rarely used it except to double as a large conference room.

It was already packed with people, dozens of families with kids hunkered down on the floor, looking like they'd been waiting to buy tickets to a sold-out show. A massive screen covered the front wall, showing detailed schematics of the array, with commentary from industry leaders and journalists.

"This is something else you got going here. You think this thing is going to work?" Scott asked Quinn.

"I guess we'll find out tomorrow," he said.

Cameron and the rest of the crew trickled in as the day turned into night. The supernova was scheduled to reach critical at 7:32 a.m. the next morning. Quinn had used all the remaining loops to perfect the array—tomorrow was all or nothing.

August 7th, 2021
Day 593.
7:32 a.m.

Quinn had spent countless years in loops. His fingers intertwined with Cameron's as they lay sprawled out on their massive bed. They'd only been awake a couple of minutes. He'd planned it that way, only giving them enough time to hold each other in case of the worst.

Once the moment arrived, the supernova gleamed, lighting up the world, but it did not end it. Like the centuries before its arrival, time galloped in with terror and uncertainty but finished with a brilliance that drowned out the worst of humanity and carried with it the promise of a brighter future at the end of a long dark tunnel.

If you enjoyed this book, please share and show your support by leaving a review.

Don't forget to visit the link below for your FREE copy of *Salvation Ship*.

https://royhuff.net/salvationship/

Printed in Great Britain
by Amazon